St Aldate's Magick

Also by this author

The Lancefield Mysteries

Salvation Hall

The Redemption

Hemlock Row

Liberation Park

The Rose Bennett Mysteries

Dead on Account

Dead Ringer

Death Duties

Death Benefit

Dead & Buried

St Aldate's Magick

A Lancefield Mystery

MARIAH KINGDOM

~ Perceda Press ~

This novel is entirely a work of fiction. Any resemblance to actual persons, living or dead, or to events, locations or premises is used in a fictious manner. Salvation Hall, the Lancefield family, the Woodlands estate, Hemlock Row, the St Aldate's estate, the Excelsior Hotel and the village of Penwithen do not and have not ever existed, except in the author's imagination.

First published in digital form 2024 by WL Fowler

Copyright © Mariah Kingdom 2024

This paperback edition Perceda Press 2024

Mariah Kingdom asserts the moral right to be identified as the author of this work.

A catalogue record for this publication is available from the British Library

All rights reserved. No part of this publication may be reproduced, stored in a retrieval system or transmitted in any form or by any means, electronic, mechanical, photocopying, recording or otherwise, without the written permission of the author and/or publisher.

ISBN 978-1-8380834-8-9

Cover design by www.ebooklaunch.com

'The bravest among them tremble at the very sight of the ragged bundle, the eggshells or Obeah bottle stuck in the thatch of a hut.'

Henry Hesketh Bell, colonial administrator, 1864-1952

1

West India Quay.

He had barely stepped onto the floating footbridge when the feathers caught his eye – gaudy shreds of yellow, blue and red eddying gently in the water at the other side of the dock; the fibres glinting sharply, almost defiantly in the early-morning East London sunlight.

Of course, he didn't know at that point that they were feathers. They were too far away to be anything other than flashes of colour. A closer investigation might prove them to be a child's toy, lost on a daytime visit to the nearby museum. Or perhaps a piece of fancy dress discarded by a late-night reveller, careless after one too many overpriced Bacardi and Cokes in one of the many dockside bars. Either way, it hardly mattered to him. It wasn't in his job description to fish rubbish out of the North Dock's murky depths.

He lifted his gaze and fixed youthful eyes above the waterline, quickening his step. It wouldn't be in his job description to do anything very much if he was late for work again. He'd been pulled up on his timekeeping twice already that week and jobs as good as his were hard to come by. Shifts at the restaurant that employed him were long and tiring, but the boss was cool and the perks were good. And that was before he thought about Isabella.

Before he thought about her? These days, truth be told, thinking about the lovely Isabella occupied most of his waking hours. They'd been working the same shift pattern in the restaurant for over three weeks now and it was only a matter of time before he dared to ask her for a date. Perhaps only a matter of hours, if he could find the courage to do it that day.

He was almost at the end of the footbridge now, carried along by his fantasies, and it suddenly struck him that the weather was turning. He glanced back over his shoulder towards Canary Wharf and spun his eyes upwards. Dark clouds had begun to swirl above the towering columns of glass and concrete that housed the City's movers and shakers, blocking out the sun and threatening to douse the world beneath them with an unexpected downpour.

He turned his attention forwards again just as the first soft, heavy raindrop landed silently on his temple to trickle lazily down the side of his face towards his neck. He lifted a hand and brushed it away with the sleeve of his jacket, cursing quietly. Any minute now, he thought, the clouds would break and his fate would be sealed. And the last thing he needed was to be soaked to the skin at the start of an eight-hour shift.

He took hold of the bridge's cold, metal handrail and swung his lean frame left to step briskly off the bridge and onto the pavement, casting a nonchalant glance down into the grey, turbid waters below. The shreds of yellow, blue and red were just beneath his gaze now and he caught his breath at the sight of them.

At the sight of what lay just beneath them.

He tightened his grip on the handrail to steady himself and swallowed hard in the hope that his hastily consumed breakfast would stay safely within the confines of his stomach.

It looked like a body.

His heart skipped a beat and he craned his neck forward, half-fearing the horror of the early-morning discovery and yet helplessly drawn to the sight by a morbid, inescapable curiosity.

It looked like a woman's body.

Face down in the water, she was bobbing gently against one of the dock's supporting pillars, her legs tucked out of sight beneath the dock edge, her right shoulder nudging softly against the visible, concrete post. Strands of blonde hair radiated in a muddied, dishevelled halo around her head and across her shoulders a spray of long, garish, synthetic feathers nestled closely against the contours of what appeared to be a stylish, chiffon blouse.

For a moment, all thought of speech escaped him and then he drew his eyes away from the body. Away in the distance to his left, a short, elderly man in overalls was sweeping the outdoor seating area of a popular Italian restaurant. To the right, a straggle of reluctant weekend commuters were making their way towards the nearby station to board the Docklands Light Railway. Behind him, the footbridge was empty. No one else was aware of the woman in the water.

No one knew she was there but him.

He cast another furtive glance to the left. In a heartbeat, he could be safe inside the restaurant that employed him, on time for his shift and without the risk of yet another reprimand. He could walk away now, distance himself from the drama, and no one would be any the wiser. He straightened his back and took his hand slowly away from the handrail.

And then he remembered the cameras: the all-seeing eyes of the broader Canary Wharf Estate. It was impossible to move in this part of the City without those movements being captured on film. If he walked away now, of course someone else would know. They might not know immediately, but sooner or later, when the police were notified of the body and got around to examining the footage from all the nearby CCTV cameras…

He accepted the inevitable with a sigh; fingers trembling, he slipped his right hand slowly into the back pocket of his jeans and pulled out his mobile phone. The rain was falling steadily now, heavy drops landing silently on the screen as his moistened fingers punched the obvious number into the keypad. His hand shook as he lifted the phone to his ear. He'd never had to call the emergency services before.

And he truly hoped to God that, after that day, he would never have to do it again.

*

'How did you get on at Palmerston Place?' Kathryn Clifton pulled her chair a little closer to the kitchen table, and rested her hands gently in her lap. 'I didn't like to ask yesterday evening. It was so late when you arrived, and you looked so tired.'

'Tired?' At the other side of the table, Barbara Gee parroted the word with an air of weary resignation. 'Not the word I would have used. When I agreed to help David clear Stella's things out of the house I didn't expect it to be such an emotionally draining experience.' She picked up a teaspoon and swirled it around in her coffee as she spoke. 'All things considered, David coped very well. I think he has an inner well of strength, you know, that nobody gives him credit for.'

Kathryn couldn't argue with that. In the few short months that she'd known him, David Lancefield had experienced his daughter's murder, the indictment and trial of his stepson for the crime and the gunning down of his wife by a local delinquent who was still on the run. It was a tally of trauma that would have devastated the strongest of men. And yet the gentle and unassuming David had shown no sign yet of buckling under the pressure. 'Is he still determined to sell the house?'

'It's already on the market.' Barbara slipped a plump finger into the handle of her mug and lifted it from the table. 'He gave the instruction to his solicitor on Thursday, before he left for St Felix. Stella's clothes and books and any day-to-day personal items have been taken to a variety of charity shops, and her jewellery has been deposited at the solicitor's office for safekeeping in the short term. The solicitor has the keys to the house now and will manage any viewings.'

'And David's belongings?'

'All packaged up for transportation down here to Salvation Hall. The removal firm collected them early yesterday morning, though I don't expect them to arrive until Monday.' Barbara blew gently on her coffee to cool it. 'It's mostly books and paintings. The furniture will stay in the house until it's sold. The solicitor has an inventory of which items are to be disposed of and the rest will be shipped down here to Penwithen.'

'Then he hasn't changed his mind? He's going to live permanently at Salvation Hall?'

'That seems to be the plan.' The reply came with a wry smile. 'Although, I think he might come to regret the decision. He and Stella were so happy with their life up in Edinburgh and giving up the house means giving up the memories.' The wry smile softened. 'Of course, he still has Eva up there. We had dinner with her on Wednesday evening. She was in good spirits and looking forward to flying out to St Felix next month, to visit Marcus.'

So, despite the pain it was all finally beginning to come together. David had lost his wife but found a surrogate sister in his distant cousin, Barbara. He had lost his daughter but found a new protégé in his Scottish cousin, Eva. His stepson, Marcus, was stepping up to take over the running of the Lancefield family's estates on the Caribbean island of St Felix. And the growing bond between Eva and Marcus just promised to be the icing on the Lancefield family's cake.

If it weren't for the lingering shadows.

Kathryn's brow furrowed, but she cast the thought aside. 'And what about your own plans, Barbara? Have you given any more thought to Richard's suggestion that you move to Salvation Hall?'

'I won't deny that it's very tempting. It's not every day that you're invited to swap a modest semi-detached in Liverpool for a suite in a Cornish manor house. But I've only known the family since last November.' Barbara leaned a little closer to Kathryn. 'Don't get me wrong. There isn't a day goes by that I'm not grateful to have forged a connection with Richard and David. And when I gave Richard my word that I would always be there for David, I didn't give it lightly. I'll be in David's life for as long as he needs me. But…'

'But, it's all still a little too much, a little too soon?'

'I knew you would understand. Though I could almost ask the same question of you. I can't believe that Richard hasn't already made some attempt to persuade you to move to Penwithen on a permanent basis.'

'And you would be right, though I'm not sure that my involvement with the family going forward would merit it. After all, I'm not a relative. I'm just employed to curate and document the family's history. Once that work is complete I'll remain an executor of Richard's will, and I'll be happy to help David and Marcus with the estates on an advisory basis, if they want me to. But I don't need to move to Cornwall to do that.'

'And does DCI Price agree with you?'

The question caught Kathryn off guard and she felt her cheeks flush pink. And then she laughed. 'It's one of those conversations that we come dangerously close to on a regular basis.' But, somehow, neither of them ever seemed able to get the words out. 'I've always known that my time here would be limited. To be honest, when I arrived last September I didn't expect the commission to last more than a couple of months at the most.' Any more than she had expected to witness the fallout from no less than six murders in just as many months, let alone forge a deep and affectionate friendship with the detective chief inspector put in place to investigate the crimes. 'But things are coming to a close for me now. I understand why David wants to ship all of the family's historical documents and artefacts back to the Woodlands estate, and I'm more than happy to prepare an inventory and package everything up. But…'

'You'll be sad to see it all go.' Barbara nodded to herself. 'Times are changing for all of us. But it doesn't have to end, Kathryn. I might not have known you for very long, but I couldn't imagine the Lancefield family coping without you now.' She sipped slowly on her coffee. 'And, in all honesty, I can't really see any reason why they would have to.'

*

Becca Smith slipped the fingers of her right hand under the edge of the living room curtain and carefully teased it away from the window. She tilted her head to peer through the gap between curtain and glass, and then drew back sharply with an exasperated hiss. The bastards must have been out there all night.

Again.

She let go of the curtain and slumped against the wall, folding her arms across her chest to steady herself. What the hell was the point in trying to make a fresh start if she was always going to be under police surveillance? Were they going to do this to her after she'd made the move to Truro? Were they going to camp out on the doorstep of the smart little new-build she'd moved heaven and earth to afford?

Of course they were.

She pursed her full lips inward and banged her fist against the wall. All she wanted was a chance to start again, to leave the drab little council house on the outskirts of Penzance and forge a new, more optimistic life for herself and her daughter, Frankie. It wasn't her fault that her brother had decided to take a potshot at the Lancefield's Scottish cousin, Eva McWhinney. Any more than it was her fault that Zak had clumsily missed his target not just once, but twice, managing to murder both a complete stranger and David Lancefield's obnoxious wife, Stella, in the process.

What a bloody mess.

It was still inconceivable to Becca that Zak could have been quite so stupid. Stupid enough to drive all the way to Edinburgh to murder a woman that he didn't know. Stupid enough to murder an innocent woman by mistake. And stupid enough to go on the run. But then he had been impervious to the toll it had taken on his family: his brothers charged with false representation and fraud for hiring the van that he had used to drive to Edinburgh; his mother, Sadie, her heart broken, charged with assisting an offender for simply allowing her own son to stay safely under her roof. And Becca…

Well, in some respects Becca knew that she had got away with things more lightly. If having her home regularly staked out by the police and her every move monitored could be called getting away with things more lightly. They had hoped to charge her with providing a false alibi for Zak, but they couldn't tie the alibi to the murders securely enough to make the charge stick. Keeping her under surveillance was the only avenue left to them. She knew they were convinced that Zak would make contact with her sooner or later. Just as they knew that any other member of the Smith family wouldn't hesitate now to turn him in.

She pushed herself away from the wall and took another furtive peek out from behind the curtain. The non-descript, grey Ford Mondeo occupied by two stony-faced detectives was still parked across the road on the spot it had monopolised ever since Zak had gone on the run. But now it had been joined by a second vehicle, an unfamiliar silver luxury saloon that looked completely out of place amid the ageing, dilapidated rust-buckets that most of her neighbours dared to call 'a car'. The sleek, highly polished Mazda had pulled parallel to the Mondeo, and the driver had lowered his window to speak to the detectives. Becca's heart sank at the sight of a car she didn't recognise. Had the driver come to advise his colleagues of a development in the case? Had Zak been found? Was the nightmare nearly over? Or was it just about to begin?

A momentary panic gripped her and she turned back to the room, and the small and untidy collection of battered cardboard boxes that were holding her few, unremarkable possessions. In a couple of hours, Robin would be calling for her in his van. While their mother looked after Frankie, they would ferry those boxes to the new house over in Truro. The new house that would be paid for with the wages from her new job as a cleaner at the Royal Cornwall Hospital. The new job that was going to support her while she left the past behind, settled Frankie into a new nursery, made new friends. Friends who wouldn't know about her brother: that he'd murdered a stranger, that he'd murdered a Lancefield, that he was still on the run.

Friends who wouldn't know that he'd mired his family in shame, and was content to let them all share in the burden of his cold-blooded crimes without a single word of contrition.

A lone, salty tear made its way down Becca's face and she smeared it away with the back of her hand. The police weren't going to give her a moment's peace as long as her brother remained on the run. But Zak wasn't going to give himself up any time soon, and she knew they would never find him where he was hiding.

She sniffed back a second tear. They would never find him, and however long the police were determined to go on watching her she would never give him up.

She would never give him up. Not even if her life depended on it.

2

Detective Chief Inspector Chris Greenway stared down at the waterlogged body. 'What's with the feathers and flowers?'

'Who knows? They're threaded on a cord that's been hung around her neck. Like some sort of garland.' Detective Sergeant Bob Marwick raised a thick, greying eyebrow. 'If you look closely, you'll see a small glass bottle behind the feathers. And something else... I think it's a plastic replica. At least,' he frowned, 'I hope it's a plastic replica.' He pointed to the victim's right shoulder. 'Just there, in the crook of her neck.'

Greenway bent his head forward to examine the item. 'What the hell is it?' Something small and white, anyway. 'It looks like some sort of skull.' He flicked incredulous eyes towards the sergeant. 'Any ideas?'

'It looks like a small mammal. A cat, maybe. Or a small dog?'

'Not the animal.' Greenway cursed under his breath. 'The reason for the garland being hung around her neck.' He hitched up the knees of his trousers and crouched down on his haunches beside the body. 'Cheap nylon cord. Washing line, maybe.' He slipped a cautious finger under the bright orange twine to pull it away from her flesh. 'And the feathers look synthetic.' He stared hard at the tawdry collection of objects. 'A garland made of imitation feathers, artificial flowers, an empty bottle and a plastic skull. Some sort of prank?'

'If it was, sir, I doubt that she was in on it. She looks too well-dressed to be a game-player.'

There was no question of that. Greenway ran an appraising eye across the victim. She was lying face-up on a stretcher, her once-pretty face now blue and bloated from the water. 'Age? Maybe in her mid-thirties?' She was wearing slim, navy woollen trousers and a long-sleeved chiffon blouse with frills at the cuffs and neck. 'It wasn't a robbery. She's wearing a ton of gold jewellery.' Generous teardrop earrings still hung from her ears and an antique belcher chain was visible just above the neckline of her blouse. 'That gold cuff on her wrist would have come off quite easily, even if the assailant didn't have time to remove her rings.'

'We haven't located her shoes yet, sir. Or a handbag. A mugger could have made off with that.'

'Grabbed the bag and pushed her in?' Greenway screwed up his nose. 'Unlikely. If it was a simple mugging, where did the garland come from?' Still crouching, he drew a pair of latex gloves from the pocket of his jacket and pulled them onto his hands. 'Excuse me, sweetheart.' He slipped gentle fingers into the right-hand pocket of her trousers. 'Nothing in there.' He repeated the exercise with the left-hand pocket. 'And nothing in there. So, at this point we have nothing at all to identify her.' He looked up at his colleague. 'Do we know yet how long she was in the water?'

'Dr Davis was fairly noncommittal. He wants the body moving as soon as possible so he can do a full examination. But he reckoned no longer than twelve hours, which we can narrow down much further with a bit of common sense. This place is usually buzzing until the early hours of the morning, so I would guess she went into the dock no more than eight hours ago.' Marwick sniffed. 'He wouldn't commit to a cause of death at this stage, either. It's possible that she was dead before she went into the water.'

Greenway pushed himself to his feet and smoothed out the knees of his trousers, then turned to the buildings that lined the dockside: restaurant after restaurant, each with its own elaborately furnished outdoor seating area. 'She was smartly dressed and probably here for a dinner date.' He shook his head. 'Bob, we're missing something. This is West India Quay. It's part of the Canary Wharf Estate.' He lifted a finger to point upwards. 'There are CCTV cameras everywhere. There are even bloody signs to *tell* you that there are CCTV cameras everywhere. Twenty-four-hour surveillance.' His sandy brows beetled forward. 'If she went into the water anywhere along the quayside – and, given the layout of the dock, it's unlikely that she drifted from another location – it must have been captured on CCTV.' He spun back around to look at Marwick. 'No one who knew the area would be crazy enough to carry out an attack with all these cameras watching. Does that mean the killer wasn't local?'

Marwick shrugged and walked a couple of steps towards the water's edge. 'How would you get a body over these railings?' They were constructed of twisted wire strung between metal posts, with a solid metal upper edge. 'They're angled inwards, towards the pavement. You couldn't just push someone over them, you would have to lift the body over and drop it into the water. If she was still alive, she wouldn't have gone over without a struggle. And if she was dead, or even unconscious, it wouldn't be easy to get a dead weight up and over this.' He grasped at the top rail with both hands and stared out across the water. 'How would she have travelled here? By tube to Canary Wharf, and then on foot across the floating bridge? Or by the DLR to West India Quay?'

Either way there would be yet more CCTV footage to

check. 'Who found the body?'

'A young man called Jamie Bradley. He crossed the bridge at around seven forty-five this morning, on his way in to work, and he spotted the body as he came to the end of the footbridge.'

'And he put the call in to us?'

'Yes. He said it was the feathers that caught his attention. He thought they might be part of a child's toy that had gone into the water.'

Some toy. Greenway peeled off the latex gloves and stuffed them back into his pocket. 'Right, then, Bob. Let's get our mystery blonde into the tender hands of Dr Davis, and then we can make a start on questioning the staff of the surrounding restaurants for any possible sighting of her yesterday evening. I want the CCTV footage for last night from any business along the quayside that has it, and for the street cameras on the outside of these buildings.' He closed his eyes for a moment, and then opened them to crouch back down beside the blonde. 'Don't worry, sweetheart.' He pulled a thin strand of seaweed almost tenderly from the dead woman's hair. 'Whoever did this to you won't be on the loose for long. Because I give you my word that we're not going to rest until we catch the bastard.'

*

Richard Lancefield settled into his favourite armchair beside the library fire and rested his elbows on the chair's arms. 'I hope you're not too disappointed, Kathryn, that everything is to be shipped back to St Felix?'

Kathryn, comfortable in the fine captain's chair beside the desk, swivelled the seat on its castors to face the old man. 'I suppose I was a little disappointed at first. We had spoken of the possibility of donating everything to a museum or university in this country. But the more I think about it, the more I see that it's the right thing to do. I can understand that you don't want the items to leave the family's possession. And given that they came from St Felix and are a part of its history, it's only right that they should go back.'

'Thank you, my dear. I would not have wanted to displease you after everything you have done to help us.' The old man sounded relieved. 'How much longer do you think you will need access to the family's original papers?'

'Well, I have almost completed my work on the Payne connection, so I should be able to pack up those papers in the next day or two. Most of the other documents are already back in their packing cases.' She retrieved a small sheaf of papers from the desk. 'I've taken digital images of most of the estate registers and I'll try to complete the last two volumes this week.' She ran her eyes down the top sheet of paper. 'Packing up the items in the storeroom is going to be the real challenge. I'll need Nancy's help to do that. She knows how everything was packed when it was shipped over from St Felix.'

'Whatever is necessary.' Richard steepled his fingers. 'I had a video call with David and Marcus yesterday evening.' A faint smile began to play around his lips. 'Marcus is settling in so well, much better than I had dared to hope. In fact, he seems to have taken to the lifestyle out there like the proverbial duck to water. He's putting down roots much more quickly than I expected and is in no rush at the moment to come back.'

'And David?'

'Still a little tired from the flight over. But I'm confident that the rest will do him good. He needs to get away for a while.' Richard's face clouded. 'You know, the sooner they catch Zak Smith and bring him to justice, the happier I shall be.'

And so would they all. Kathryn swayed the captain's chair gently to and fro, thinking, and then she asked, 'What will happen to the documents and artefacts when they arrive back at Woodlands? Are they destined to go back into storage?'

'Good heavens, no. David has proposed that we set up a charitable foundation: a museum and research centre on the Woodlands estate. It would house everything relating to the plantation's history and be available to anyone who wishes to make use of it.' Richard turned his head towards her. 'I have not forgotten, my dear, our original agreement. I promised you unfettered and exclusive access to all of our precious belongings. I hope it goes without saying that you will always have full access to everything. The estate will fund any travel you wish to make to St Felix. As to the exclusivity…'

'The opportunity to discover all of that heritage before anyone else set eyes on it was more than enough for me, Richard.' An opportunity for which she would always be grateful. 'Do you have a timescale in mind for things to be sent back?'

'As soon as is reasonably possible. There are some redundant buildings on the estate which Marcus thinks might be renovated to house the collection. I have asked him to investigate the possibilities. In the meantime, I would appreciate your opinion of my plan to appoint a caretaker for the collection.' Richard looked down at his fingers as he spoke. 'I am proposing that Nancy should take ownership of it.'

'Why Richard, that's wonderful. I had no idea. Is she pleased?'

'I trust she will be, when I tell her.'

'Tell her? Surely you mean "ask her"? You wouldn't want her to take on the task if she didn't want to do it?'

His thin lips pursed. 'I don't consider it a matter of choice. It is my wish that Nancy should take ownership of the family's heritage when she returns to St Felix on a permanent basis. It will be a wonderful opportunity for her. And I am pleased that you agree with me.'

'I agree that it's an opportunity.' Kathryn's frown

deepened. 'So, she is definitely to return?'

'After Stella died, I made it clear that we would take some time to wind up Nancy's responsibilities at Salvation Hall. I had considered asking her to take on a role at Woodlands as second-in-command to Marcus, to assist in running the estate. But I think it may be more pragmatic to give her a project of her own. Assuming that you consider she is up to the task?'

'Of course she's up to it. You know how interested she is in the family's heritage, and how hard she has been working to compile her own family tree.' That wasn't really the issue. 'Richard, I don't want to speak out of turn, but I have to ask: do you think it's fair that management of the estate should go to Marcus, when he isn't a member of the Lancefield family?'

'Fair?' Richard repeated the word slowly, as if he didn't quite understand the implication. 'Marcus may not be a Lancefield by blood, but he is David's stepson.'

'And Nancy isn't just your secretary, she's your granddaughter.'

'Which is why I am entrusting the family's heritage to her.'

'But not the estate.'

'The family's heritage is very precious to me, Kathryn. This much you have always known.'

'I know. But one day Nancy may come to know that she is a Lancefield by blood. And how do you think she will feel then, knowing that you could have recognised her? Knowing that you could have entrusted the running of Woodlands to her but chose, instead, to give it to Marcus?'

The old man closed his eyes and jutted out his chin. 'Am I being chastised, Kathryn?'

'Good heavens, no. Challenged, perhaps. But not chastised. It is not my place to chastise you.' She steadied the captain's chair and rose to her feet. 'Have you ever stopped to think that this isn't just about Nancy?' She crossed the room and knelt down beside Richard's chair. 'Have you ever stopped to think that one day David might discover the truth?'

*

Detective Chief Inspector Ennor Price folded his arms on the desk and ran his eyes wearily down a page of handwritten notes. Unpaid overtime on a Saturday had become a regular occurrence since the murder of Stella Lancefield, though as Kathryn was frequently at pains to point out, it did little to assuage his guilt.

Nor had it got him much further in the search to find her killer. Zak Smith had been on the run for the best part of eleven weeks now: seventy-seven excruciating days of false sightings, fruitless searches and – at least as far as Price was concerned – ceaseless self-recrimination. Eleven weeks since the man had casually admitted to the Lancefield's cousin that his attempts to murder her had instead led him to murder two completely innocent women. Eleven weeks since he had backed away into the darkness, claiming that Marcus Drake had offered to pay him twenty thousand pounds to send Eva McWhinney to her maker.

The detective put a hand up to rub at a greying temple that was growing greyer with each day that passed. In all the years he'd known of Smith, it had never occurred to him that the man was anything more than a petty chancer. Poaching, drunk and disorderly behaviour, harassment against the Lancefield family: all of this was well within his capabilities. But murder? No, *double* murder? Even the case-hardened Price hadn't seen that one coming.

And as to whether Marcus Drake really *had* offered Smith the money to drive all the way to Edinburgh to commit the crime: well, Price really couldn't see that, either. Although it probably hadn't surprised him to learn that Smith had been reckless enough to murder the wrong woman.

Geraldine Morton had been making her way back to Eva McWhinney's house in Hemlock Row when Smith mistook her for Eva. Dragging her into the mews lane behind the house to strangle her without checking that he had targeted the right blonde was just the sort of thing that the arrogant, overconfident Smith *would* do.

Price shivered, and pulled on his ear. Maybe Smith wasn't the only one who could be arrogant and overconfident. Maybe he could lay claim to the epithet himself. Looking back, he could hardly believe his own stupidity. Within twenty-four hours of Gerladine's death, he had encouraged Eva McWhinney to visit her Lancefield cousins at Salvation Hall. He had actually believed that if Smith were to make another attempt on Eva's life, it would be so badly executed it would lead to his capture. It had never occurred to Price that Smith would succeed in breaking into the grounds of Salvation Hall to take a potshot at his victim, and that a cruel twist of fate would lead to the shot hitting Stella Lancefield instead.

The policeman felt the muscles in his throat tighten. It was a serious error of judgement that had cost David Lancefield his wife and left Price's career on the line. Thirty-odd years of exemplary service wrecked by a monumental misstep for which he had no one to blame but himself. And now the burden was on him to find Zak Smith and bring him to justice. That much he owed not just to the Lancefield family, but to the family of Geraldine Morton and the Edinburgh detectives who wanted to bring her killer to justice.

He glanced sideways to the small brass clock on his desk. In another ten minutes or so he would be taking a call from Alyson Grant, the Edinburgh DCI investigating Geraldine Morton's murder. Their daily calls had become a habit, borne more out of shared frustration than any real belief that they were moving the investigation forward.

Despite the situation, Grant had proven herself to be a much-needed ally; always encouraging, always willing to talk through the disappointments, the possibilities, the setbacks.

At least today Price had a sliver of good news for her. The forensic evidence they needed to bring a cast-iron case against Smith was building nicely. Thanks to Amber Kimbrall, they had the shotgun he had used to murder Stella, and a thorough search of his lockup garage had produced a dark blue, woollen overcoat with not just one, but two magnificent blonde hairs which came from the head of Geraldine Morton. Now, to seal that case, Price was able to confirm that tiny blue fibres found under the innocent girl's fingernails were a perfect match for the fibres of Smith's overcoat. It was painful to think how those same tiny blue fibres came adrift from their mooring; the victim must have clawed at the killer's sleeves as she struggled to fight him off. But there was no question now that killer and victim had each left their mark on each other. It would give Grant the evidence she needed to secure a conviction.

But what good was the forensic evidence needed to secure a conviction if you couldn't find the killer to convict? Deep down Price knew that, though she would be grateful for the evidence, what Grant really wanted to hear was that Smith was in custody. And today the only answer he had for her was the same as the answer he had for her the day before, and the day before that, and the day before that...

We're still no closer to bringing him in.

3

'Who's the dish?' Marlie Connor whispered the question as she passed behind her colleague. 'Over on the right, fiddling with his cufflinks.'

Lesley tilted her head back to reply. 'A non-resident. He came in about fifteen minutes ago, looking for his cousin.' Her eyes were still trained on the dish in question. Tall, dark, and expensively dressed he was sitting on a low, leather sofa just a few feet away from the hotel's reception desk. 'She was supposed to call him first thing this morning to arrange a time for lunch and he hasn't heard from her. He's tried her mobile but she isn't answering.'

'When did he last see her?'

'Yesterday evening. She checked in here late yesterday afternoon and the two of them had dinner at Vincenzo's. He said something about meeting up on family business.'

'And she hasn't just checked out?'

'No. She's booked in for two nights. She's not due to leave until tomorrow.'

Marlie whistled through perfect teeth. 'Does he know about the body in the dock?'

'I don't think so. He didn't mention it.' Lesley gave Marlie a knowing look. 'Anna tried calling up to the room through the switchboard but there was no answer, so she's gone up to check that everything's okay.'

'I thought the police had asked us to check on all solo female guests, to make sure they were accounted for?'

'They did.' A faint blush appeared in Lesley's cheek. 'But there are seventeen on the list, and we've had so many guests checking out this morning that we've only had time to follow up on a handful.'

Both women turned their eyes back towards the waiting man. Unaware of being watched, his own gaze was fixed intently on the doors of a lift at the far side of the hotel's lobby. 'I suppose he's waiting for Anna to come down. I wish he was waiting for me. He's got lovely eyes.' Marlie sighed, and nudged her colleague's arm. 'I'd better go, I'm supposed to be preparing the main conference room in readiness for Monday. Let me know if you hear anything.'

Lesley mumbled her agreement as Marlie went on her way, though what she might hear that would be worth the repeating was anyone's guess. Tragedies didn't happen at the Excelsior Hotel. It just wasn't that sort of establishment. It was a chrome-and-marbled-filled hostelry for businessmen and overseas travellers, luxurious enough to justify its price tag but just too pedestrian to attract scandal or gossip or murder.

Murder? The receptionist shivered, startled by the unexpected thought. Did the policeman who briefed them this morning actually say that the woman in the dock had been murdered? On reflection, she couldn't be sure that he had. Only that a woman's body had been found and the circumstances were so far unknown. Just like the woman's identity. Which was why Lesley was meant to be checking through the guest list in the first place.

She dragged her eyes back to her computer screen in readiness for resuming the task. But as she did so, the lift bell pinged and the doors slid open to reveal the hotel's assistant manager. Lesley watched as Anna stepped out of the lift to make her way towards the waiting man, and nodded when the woman cast a worried glance in her direction, raising an index finger in a familiar, silent gesture of entreaty for the receptionist to join her. Whatever it was that Anna had to tell the man, she clearly wanted a witness.

'I'm afraid your cousin isn't in her room, Mr Payne.' The manager sat down on the sofa beside him as Lesley approached. 'And it looks as though her bed hasn't been slept in.' She flicked concerned eyes up to Lesley. 'But all of her belongings are still there. Her suitcase, clothing, cosmetics…'

Lesley took her cue. 'Did you walk your cousin back to the hotel yesterday evening, Mr Payne?'

'Walk her back?' Puzzled, he scratched at his forehead. 'We walked together to the footbridge behind the hotel. She told me that she was happy to walk the last few yards by herself. She only had to walk down the side of the building and round the corner to reach the front door.' He looked up at Lesley with deep blue eyes. 'I don't understand what's happened to her. She could hardly just vanish into thin air, could she?'

*

Kathryn, a small sheaf of documents in hand, looked up from the desk as the library door opened and greeted the incomer with a smile. 'Were you looking for me?'

'Yes.' Nancy paused in the doorway. 'I came to ask if you were taking lunch in here. Richard and Barbara are taking theirs in the Dower House after their walk.' Her eyes wandered to a sturdy cardboard box on the desk. 'Are you packing up documents?'

'I'm afraid so.' Kathryn dropped the papers in her hand gently into the box. 'This one is nearly full.' She tapped a slim finger on the side. 'Only another few hundred to go.'

The attempt at humour fell flat. Nancy murmured, and let the door swing shut behind her. 'Won't you need to access these documents again at some point?' She crossed the room and sat down on the chair beside the desk. 'And what do you mean by "only another few hundred to go"?'

Kathryn lifted her reading glasses from her nose and pretended to examine them. 'Richard and David have decided to send everything back to St Felix.' She rubbed at the tortoiseshell frame, pausing to let the information register, and then added, 'I was hoping that you might be able to help me after lunch. I've already identified several more sets that are ready to pack.'

The girl's dark eyes widened. 'Everything? Everything is to go back? But how are you to complete your work? How am *I* supposed to continue work on my own family tree if they send everything back?'

Now wasn't the time for Kathryn to suggest that 'everything' going back to St Felix might include Nancy herself. It was enough that she had agreed to assist Richard by warming Nancy up to the idea. 'I've been making digital copies of the documents as I worked. We can both work from those.'

'But there are so many. I will need copies of the annual slave inventories, the chapel records, the hospital records…' Nancy threw up her hands. 'And how many volumes of the estate daybook are there? One for every year since 1736. You can't possibly have made copies of all of those.' An exasperated laugh escaped her lips. 'And what about the records that I don't know I need? All those opportunities for a chance finding, a snippet of information we couldn't have guessed was there?'

'Well, you'll be able to look at those when you visit St Felix. It's not as if you won't ever be there again, is it?' And sooner than she might think, if Richard had his way. 'Don't take it to heart, Nancy. It's not as if the documents are leaving the family's possession.'

'But why has this been decided?'

'I don't know all the details. You'll have to ask Richard. But it's going to happen, whether you like it or not. He's quite made up his mind.' Kathryn lowered her spectacles and let them drop gently to the end of their chain. 'Barbara has agreed to help me with the packing, and I hope I can count on your help too.'

'Do I have a choice?'

'Heavens, Nancy, you always have a choice. Just say if you don't want to help.'

'And then I will look churlish.' Petulant, the girl rolled her dark eyes and brought them to rest on Kathryn's face. 'Of course I will help you. But it is very annoying all the same. I am so close to resolving a conundrum in my family tree and now the documents will be removed before I can get to the bottom of it.'

'Is it something I can help with?'

'Perhaps.' Nancy relaxed a little. 'I've traced my maternal grandmother's line back to a house servant at Woodlands: her name was Millie, and her birth in 1758 is recorded in the family's Bible. She had an older brother, Anthony, who was sold to a neighbouring plantation. And a sister, Abigail, who was born in 1760. I can find details of both girls in the annual inventory of slaves on the estate for every year up to and including 1777. But I cannot find any reference to Abigail after that. She doesn't appear on the inventory for 1778.'

'Have you tried looking in the daybook to see if she was sold? Or the hospital records to see if she suffered an illness or injury?'

'Yes. I have tried both of those.'

'And there is no reference in the family Bible of a marriage? Could she have married out to another plantation?'

'I can find no mention of a marriage or death, as I have for Millie.'

'Then we'll have to give the matter some additional thought. I suppose it's possible she was liberated for some reason, but I haven't seen any evidence of it. Could we discuss it again after lunch?'

'I would like that very much.' Nancy, momentarily

appeased, offered up a warmer smile. 'Would you also have some time to help me examine my maternal grandfather's line? We haven't really looked at Addison's side of the family yet.'

'Addison?' Kathryn shivered, uneasy. She already knew that Addison Woodlands was Nancy's grandfather in name only, the man encouraged to marry her grandmother and bring up her illegitimate child as his own. It was the reason she had so far done everything she could to avoid looking at Addison's extended family tree. It would be a monumental lie to produce that line and call it Nancy's.

But maybe the avoidance in itself might give the game away. What possible reason could she have for *not* looking at it? None that she could think of, save for keeping the truth a secret. 'I'd love to help with that, but perhaps another time? Richard is quite keen that we should make a start on packing up the documents.' She knew the excuse sounded feeble. Because it was.

'I can't help wondering' — Nancy arched a suspicious eyebrow as she spoke — 'whether you already know something of Addison's line, Kathryn. Are you afraid there is something contentious in there? Something that might cause me some discomfort?'

'Far from it.' Kathryn met the challenge with as serene a smile as she could muster. 'I can't claim to know anything at all about Addison apart from his marriage.' That, at least, was the truth. 'All I can suggest is that we look for information on both Abigal and Addison as we work our way through the packing of the documents. And if you're very good, and can help me to work out how to pack up all the items in the storeroom for shipping, as well as the documents, I might even help you to document anything that we find.'

The deflection took Nancy by surprise. 'The items in the storeroom are also to be returned? Do you have any idea, Kathryn, of the effort it took to pack all of those items up in the first place because Richard insisted on shipping them over here to England?' She rose to her feet with a groan. 'I suppose I'd better make a start on lunch.' She turned and made for the door, then hesitated as her hand reached for the doorknob. '*All* of the items in the storeroom?'

'I'm afraid so.'

'But why on earth does he want to ship them back?'

'I'm afraid that's another of life's little mysteries.' Kathryn lifted her reading glasses and placed them back onto her nose. 'Perhaps you could ask Richard that question yourself.'

*

Barbara dug her hands into the deep pockets of her green woollen coat and lifted her head to breathe in the crisp Cornish air. 'Do you think it will rain?' She cast the question over her shoulder as she strode off towards the lake. 'Perhaps we should have brought an umbrella.'

'Nonsense. A drop of honest rainwater never hurt a soul.' Richard chuckled throatily as he followed in her wake. 'Samson and I frequently get wet, don't we, boy?' He snapped his fingers at the terrier trotting along beside him. 'Nancy often chides me about it. She says my bones are too old to stand the damp. I say my bones are so old now it hardly matters. One way or another, God will get me in the end.'

'She's only thinking of your welfare.' Barbara halted, waiting until he was beside her, and then slipped her arm into his. 'She cares very much about you and David. You should be grateful.'

'Perhaps.' And perhaps not. 'Our beloved Nancy is a bag of contradictions, Barbara, as you will see when you get to know her better.'

'I rather thought I had spent enough time with her already to get the measure of her. What have I missed?'

'Well, Nancy can be a little…' He hesitated, searching for the right words. 'A little overconfident of her importance within the household.' He felt Barbara's fingers tighten on his arm and he lifted his free hand to wrap it over her own. 'Don't misunderstand me, my dear. The girl is much loved. I have known her since she was a babe-in-arms and watched her growth with a great deal of pride. As I have for dozens born on the Woodlands estate.' He ran his tongue around his teeth. 'I knew Nancy was special from her earliest years. She has a presence, an inner strength which does her credit. And it has been a great pleasure to have her here at Salvation Hall as my secretary. But there are times when she can overstep the mark, and those times are becoming more frequent. Which is why I think the time has come for her to return to St Felix.'

'Good heavens. I thought she would stay here indefinitely, to support both you and David.'

Richard patted Barbara's hand. 'I'm hoping that you will be here to do that, my dear.' They had reached the water's edge now, and they turned left along the narrow path that led around the lake. 'Has Kathryn told you that everything relating to Woodlands is to be packed up and shipped back to St Felix?'

'Yes. She tells me that you plan to set up some sort of museum.'

'It's David's plan and I have given it my full support. If he is to take the estates forward, then I need to give him the freedom to make such decisions.' Richard lowered his head, closer to Barbara's. 'I hope Kathryn isn't upset by the decision. She tells me that she understands, but I know how attached she has become to our fusty old documents.'

'As far as I can tell, Kathryn is fine with the decision. And she's very touched by your offer of funding her travel to St Felix, if she ever wishes to visit.'

The old man nodded, content. 'And you, Barbara? How do you feel about it? I know that you have strong views of your own on the way our family made its fortunes.'

'It's not for me to agree or disagree. The decision is yours and David's to make. But, if pushed, I will admit that I can't help wondering whether David is simply trying to bury the past by shipping it back to St Felix. He's always felt uncomfortable about the Lancefield heritage, hasn't he? And in a sense I can understand that he might just want to send everything back to the Caribbean so that he doesn't have to be reminded.'

'You don't agree that the items belong in St Felix?'

'I didn't say that. It's just that the family's history is an important part of British history too. How will people here really come to understand what happened in the past if all the evidence is hidden away where it can't be seen?'

'I don't think that particular consideration is at the forefront of David's mind.' They had reached the farthest point of the lake, and Richard slowed his step to turn and look back at the house. 'How was David when you last saw him? He seemed well enough to me when I spoke to him yesterday evening, but I couldn't help wondering if it was an act.'

'I don't know. I know that he found it difficult to clear out Stella's belongings, and he still has angry moments when he rails against the unfairness of it all. But most of the time he just seems sad. And a little lonely.' She narrowed her eyes. 'But the grieving process isn't linear, is it? All that anger is still in him, just waiting for the moment that they finally run her killer to ground.' She leaned a little closer to Richard. 'Do you think they are any closer to catching Zak Smith?'

'I doubt it. I'm sure that Inspector Price is doing everything he can, but Smith is a slippery beggar. He has all the cunning of a poacher; he knows how to keep his head down, how to stay out of sight, even how to live rough under the stars if necessary. And I doubt that his family would give him away. But they can hardly be blamed for that. They have endured losses of their own.' Richard looked up at the sky, and the gathering clouds. 'Perhaps we should make our way back to the house.' He began to walk slowly along the path, Barbara in tandem beside him. 'There is no question that Stella's death has changed David, and it is a relief that he has not descended into self-pity. But I hope that he will not become too cold. Too hard.' It had never occurred to Richard that those softer qualities he once despised in his son – the kind gentleness of his nature – would be something he would want to preserve. 'I suppose a death must change all of us, one way and another.' And lead to new beginnings. 'Tell me, Barbara, have you given any more thought to the idea of moving to Penwithen?'

Barbara's lips curled into an inscrutable smile and she pulled mischievously on Richard's arm. 'If I say "no" to your offer of a permanent home at Salvation Hall, will you still send Nancy back to St Felix?'

4

DS Marwick watched as Laurence Payne took the seat opposite, and tried to measure him up. Forty, maybe forty-five; tall, with pale skin, thick dark hair and piercing, almost mesmeric, blue eyes. Groomed and well-heeled – the policeman thought he could detect a trace of Jermyn Street in the blue paisley shirt and cashmere jacket – the hand he extended for Marwick to shake was soft and manicured, but his grasp was a firm one.

They were sitting at a corner table in the Firkin and Frog, one of the popular wine bars that lined the gentrified quayside, and Marwick gave an almost apologetic tilt of the head as he spoke. 'Sorry about the informal surroundings, Mr Payne. The manager has been good enough to give us free use of the premises for the rest of the day, as a temporary base.' He pointed towards the bar. 'Can I get you a coffee, while we chat?'

Payne put up a hand. 'No, I'm fine, thanks.' His voice was rich and smooth, with a hint of anxiety. 'I hope our chat will be a brief one. I only came down here because the staff at the Excelsior suggested it.' He drew in a breath, and blew it out again slowly. 'I'm looking for my cousin. She failed to call me this morning, as arranged, and she seems to have disappeared from her hotel. They tell me that her bed hasn't been slept in.' He looked down at his manicured fingernails. 'They also told me that you've found a woman's body in the dock.' He let out a short, low-pitched laugh. 'I'm sure it can't be her, but…'

'But you have no other explanation?' Marwick felt a little thrill of anticipation. 'Could you describe your cousin for me, Mr Payne?'

'Of course. She's in her early thirties, slim build, medium height, blonde.' He hesitated. 'Do you think it might be her?'

The sergeant swerved the question. 'Can I ask when you last saw her?'

'Yesterday evening, just after midnight. We had dinner at a restaurant farther along the quayside. At Vincenzo's.'

'And what she was wearing?'

'Navy woollen trousers and a chiffon blouse. It had frills at the collar and cuffs.'

'Was she wearing a coat?'

'No. She had a shawl, one of those pashmina things. Burnt orange. The same colour as her handbag.'

Marwick pulled a small notebook and a pen from his jacket pocket. 'Can you describe the bag for me?' He flipped the notebook open and began to write. 'Was it large or small?'

'Quite a large one. Soft leather.'

'With a shoulder strap?'

'No. It was a handbag, not a shoulder bag.' Laurence Payne leaned across the table. 'I would like to know if the body you have found is my cousin.'

'You said she was staying at the Excelsior. Did you walk her back to the hotel after you had dinner?'

'Yes.'

'Did you see her go into the hotel?'

'No. The entrance is at the front of the building.' Payne licked his lips. 'When I say I walked her to the hotel, I walked her along the quayside to the rear of the hotel. We parted company at the footbridge. She was happy to go the last few yards on her own. She only had to walk down the side of the hotel and round the corner of the building.'

'And where did you go?'

'Back to my flat, of course.'

'And where is that?'

'Canary Wharf. Around a ten-minute walk from here.' Payne's handsome face paled. 'It's her, isn't it?'

Marwick's pen stopped moving, and he put it down on top of the notebook with a sigh. 'With regret, based on the information that you've just given me, I think it's possible.'

'Possible, or probable?'

There was no easy way to answer. 'Probable.'

Payne slumped forward in his seat and covered his face with trembling hands. Eventually he lifted his head and said, 'Where is she now?'

'The body's been taken to the local mortuary.' Marwick spoke very quietly. 'Mr Payne, would you be prepared to identify her for us?'

'Of course I would.' The man's composure was returning. 'If, in return, you would stop referring to her as "the body".'

The policeman picked up his notebook and pen and slipped them back into his pocket. 'I'm sorry if it sounds disrespectful. I'm afraid I can't use her name until we have a positive identification.' He pushed his chair away from the table and stood up. 'I can drive you over to the mortuary now, if you're prepared to come with me?' The words sounded brusque and he felt a sudden pang of shame. 'It's only routine, Mr Payne, and I'm sorry if it sounds insensitive.' He placed a hand on the man's shoulder. 'What *was* your cousin's name?'

*

'I do think you might have told me first.' Nancy scowled her disappointment and leaned against the doorframe, her hands clasped loosely in front of her. 'After all, I am still your secretary.'

'And Kathryn is currently responsible for the family's heritage and history. That will not always be the case. But while it is, I would like her to manage things.' Richard clicked his teeth. 'And if you are coming into the orchid house to speak to me, Nancy, please do so. You are letting the warm air out, and the cold air in.' He waved a hand towards the crumbling Lloyd Loom chair beside the door. 'You are welcome to sit.'

Chastened, Nancy stepped forward to let the door swing shut behind her. 'It isn't just the telling of things. How am I to complete my own research, with all the documents in St Felix?' She sank onto the chair. 'I'm making such good progress, and Kathryn agrees with me that we should produce a composite family tree: one showing not just the legitimate Lancefield family tree for the Woodlands estate, but the illegitimate members too.'

The old man bristled, and turned his head slowly to look at her. 'And what, pray, do you mean to infer by that statement?'

She lifted her chin with a mischievous smile. 'That Kathryn and I are in accord.'

'Please do not be insolent. You know very well that is not what I meant.'

Her face crumpled. 'Forgive me, Richard. It was not my intention.' She glowered down at her fingers. 'But you know as well as I, that the families belonging to Woodlands are connected in many ways. There has never been any secret that your ancestor, Benedict Lancefield, took a Creole lady's maid for his mistress. And his granddaughter, Isabella, ran off with…'

'Tush.' Richard shook his head and put down the orchid he was tending. 'You are saying these things to annoy me, and it will not do.' He pulled a small wooden stool out from under the potting bench and sat down on it. 'Now, what is this really about?' As if he couldn't guess.

'You are sending all evidence of St Felix back to the island. After I took such time and care to help you bring it over to England. And I do not understand why.'

'There are plans afoot of which you are not yet aware. The documents and artefacts are being shipped back because it is David's wish. And it is *my* wish that you should take care of them for us in the future.'

The implications of the simple statement took a few moments to register. And then Nancy's eyes widened almost imperceptibly and she arched her neck. 'But in order to do that, I would have to return to St Felix.'

'And that should not be a hardship for you. St Felix is your home. It is where you belong. You knew when I invited you to work here as my secretary that the role was not open-ended. You knew that one day it would be time for you to return home.'

'But it's been ten years. I have built a life here in England now. A life with you. And with David.'

'Perhaps.' Richard ran his tongue thoughtfully around his teeth. 'But you have always told me that it is your pleasure to serve the family. And it is my belief now that you can best serve us in St Felix.'

'Is Marcus unhappy with his new role running the estate?'

'No. But he will not have time to manage our new venture on top of everything else. We intend to establish a museum and educational facility on the island. And it is my express wish that you should manage both the creation and future of that facility.'

'A museum and educational facility?' Doubt flickered into the dark, expressive eyes. 'You want me to go home to St Felix to create a museum?'

'I want you to *own* the family's history and heritage. The w*hole* family's history and heritage. I will give you carte blanche to create a museum and centre of learning to your own specification, on condition that it brings maximum benefit to the people of St Felix.' The old man relaxed forward and dropped his forearms onto his knees. 'Nancy, this is bigger than the family. The project needs your expertise. You are a native of St Felix, you understand the island and its people and you have an in-depth knowledge of the family's heritage.' He studied her face as he spoke. Her features were impassive, but he knew that the cogs in that quick, sharp brain were turning to consider the opportunity. And he gave one last, gentle push. '*All* of the family's heritage.'

'I see.' Her brow wrinkled. 'Would Marcus have ultimate responsibility for the project? As the estate's manager?'

'No. The project will be funded by the estate, but we hope it will proceed in collaboration with other bodies on the island. David is planning to sound out the board of education and some of the neighbouring plantation owners this week, while he is out there. We intend it to benefit the whole island, not just Woodlands. And you would have sole responsibility on our behalf.' He still couldn't tell if she had taken the bait. 'Of course, you will need time to consider.'

'Of course.' Nancy repeated his words with a lick of the lips. 'And where would Eva fit in to this proposed scenario?'

Ah, the inevitable question. 'We have no plans to offer Eva any formal role on the Woodlands estate. Why would we? Eva has a significant career of her own, and no intention of relinquishing it.' At least not for a job. Richard hadn't yet given up on the hope that Eva's blossoming romance with Marcus might lead to a very different sort of role for her. But that was nothing to do with Nancy. 'Does that answer your question?'

Not if the girl's expression was anything to go by. 'You know that my first thought is always to serve the family. But I hoped to always be here in Penwithen, to support you.'

It was a pretty sentiment and, he was sure, a sincere

one. 'You will always be welcome to visit Salvation Hall whenever you wish, Nancy.' More than that he was not prepared to say.

At least, until the time was right.

*

The thin, gold bangles around Amber Kimbrall's wrist jangled musically as she lifted the pint of best Cornish ale and slid it across the bar. 'We don't normally see you in here when you're off duty, Inspector Price. Always assuming that you are off duty.'

Price dug his hand into the back pocket of his jeans and pulled out his wallet. 'Even a policeman needs a kind word and a pint now and again.'

She put up a hand as he pulled a note from the wallet. 'No, this one's on the house. I'm feeling generous today.' She offered him a coy smile. 'Didn't you see the new nameplate above the door when you came in?'

'Amber Kimbrall, Licensee?' Price grinned. 'Of course I saw it.' And a fine choice Richard Lancefield had made when he decided to put her in charge of The Lancefield Arms. According to Kathryn, it had been the old man's way of thanking the girl for the bravery she had shown in trying to bring his daughter-in-law's killer to justice. 'Your very good health, Amber. I hope it works out for you.' He sipped thoughtfully on the ale. 'What happened to Harry?'

'They gave him three months' notice to quit, and I can't say he took it well. But he lined up a new place quickly, and they let him go early. He's got the tenancy of The Black Swan.'

'That place on the Newlyn road that's just been refurbished?'

'Yes, that's the one.' She leaned an arm on the bar and craned her neck forward, enveloping the detective in a cloud of familiar, musky perfume. 'But you didn't answer my question. About being off duty.'

It was a fair cop. 'Officially, I'm off duty. Though unofficially, it never really happens. I came in because I was hoping to have a quiet word with you.'

'With me?' The suggestion seemed to puzzle her, and then her eyes grew wary. 'Is this about Zak? You haven't found him?'

'No.' How he wished the answer could be yes. 'I wanted to know if you'd heard anything from him?'

Now she laughed. 'Me? He won't contact me, Inspector Price. I'm the woman who took his gun away and called the police while he was sleeping.'

'And very brave you were. If it hadn't been for you, we would never have had the gun that killed Stella Lancefield. You gave us the forensic evidence to tie that crime to Zak, Amber. And I'll never forget that.'

'Well, I couldn't let him get away with it, could I?' Her plump cheeks dimpled. 'But the evidence alone isn't enough, is it? You still have to catch him.'

As if he needed reminding. 'It's not as if we haven't tried.' In the months that Smith had been on the run they had scoured most of Cornwall and half of Devon, and stretched out feelers into Somerset and Dorset, but all to no avail. 'I suppose that's really why I wanted to have a word with you. Apart from his family, you're probably the person who knows Zak the best. If anyone knows what I've missed, it's likely to be you.'

She let out a sigh. 'I've already told you everything I can think of, Inspector Price. You've searched his lockup. And I've given you the names and addresses of as many of his dodgy contacts as I could remember.'

'But where do *you* think he is? I can't believe that you don't think about him. Wonder where he went.' Price couldn't bring himself to say, wonder if he's going to come back for you. 'He can't just disappear into thin air. And my guess is that someone is shielding him.' He watched her face as she considered the possibility. 'Did you know that

Becca Smith is leaving Penzance and moving to Truro?'

'I heard on the grapevine. She doesn't speak to me now, so I won't hold my breath for an invitation to the housewarming party.' Amber gave a shrug. 'But good luck to her, I say. She's had her fair share of pain in all of this, losing Philip the way she did. She can't help what her brother is.' The landlady shook her head. 'You know, Zak was a lot of things, but I never had him down as a killer. And it shakes you up, Inspector Price, realising that you've shared your bed with a man who's capable of taking a life.'

Of taking more than one life. 'What do you think made him do it? What would make him kill? Do you believe his story, that Marcus Drake offered him twenty thousand to murder Eva McWhinney?'

'I couldn't imagine Zak doing anything for Marcus Drake. He hated him. Unless he could think of a way to take the money and stitch Marcus up in the process. The money alone might not have been enough, but maybe the feeling of power... of getting one over on Marcus.' She looked suddenly crestfallen. 'It's only now that I realise how abusive he was. How dangerous he was. He never raised his hand to me – except that one time when I tried to hand him over to the police. But I suppose deep down I knew he was capable of it.' She shook her head with a sigh. 'If anyone in the family is shielding him, it could only be Becca. I had Robin Smith in here last week. He's a nice boy, too good for that family. He called in to see how I was. And he told me that if he had his way, Zak would hand himself in. The whole family has been affected. Mick's wife is threatening to leave him and take the kids with her. She doesn't want to be mixed up with a murderer's family. And their mother is heartbroken. No, I think he's burnt his bridges now where his family is concerned.' Amber let her words settle, and then pointed to Price's emptying glass. 'Can I get you a refill?'

He shook his head and drained off the dregs. 'Another time. I need to keep a clear head today. But I appreciated this one.' He put the glass down on the bar. 'We're doing everything we can to find him, Amber. And when we do, you'll be among the first to know. But until that happens, please look after yourself.'

5

Laurence Payne put his hands on the back of a nearby chair to steady himself. 'I'm sorry. It's the shock.' And shock it had clearly been, for the man to see his cousin lying dead on a mortuary table.

Bob Marwick put a hand into his jacket pocket and fished out a packet of mints. 'Take your time, Mr Payne. It might help if you take a seat.' He offered the packet to Laurence.

'Thank you, no.' They were in a small, clinical waiting room and Laurence pulled the chair away from the only table and sat down on it. 'Nothing prepares you for death, does it? I can hardly believe that I was having dinner with her yesterday evening, and now she's gone. She was so... alive. So animated. There was no reason...'

The sergeant shoved the mints back into his pocket and pulled out his notebook and pen. 'Would you mind?' He sat down at the table without waiting for an answer, flipping open the notebook. 'Anything you can tell me now will be an enormous help to the investigation. Name – Eva McWhinney. Age?'

'Thirty-four, I believe.'

'Address?'

'Number three, Hemlock Row, Edinburgh.'

'Occupation.'

'She was a consultant cardiologist at the Edinburgh Royal Infirmary.'

Marwick, surprised, looked up from his notebook. 'Next of kin?'

There was an unexpected pause and then Laurence said, 'I think it's me. She's not married, her parents are dead, and she has no siblings. I'm not aware of any other cousins closer than myself. Apart from the Lancefields, and I don't know whether they are technically closer to her in kinship than I am.'

'The Lancefields?'

'Richard and David. They're very distant cousins to both of us, although I've never spoken with them directly. Eva only became aware of them towards the end of last year, but she's grown quite close to them. In fact, that's why she and I were meeting. They're trying to document the family's history, and Eva asked me to provide her with some additional information relating to my branch of the family.'

'So they knew that she was meeting with you this weekend?'

'No. She wanted it to be a surprise.'

A surprise? Marwick put down his pen. 'Why would she want to do that?'

'I don't know. Now I think about it, it does sound rather odd, though I didn't attach too much significance to it at the time.'

'So, whose idea was it to actually meet up in person?'

The question appeared to throw Laurence Payne. He considered it for a moment, the mesmeric eyes glazed, and then said, 'It was Eva's.'

'And to the best of your knowledge, no one else of her acquaintance knew that she was going to be in London?'

'I don't know. I can't speak for her work colleagues or her friends. I only know that the Lancefields didn't know she was coming.' He fixed Marwick with a penetrating gaze. 'Do you have any idea at all what happened to her? Did she fall into the quay? Did she drown?'

'I'm afraid I can't release any details of her death at the moment.' Marwick pushed his chair backwards, away from the table. 'But there is something I can share with you. In fact, I'd be interested to know what you make of it.' He stood up and crossed the room to a small cupboard. 'When Eva was found, this was around her neck.' He lifted a large, clear plastic bag from the cupboard's top, and carried it over to Laurence. 'We don't understand the relevance of it. But I'm guessing that she wasn't wearing it the last time you saw her.' He placed the bag down on the table.

The effect on Laurence was profound. His chiselled face contorted, and for a moment it looked as though he might be sick. And then he raised his eyes to the policeman's face. 'You say this was around her neck?'

'Yes.'

'While she was in the water?'

'Yes.'

Laurence puffed out a breath to steady himself and pulled the bag towards him to examine the contents more closely. 'Seven feathers and five flowers, garlanded. A small glass bottle. And a monkey's skull.'

'You talk as if you recognise it.'

'I do.' He turned the bag over. 'At least, I recognise what I think it is intended to represent.'

'Which is?'

'An Obeah garland.'

'I'm sorry?'

'It's a poor imitation, of course. The feathers appear to be synthetic, as do the flowers. And the bottle seems only to contain liquid. There would normally be some sort of insect in there, usually a cockroach.' Laurence pulled gently on the plastic bag, teasing it away from the contents. 'And the skull is obviously a plastic replica. I suppose it might have come from an educational establishment, something designed for use in veterinary study?' He turned inquisitive eyes to the policeman. 'This was definitely around Eva's neck?'

'Yes. I'm sorry, you said "Obeah".' Marwick was beginning to lose the thread. 'What is that, exactly?'

'It's magic, Sergeant Marwick. Caribbean witchcraft.'

The policeman's laugh was spontaneous: a loud, dismissive snort of incredulity. 'Witchcraft? What kind of a joke is that?'

Laurence pouted, and pushed the bag away again. 'I can assure you, there is nothing amusing about this. Quite the contrary, I would suggest. At best, it is an omen of ill fortune.'

'And at worst?'

'A warning of evil intent.'

Marwick leaned back in his seat and folded his arms. 'Is this some sort of a game, Mr Payne?'

'I have never been more serious in my life.'

Could the policeman believe him? 'Would your cousin, Eva, have known what this was?'

'I very much doubt it. Her line of the family were medical people, and far more rooted in the scientific.'

'While your line of the family…?'

'Had two strings to their bow, Sergeant Marwick. Their primary skill was in making money. Vast amounts of money that they used to fund their other interests.' Payne shifted in his seat. 'Those other interests were a little less conventional. My family have always had very close connections to the esoteric.'

'I'm sorry?'

'The occult, Sergeant. My family have always been experts in the mystical and the arcane. So if anyone should recognise this garland, it wouldn't be Eva. It would be me.'

*

The garden storeroom at Salvation Hall was damp and smelled of decay.

'There's no heating in here, is there? And not much in the way of light.' Barbara gave a tentative sniff and wrinkled her nose in disapproval. 'You know, I haven't been in here since David first showed me around the Salvation Hall estate. I can't say I've been keen to come back.' She shivered at the thought. 'I took one look at a set of iron manacles and that was it. I couldn't get out of the place quickly enough.'

'And now I've coaxed you back in here to help me.' Kathryn, behind her, had begun to rifle through a tea chest. 'Try to think of those things against the wall as nothing more than rusty old agricultural tools. Because for the most part, that's what they are. Just things that were used for growing and harvesting sugar cane.'

'You make it sound so innocent.' Barbara turned to look at the tools in question. 'For pity's sake, is that a machete?' She picked up the offending item and examined it a little more closely. 'Why on earth did Richard ship this over here? It's barbaric.'

'It's not barbaric. It was used for cutting the sugar cane.' Kathryn lifted her eyes from the tea chest. 'He brought it because he intended to document everything relevant to Woodlands – not just the family's history, but how the plantation operated.' She pulled a small cardboard box out of the chest and peered into it. 'I think this crate is full of china. We'll probably have to repack everything. I wouldn't want any of it to break on the way back to St Felix.' She glanced across at Barbara. 'Do you know much about sugar production in the eighteenth and nineteenth centuries?'

Barbara gave her a withering look. 'I can't say it's ever been on my radar.'

'It was very labour-intensive. They had to dig deep holes or trenches to plant the canes, and then fertilise them by hand using animal manure. Then, once the cane had grown and matured, it had to be cut by hand with machetes like the one you're holding, and loaded onto a cart for transporting to the mill.'

'By slaves.'

'Yes, by slaves.' Kathryn sighed. 'The cane had to be crushed in the mill to extract the juice…'

'Please don't tell me that they used slave-labour to power the mill.'

'Heavens, no. They used horses or cattle in the early days, then as they became more established plantations would build a windmill. In later years, some even invested in steam engines.'

Barbara put the machete back on the floor, leaning it gently against the wall. 'When I was a little girl, my granny used to talk about the family's fortune being lost in a game of cards. The family we were descended from were very wealthy, she said, but their business was a secret. They traded in precious goods to the West Indies, but they couldn't talk about it. I had no idea, until I discovered our link to the Lancefields, that the precious cargo was human flesh. And that far from being lost in a game of cards, our share of the fortune went to another branch of the family because our Lancefield ancestor had the basic human decency to turn his back on the slave trade.'

'I know it was a shock to you to learn the truth.' Kathryn straightened her back and rubbed at the bottom of her spine with her fingers. 'There is so much to do here. All of these tea chests to be emptied and repacked. And that's before we tackle the ironwork.' She glanced around her. 'I think we might have to ask Ennor to help with that. It's not the sort of thing you could ask a stranger to help with.'

Barbara sat down on the edge of a sturdy packing crate. 'Do you think that Richard is right to ask Nancy to take care of all of this?'

'It depends what you mean by "right".' Though Kathryn had to admit she had been asking herself the same question. 'She certainly has the ability to set up the foundation, and it will be a fantastic opportunity for her. She loves the family's heritage and doesn't share your squeamishness at the more disagreeable items. The question really is how she feels about going back. I think she was hoping to stay on here, at Salvation Hall.'

'Does Marcus know that she'll be returning to Woodlands for good?'

'I don't know. But I hope so.'

'There's an awkwardness between them now, isn't there?'

That was one word for it. 'They haven't always seen eye to eye. But I try not to think about it. They muddle through, somehow.' Kathryn moved on to the next packing case. 'Has Richard said any more about you moving to Penwithen?' It was a clumsy attempt to change the subject.

'Yes, he's offered to refurbish Holly Cottage for me, so that I could have my privacy.'

'And does that make a difference?'

'Possibly. If I accepted, I would probably rent out my home in Liverpool, just in case it didn't work out and I wanted to go back. Though now that Dennis is gone and Jason is in prison, I'm not sure what I would go back for. Perhaps I just have to accept that Richard and David are my family now. And Nancy.' She cast a sideways glance at Kathryn. 'Nancy is really a part of the family too, isn't she? She's much more than a secretary.'

Was Barbara fishing, or had Richard already shared the secret with her? Kathryn shrugged the question away, and began to examine the contents of the packing case. 'The way Nancy sees it, everyone at Woodlands is part of one large, extended family. And in so many ways she is right. The lives and relationships of everyone on the estate are so tightly interwoven.'

'That doesn't extend to Eva, though, does it? Nancy can't hide the way she feels about her. It's in her eyes, the way she looks at her. I wondered if it was because Eva and Marcus were growing close. That perhaps Nancy had feelings for Marcus herself, and that's why they were so awkward together?'

*

'Two calls in one day?' DCI Price, back home in the comfort of his study, welcomed the caller with an unseen smile. 'What have I done to deserve that?'

'I just wanted to make sure you weren't napping on the job.' DCI Grant's gravelly Scottish burr purred down the phone line. 'That, and I wanted to sound you out about something.' She sounded hesitant. 'My boss wants me to make another trip to Cornwall.'

Price took a moment to think about it. And then he said, 'Not that we wouldn't be delighted to see you, Alyson, but what does he think that would achieve?' Given that her last two trips hadn't brought them any closer to finding Zak Smith.

She snuffled a laugh. 'Who knows? He's just getting twitchy. I gave him an update this afternoon, and he's delighted that you've given us more evidence to build a case, but he's bending my ear about not having a suspect in custody to pin it on. I think he thinks a miracle will occur if I travel down to Penwithen.'

'And what do you think?'

'I know that you're doing everything you can. But I have to be seen to make an effort. Smith committed a cold-blooded murder on our patch, and we have no control over the search for him because he's on yours.' She sniffed loudly. 'And it is meant to be a joint investigation.'

He couldn't argue with that. 'I still feel the pressure is on me, Alyson. It isn't your fault that Smith slipped through my fingers.' Or that Price might be facing an investigation into his conduct for a serious lapse of judgement by tethering Eva McWhinney to Salvation Hall in the hope of drawing out a killer. He pushed the thought from his mind. 'I spoke to Amber Kimbrall again this afternoon. She knows Smith better than most, and I thought she might be able to give me more insight into how his mind works. But she's as stumped as we are. She can't think of any reason he would target Eva, and she has no idea where he might be holed up.'

'How the hell has he managed to keep his head down for so long?'

'He's had plenty of practice. He's lived such an itinerant lifestyle that going on the run would be easy for him. He's always given his mother's address as his permanent residence, but he mostly spent his time either sleeping at Amber's or dossing down on other people's sofas after drinking sessions.' They had even found a grubby pillow and duvet at his lockup, which suggested that he thought nothing of sleeping on the shabby recliner in the garage when the need arose. 'Add that to his love of the outdoors, his skills as a nighttime poacher...'

'And you've checked with everyone and anyone who might be shielding him? Family and friends?'

'We've checked out the homes and workplaces of anyone who's been known to give him houseroom in the past. But even most of his family don't want to know.' At least, that was the story they were peddling. Price blew out his frustration and stared down at the notes on his desk, a handwritten catalogue of ideas and disappointments. 'The lockup is off limits to him now we've secured it. So he's either sleeping rough, or he's in a hotel or doss house somewhere.' They had scoured every possibility from Lands End to the county's border. Even a half-hearted push into Devon had yielded nothing for Price but a reprimand for his failure to manage the overtime budget. 'The bastard could be anywhere.'

'He would need money to pay for accommodation. Where would he get that?'

'Who knows? On the night he went missing, he drew five hundred pounds – the maximum possible – from each of his two bank accounts at a cash machine in Helston.' Though how the hell he had travelled the fourteen miles to get there was anybody's guess. 'That thousand pounds wouldn't have lasted long, but neither of his bank accounts, nor his credit card, have been used since. We left the accounts open under close monitoring, but he wouldn't dare use them. He's not particularly bright, but streetwise enough to know that we'll be watching.'

'I suppose someone could be funding him? Just because his family and friends won't give him houseroom doesn't mean one of them wouldn't help him out with some cash. They might even be paying him to stay away, to avoid causing more distress for the family. After all, most of them are giving the impression that they're shunning him, but they're not squealing, either. What about his sister?'

'We still have her under surveillance. She moved to a new address in Truro this afternoon. We kept tabs on her, but there was nothing to report. Her brother, Robin, drove her over there.' Another chunk of the overtime budget spent in vain. Price drummed his fingers impatiently on the desk. 'And before you ask, we're still all over the family's mobile phone records.'

'I thought you said he hadn't used his mobile phone since the night of Stella Lancefield's murder?'

'He hasn't. We're assuming he's acquired a burner phone, though we haven't any evidence so far of any of his family taking or making calls from an unrecognised number.' *A burner phone?* Price winced, and his spirits sank. 'And that's your cue.'

'I know.' Grant sounded almost apologetic. 'Only you didn't mention it when we spoke earlier, so you know I have to ask.'

'Of course I know.' There was nothing to be served by playing dumb. 'You're going to ask me now if we've traced the original burner phone.'

6

'So, this Laurence Payne and the victim are cousins. They've only exchanged Christmas cards in the past, they've never met before this weekend, and the first time she comes to London to meet up with him she ends up in the North Dock?' DCI Greenway whistled under his breath. 'How does that sound to you, Bob?'

'Unlucky?' Marwick knew it wasn't the word that Greenway was looking for, but the day had been a long one, and he was in no mood to say 'suspicious' just to offer Payne up as a convenient scapegoat. Not after putting in the lion's share of the legwork while Chris Greenway kicked his heels in the office. 'He reckons it was her idea to meet up. She wanted to know something about their shared family history.'

'She travelled all the way from Edinburgh to London to talk to a virtual stranger about dead people?'

The sergeant nodded as he consulted his notebook. 'She and Laurence Payne are distantly related to a family called Lancefield, who live in Cornwall. She wanted information about Payne's line of the family to pass on to them.'

'Because?'

'The head of the family, Richard Lancefield, is

documenting his family history.' Marwick turned the page in his notebook. 'Payne doesn't know much about them, other than there is just a father and son, Richard and David, and they are wealthy, influential and connected to him by a common ancestor.'

'In Cornwall?'

'In the Caribbean. An island called St Felix.'

Greenway folded his arms across his chest. 'It all sounds a bit fanciful, doesn't it? Still, we've got a positive ID and a name and address to be going on with. What about next of kin?'

'He isn't sure. She was single and an only child, and her parents died several years ago. So, it's either himself, or the Lancefields.'

'No other family? Aunts, uncles, cousins?'

'No. That's why she was so keen to hook up with the Lancefields. She doesn't have anyone else.'

'Apart from Laurence Payne.'

'And a possible boyfriend. She told Payne yesterday evening that she's grown close to David Lancefield's stepson.' He glanced down again at his notebook. 'Marcus Drake.'

'And he's in Cornwall?'

'At the moment he's in the Caribbean, managing a plantation estate for the family.'

Greenway grunted. 'Alright for some.' He ran his tongue thoughtfully around his teeth. 'Have we had any luck at the hotel?'

'Nothing that gives us a lead. Her room has been searched and nothing obvious found. All of her belongings are there, with three notable exceptions – the pashmina and handbag she was using yesterday evening when she met with her cousin, and her mobile phone, which we're assuming was in the handbag. Though we do have the number now, thanks to Laurence Payne, so we can try for a trace and follow up on her phone records.'

'Nothing out of the ordinary reported by the hotel

staff?'

'No. The manager I spoke to confirmed Payne's story: that he visited the hotel to look for Eva, and after confirming that her room was empty they advised him to speak to us.'

Greenway stared into space for a moment, and then he bent forward and rested his elbows on the desk. 'Any sniff of a motive?'

'Not a motive. But he knew something about that paraphernalia that was draped around her neck.'

'The feathers?'

'He reckons they are something to do with Obeah.'

'Come again?'

'Obeah. It's some sort of Caribbean witchcraft.'

The inspector coughed out a laugh. 'Bloody hell, Bob, I know it's been a long day, but… witchcraft? Is that some sort of wind-up?'

'No, he was deadly serious. He claims to be an expert in the occult. He's studied it widely, written about it, even acted as a consultant on occasion.'

'Who the hell needs a consultant in the occult?'

Marwick didn't have the answer. 'He identified the garland straight away. He said it was a replica of a charm used on St Felix in the eighteenth and nineteenth centuries. The original would have used feathers from a parrot or a parakeet, and hibiscus flowers. The bottle of liquid would have contained rum and an insect, probably a cockroach.'

'And the skull?'

'Usually a rat or a mongoose. And it wasn't a benevolent charm. It was a hex. A curse to bring ill fortune.'

'How the hell can he be so certain?'

'Because as well as being an expert in the subject, his Caribbean ancestors had to deal with Obeah, and it's documented in family papers still in his possession.'

'Did Eva know about that?'

'He didn't think so.'

Greenway smiled, a slow curve of the lips. 'So, let me see if I've got this right. The victim had never met her cousin before yesterday, no one knew she was going to meet him, at this point we believe he was the last person to see her alive, and he has the specialised knowledge to identify that thing that was hanging around her neck. A thing so unusual that we'd probably have to go all the way to the Caribbean to find anyone else who might have a clue what it was?'

'It's too obvious, boss. And why hang the thing around her neck at all? He'd just be drawing attention to himself.'

'Why claim that it's some sort of hex, as if he's an expert in it, when for all we know if could be a complete piece of hokum designed by her killer to throw us off the scent? How do we know that Laurence Payne didn't just make all that rubbish up to cover up what could be a very simple, very uncomplicated case of murder?'

*

Richard pressed the remote control with his thumb and squinted at the television as the grainy black and white image filled the screen. 'Barbara, my dear, you will have to take charge of these controls.' She was sitting on the sofa, and he leaned out of his armchair towards her. 'My old fingers are simply not deft enough for the job.'

She took the remote from him with a smile. 'I must admit to being intrigued. When you invited me over to the Dower House for supper, I thought we were just going to spend the evening chatting. I had no idea we were going to watch home movies.' She pressed the play button before settling back against the sofa's cushions. 'When was this film made?'

'In nineteen thirty-four. I was just a toddler then.' He pointed at the screen. 'Now, look at that. Isn't that marvellous?' He let out a sigh. 'That's the front elevation of the plantation house. And that's my father standing on the steps, with me in his arms.'

Barbara paused the film and turned to look at him. 'You must have seen this film before?'

'Not for many a year. Kathryn found the old reel of cine film in a packing crate in the storeroom, and had it copied onto a disc for me so that I could watch it again. I couldn't have been more pleased when she told me.' The old man's eyes were still fixed on the television's screen. 'My father was a fine man, in his own way. Not harsh, but distant, you know? Children were to be seen and not heard.'

'And your mother?'

'The same.' He spoke without any hint of resentment. 'They weren't unkind, you understand? Just the product of their time. But it was a lonely upbringing for an only child. I had a nanny, Delia, when I was a small boy. And then a governess, Alice, who travelled everywhere with me. Both very kind. But they were not my mother.' The words were tinged with sadness. 'I suppose my parents were just repeating a pattern. In their circles, children were necessary to carry on the line, the family name. Not something to be loved and enjoyed. They tried for a second child to support me, I believe, but it didn't happen for them.' His voice took on a wistful note. 'I worry sometimes that I have visited the same disadvantage upon David. I have seen him too much as the future of the estates, and not the man he is.'

'If that truly worries you, there is still time to make up for it.'

'Which is why I am giving him the opportunity to make his own decisions about the future of the estates. I see now that he has to own them in more than name only, in order to take them forward.'

'And I'm sure he will make a splendid job of it.' Barbara flicked the remote control at the screen again, entranced as the film crackled into life and the infant Richard waved at the camera with an uncertain smile. 'You looked like a very solemn little boy.' The image panned out to show the wide, canopied porch that ran the length of the plantation house and then cut to a different scene: an idyllic, sandy bay fringed with rocks and palm trees. 'Oh, that looks wonderful. What a pity it's only in black and white.'

'That's Quintard Bay. Where your ancestor Digory Banks anchored The Redemption when he was refused permission to bring his cargo ashore.' Richard lowered his head. 'It was a sorry episode, Barbara. And I quite understand why it would cloud your opinion of the family. But we cannot change the past. Only live in the present and resolve to do better in the future.'

She couldn't argue with the sentiment. 'You miss St Felix very much, don't you?'

'With all of my heart. I was born on the island and it's my true home. I haven't been able to visit for several years now. My doctor has forbidden me to make the journey, though I'm sure he has my best interests at heart.'

'Have you ever thought of disobeying him?'

'Oh, many times.' The old man laughed. 'Have you given any more thought to the idea of moving into Holly Cottage?'

'Touché.' Barbara paused the film a second time. 'I was rather hoping for a little time to think about it. You only made the suggestion this afternoon.'

'I know. But it's much on my mind.' He studied her face. 'You know that I'll wear you down until you say "yes".'

'And you know that I'll probably agree in the end. But I have to be sure. It's a big decision, and I have to be sure that I'm doing it for the right reasons.'

'I would hope that David would be the right reason. I know that the family's wealth doesn't interest you, Barbara, and that does you great credit. You may not want the material wealth that the Lancefields can offer you, but David is your cousin. Your family. Surely that is worth having.'

Worth having? When she had lost her beloved Dennis, the cousin so cruelly taken from her by the greed of the young man he loved like his own son? 'Richard, you're an old rogue. You know there is a Dennis-shaped hole in my life that David could fill.' If he hadn't already begun to fill it. 'Tell me, if Nancy is to go back to St Felix for good, who is going to fill the Nancy-shaped hole in *your* life?'

He gave an enigmatic smile. 'If a replacement was necessary, I would hope it would be Kathryn.'

'And will Kathryn cook your supper, as well as walking the dog and acting as your secretary?'

'Of course not. But I am encouraging Amber Kimbrall to improve the kitchen at The Lancefield Arms. Then we can all send down to the village for our supper.' He was teasing her now. 'Unless you were thinking of volunteering your own services?'

'And you expect me to dignify that question with an answer?' Her tone was suddenly gentle. 'When we both know that you don't intend to be here to enjoy my cooking?'

The question was met with a momentary silence. 'So, you have guessed my secret.' The old man's face straightened. 'Would you judge me harshly for wanting to grow orchids in St Felix while I still have the time? Would it be such an awful thing, Barbara, for me to admit that I want to go home?'

*

Ennor Price put down his fork and pushed his plate away. 'Why do I always eat too much when we come to a tapas bar? I thought tapas was meant to the light option?' He stretched out a hand to his glass of wine. 'I hope you're going to eat that last meatball, by the way.'

Kathryn stifled a smile, and skewered the meatball with her fork. 'It's only a light option if you don't order too many dishes. And that's the danger, isn't it? Because all the portions look small and arrive on dinky little plates, you convince yourself that you're not eating much.'

'So, it's my fault, for overindulging?'

'I wasn't criticising. In fact, I'm all for you consuming calories and building your strength. Those things in the storeroom are heavy. It's going to take some muscle to get them packed away.'

Then she had really meant it? 'You want me to pack up all those...' He struggled for the words. 'Those instruments of torture.'

'For heaven's sake.' Kathryn waggled her fork towards him, the half-eaten meatball quivering dangerously on the end. 'I'm asking you to help me pack up some historical artefacts, not suggesting that you condone what they were used for in the past. Anyone would think that I'd asked you to start using them.'

'Chains and manacles.'

'Yes. And fetters, and neck collars.' She put down her fork and took hold of his arm. 'But don't worry about the branding irons. I can probably manage those myself.' She squeezed his arm with a laugh. 'Please loosen up, Ennor. You know you'd be so much happier if those things were off your patch. I just need a bit of help to make it happen.'

'Next weekend, then.' He scowled at her over the rim of his wine glass. 'And when it's all been shipped back, what happens then? Have you given any more thought to that? Is it to be Cornwall or Cambridge?' He watched her face as he asked the question. 'Break it to me gently?'

'It looks as though Richard will need me here. He's sending Nancy back to St Felix. For good.'

Ennor felt his stomach jolt. 'She's going back permanently?'

'Yes. He feels she will be of more use to the family and

the estates if she's back at Woodlands.'

'And how does she feel about that?'

'She's not particularly happy about it. Oh, she's making all the right noises, so as not to upset Richard. But she would prefer to stay here with him and David.'

'And where does that leave Marcus? And Eva?'

Kathryn, bemused, leaned back in her seat. 'Why this sudden interest in the family's relationships?'

'I'm just curious.'

'No, you're not. You're fishing.'

'Is it a crime, now, to be interested in how things are working out for the Lancefield family? Because the last time I thought about it, I was still hunting for the man who murdered Marcus's mother and Eva's friend.'

Kathryn sucked in her cheeks. 'This is never going to go away, is it?' She fixed him with probing eyes. 'What does this have to do with Nancy returning to St Felix?'

'Well, I got the impression – from you, by the way – that Marcus and Eva were pretty loved up these days, albeit at a distance. And that the family hoped they would make some sort of commitment in the future. How does Nancy making a permanent move to St Felix fit into that scenario?'

'How *doesn't* it fit into it? Nancy and Eva are friends now. Admittedly they didn't get off on the right foot, but they've made their peace and are moving forward. Nancy protected Eva when Zak Smith confronted them, didn't she?' Kathryn frowned. 'Barbara asked me this afternoon if I thought Nancy was fond of Marcus herself. Is that what you're thinking? That she might be jealous?'

'I don't know.' Now he was confused. 'It just doesn't sit right, does it?' Was he going to have to spell it out to her? 'Nancy and Lucy were friends. Lucy was engaged to Marcus. Lucy died. Now Nancy and Eva are friends, and Eva might be engaged to Marcus in the future…'

Kathryn threw up her hands. 'Philip McKeith murdered Lucy. I thought we'd all accepted that theory?

Are you suggesting…'

'I'm not suggesting anything. I'm just saying that there are similarities in the situation.'

'Only if Eva gives up her career and moves out to St Felix. Which I very much doubt will happen. Eva is very fond of Marcus, and he's keen for her to give up her job and join him in running the plantation. And Richard and David would be delighted if that was the outcome. But I think Eva is reluctant to give up her job. She isn't just a career woman, she cares very deeply about her patients and the work she does for the hospital. It means a great deal to her.'

'I know how she feels.' Ennor tried not to sound bitter, and wasn't too sure that he succeeded. 'Mind you, her dilemma is down to personal choice. It isn't as if her career was hanging by a thread.'

'Oh, Ennor.' Kathryn took hold of his hand. 'Yours doesn't have to be hanging by a thread either, if you would let Richard help you.'

'You know I can't do that. If I let Richard Lancefield pull strings in my defence, it weakens my position as senior investigating officer. He has a vested interest in the case.' Ennor looked down at her hand. 'I'll admit we both want the same outcome – Smith under lock and key, and ready to face what's coming to him. But I don't like the idea of being beholden. I don't like the idea of being indebted to Richard Lancefield.'

'Even if it means losing your career?'

'Of course. I can't believe you don't understand that.' He stretched out his free hand to lift the bottle of Chablis from the table and topped up her glass before filling his own. 'I shouldn't have brought Eva down to Penwithen. If I'd left her in Edinburgh, Stella would still be alive. If I have to face disciplinary action for that, for not properly assessing the risk, then so be it. I should have known better.'

'And what if you catch Zak Smith?'

What if the moon was made of green cheese? 'It might go some way towards redeeming my reputation. But it won't necessarily save my job. I suppose there's always the option to resign.'

'Would you really consider that?'

'Yes. I'd have to serve three months' notice. They would probably ask Tom to step up as acting DI. It would show them what he's capable of.'

'But what would you do all day? You are the job. You said so yourself.'

Ennor took a long, slow drink from his glass. 'Go travelling. See the world. We could go together. Your work for Richard is almost complete, and you don't have to replace Nancy if you don't want to. Let Barbara do it.' He leaned forward towards her. 'I'm never going to catch Smith. I have to accept that now.' He scanned her face for any sign of understanding. 'Anyway, even if I did redeem myself and catch him, how can I go back to run-of-the-mill cases after three back-to-back murder investigations? I'd rather go out on a high.'

7

Becca Smith sat down on the edge of the new, velvet-covered sofa and looked about her. Everything in the lounge was pristine: new carpet, new bookcase, new television set, even new curtains. It had felt strange spending Richard Lancefield's money with such abandon, but he had set no restrictions on what the money was to be used for. It was compensation paid in recognition of her loss when Philip was murdered on the Salvation Hall estate. Blood money, her mother had called it, with her typical lack of sensitivity. But Becca didn't care about that. All she cared about was making a new start. She didn't bring anything from the shabby, soulless council house in Penzance, other than their clothes and personal belongings. She didn't want any of the bad memories following her to Truro.

Only the good stuff.

Her eyes wandered to the large, framed photograph on the mantelpiece: Philip and Frankie, together on the beach at St Ives, the picture taken just a few weeks before he died. Not a day went by that she didn't think about him. Not a day went by that she didn't speak to him, whispering her thoughts to the picture. Not a day went by that she didn't seethe at the knowledge that Marcus Drake had walked free.

But there was nothing, now, that she could do about it. And she could hardly take the moral high ground with the Lancefields while her brother was on the run for murdering David Lancefield's wife.

She cast anxious eyes up towards the ceiling. Somewhere above her, Frankie was sleeping soundly in her new bed, snuggled under a new duvet, cuddling in to a plush, new teddy bear. And in the morning, she would take the child into the newly fitted bathroom and bathe her in the smart, teardrop bath before wrapping her in a soft, new towel. They had never known such comfort, even when Philip was alive and they had lived together at Holly Cottage. Though that was partly down to Becca herself.

She closed her eyes, remembering. She had never really been a homemaker; the need for cleanliness and order and comfort had somehow escaped her. But now things would have to be different. This level of comfort was worth making an effort for. A fresh start didn't just mean a new home and new belongings. It meant a change of habits. A better life for her and Frankie: the clean, orderly and comfortable life that would help them turn their backs on all the sadness.

As long as it didn't turn out to be a lonely life.

She opened her eyes again and let them drift towards the small, glass-topped coffee table in front of the sofa, and the two mobile phones that rested there. She picked up the one on the left, and lifted it up to her eyes. The screen was painfully empty, save for the usual icons. No evidence of a missed call from a friend, or an unread text. But then friends had been thin on the ground since Zak's crimes came to be public knowledge. Even members of her own extended family had sought to distance themselves, not just from Zak but from his mother, brothers and sister.

She flicked her thumb across the screen and began to scroll mindlessly through the contacts list.

Amber Kimbrall.

She flinched at the first name in the list. Amber was her oldest friend: the girl she had first met at the age of five, when fate put them in adjacent desks on their first day at school. She flicked again at the screen to open up a gallery of photographs, and swiped to scroll through them until a shot of herself and Amber came into view. Teenage in years, they were smiling into the camera, arms around each other, vodka and tonics in hand. In those days they were inseparable, and it had been inconceivable that they would ever let each other down.

She stared at the screen through misty eyes. There was no denying that she missed Amber, but she could see no scope for reconciliation. Even now, she couldn't believe that Amber could have been so disloyal, that she had tried to give Zak up to the police. It was Amber's fault, she reasoned, that her brother had gone on the run. If only Amber had been prepared to cover for him, he might not have confessed to murdering Stella Lancefield.

If Amber had been prepared to cover for him the way that Becca did.

Not that it was easy to cover for a loose cannon like Zak. You could never be sure what he would do next. The only thing certain was that he would never come back to face the music. That, and the knowledge that the police were still watching her like a hawk, hoping beyond reason that she would drop her guard and give her brother's whereabouts away.

At least there was no risk of him showing up in Truro. Helping him out with cash was one thing. Harbouring him from the police was another.

She turned her eyes to the second mobile phone, still lying inactive on the coffee table. She would always take his calls, calls the police were never going to trace since he had sent her a ~~instructed her to buy a~~ second, anonymous pay-as-you-go phone. A phone that no one other than Zak had the number for. A phone that provided a lifeline between brother and sister; a means for him to send requests for cash, and for her to confirm she had sent it to him.

The thought was party to the deed. As if on cue, the phone shuddered loudly with an incoming text, and she swept it up from the coffee table.

As she ran her eyes quickly over the screen she felt a jolt in the pit of her stomach, an unbidden, unwanted stab of panic.

Because this time, the message wasn't a request for cash.

*

Ennor folded up the collar of his coat and sank his hands into the pockets. He bent his elbow towards Kathryn, his fingers still tucked into the pocket's warmth, and waited for her to take his arm. 'The temperature's dropped again. I'm sure March wasn't quite this cold last year.'

She stepped out of the restaurant's doorway and wrapped her arm around his. 'It's a pity that you can't take a holiday now. We could have made for somewhere warm. I hear St Felix is very pleasant at this time of year.'

'In your dreams.' He pulled playfully on her arm. 'I know what would happen. You'd want to get there just as all those dusty old documents arrived, and I wouldn't see you for hours. You'd be unpacking the boxes and filing everything away.'

She made no attempt to deny it. 'I'm sure that Marcus would entertain you. There are plenty of bars and beaches to enjoy. And the water sports are good.'

'If only I wasn't stuck in the middle of a murder investigation.' In the middle of *this* murder investigation. 'I think holidays will have to wait until I hear whether I still have a career.'

They walked in silence for several minutes. And then

Kathryn asked, 'Is Alyson Grant really going to come down here and interfere?'

'She is if I agree to it. And to be fair, it isn't her idea. She's getting some pressure from above.' He steered Kathryn gently around the corner of the street as he spoke. 'All things considered, she's been very supportive. She doesn't blame me for what happened. She's just frustrated that Zak Smith committed a murder on her territory, but he's holed up somewhere on mine and she doesn't have any access.' He blew out a breath. 'She was quizzing me again this afternoon about the burner phone.'

'The one that Zak made calls to on the night he murdered Stella?'

'Yes. That number called Zak when he was in The Lancefield Arms the day after Geraldine Morton was murdered, and the called pinged from a mast in Penzance. Then it called him again the following day. Both calls barely lasted thirty seconds. But the night he shot Stella, he made fourteen attempts to call that number, and none of the calls were answered. The phone was most probably switched off.'

'And it wasn't used again after that?'

'No, he made one more attempt to contact it just after he'd made his confession to Nancy and Eva. And that was the last call Zak Smith's mobile phone made to anybody. His family tried to contact him. But none of the calls were answered, and no other outgoing calls were made.'

'But what about the burner phone, as you call it? That must have made other calls.'

'Nope. We've established that it was a pay-as-you-go SIM card, and the only calls it ever made were the two made to Zak's phone.'

'And you think that it has some relevance to your case?'

Ennor frowned. 'What other explanation could there be?'

'I thought that Zak was supposed to be cheating on Amber? Couldn't that phone have belonged to the girl he was seeing?'

'But Becca admitted that he wasn't with another girl the night that Gerladine Morton was murdered. She admitted that she gave him a false alibi to cover for him.'

'That doesn't mean there wasn't another woman on the scene. Just that he wasn't with her on that particular evening. Which might be the reason they were exchanging phone calls.'

They had almost reached the corner of Morrab Place. Soon they would turn another corner and The Zoological Hotel would be only a few steps away. 'Are we having a nightcap in the hotel bar to discuss this hypothetical theory further?'

'That works for me. As long as you're not going to accuse me of throwing your investigation off course.'

As if he would have the opportunity.

As they rounded the corner, Ennor's heart sank at the sight of a now-familiar car: the sleek, silver Mazda was parked directly outside the hotel and the tall, slim figure leaning casually against it raised a hand in recognition. 'For pity's sake, what now? It's Saturday night.'

Kathryn withdrew her arm from his. 'Is that Tom?' She groaned softly under her breath, and gently rubbed Ennor's shoulder with her hand. 'Saturday night or not, it looks like that drink will have to wait.'

8

'How many murders?' DCI Greenway's Essex tones crackled incredulously down the phone line. 'Impacting one family?' There was a moment's silence and then the penny appeared to drop. 'Sorry, pal, I didn't mean to sound irreverent.'

The incoming call had been a depressing start to his Sunday morning and Price closed his eyes as he spoke, mobile phone tucked tightly into the crook of his neck. 'Be as irreverent as you like, *pal*. Nothing touches me any more when it comes to the Lancefields.' That wasn't the truth, of course. The truth was, that it was personal now, and every assault against the family felt like a twist of the knife between his own shoulder blades. 'The first case was a double murder, a domestic that was wrapped up pretty quickly. The second was also a double murder, but it didn't take much investigating because the killer surrendered and pleaded guilty.' Not least because Richard Lancefield had seduced him with a promise of the best lawyers available and a cash incentive to soften the blow when his inevitable prison sentence was spent. 'We have an outstanding investigation in place for the murders of Geraldine Morton and Stella Drake Lancefield. Geraldine was murdered in

Edinburgh when she was mistaken for Eva McWhinney, and Stella took a bullet that was meant for…'

Greenway whistled sharply down the phone line. 'Are you telling me that you already have a suspect for my murder here in London?'

Price ignored the question. He had one of his own. Dozens of them, in fact. But he would stick to the obvious. 'Do you have any idea why Eva was in London?'

'Yes, we know.' Caution crept into Greenway's voice. 'Of course, as SIO on that case you must be acquainted with her.'

'Yes. And I'm sorry that she's dead. She was a skilled medic and a decent human being.' And God knew there weren't enough of those in the world. 'She didn't tend to leave Edinburgh, unless it was to visit the family in Cornwall. So, London…?'

'She was meeting with a cousin called Laurence Payne.'

The name rang a faint bell. 'Have you spoken to him?'

'Yes. He's been very cooperative so far. He alerted us to the fact that she was missing and identified the body. And he gave us the link from Eva to the Lancefield family. But I wanted to start with you. How's your relationship with the Lancefields?'

'After six murders? What do you think?' Price closed his eyes. Whatever his relationship with them, how the hell could he deliver the news of a seventh murder to the family? It would devastate them. But better him than Greenway. 'Would you like me to speak to them on your behalf?'

'Like it? Frankly, it would be a relief.' Greenway was sounding more relaxed. 'But you didn't answer my question. About the suspect.'

'We're looking for a local man by the name of Zak Smith. He travelled to Edinburgh to murder Eva, and murdered her friend by mistake. Several days later, Eva visited the family in Penwithen and he broke into the grounds of the family home and took a potshot at her. Eva moved out of range and he hit Stella Lancefield instead. At this stage I couldn't possibly comment on whether he's a suspect in your case, though I very much doubt it. Much as I'd love to say "yes", I couldn't see him travelling into London.'

'Why not? He travelled up to Edinburgh.' Greenway's tone sharpened anew. 'And if it's an ongoing investigation and you're looking for him, you obviously don't have the bastard in custody.'

'Obviously.' The barb should have stung, but it didn't. Price was just too tired of trying to explain his failure. 'Smith went on the run in late November and we're still trying to find him.'

'But you must have a motive, if he's your prime suspect.'

'He made an informal confession to Eva McWhinney before he went on the run. He told her that he'd been offered twenty thousand to kill her, but he missed the mark twice and wasn't going to try again.'

'Who offered him the money?'

'He claimed it was David Lancefield's stepson, Marcus Drake.' Price braced himself, and said quietly, 'Marcus was responsible for the first two murders.'

The information seemed to take the wind out of Greenway's sails. 'I thought Marcus Drake was Eva's boyfriend? What motive could he have?'

'None, that I can see. In fact, their relationship only began after Smith tried to kill her.'

'And that's long distance, isn't it? I've heard that he's in the Caribbean.' Greenway paused and then said, 'And talking of the Caribbean, do you know anything about the practice of Obeah?'

'Nope, never heard of it.' Price swivelled gently in his chair. 'Would it make a difference to my investigation if I did?'

'Probably not, but it's relevant to *my* investigation. When we fished Eva out of the North Dock she had a garland around her neck, a motley collection of feathers and flowers and a plastic skull. And according to Payne, it's evidence of some sort of Caribbean witchcraft.'

'Does that make him a suspect? If he knows what the garland is meant to represent?'

'We don't know. We're keeping an open mind. I will say that he appeared genuinely concerned for her wellbeing when he reported her missing, and distressed when he identified the body.'

'But how come he knows about this Obeah stuff?'

'I know this will sound ridiculous, but he reckons it's in his blood. He said the Lancefields are a very old, illustrious family who made their money in the sugar trade, and that he's related to them by some distant ancestors who lived in the Caribbean.' Greenway laughed. 'It sounds like a load of pretentious old bollocks to me, but what do I know?'

Not much, in Price's humble opinion, but he kept the thought to himself. 'Where does the Obeah come into it?'

'He's interested in the occult. In fact, he claims that his ancestors in the Caribbean had first-hand knowledge of Obeah, and that mysticism has always been a curiosity in his family.'

Price lifted his mobile phone away from his neck and placed it gently down on the desk, tapping at the screen to switch on the loudspeaker. 'I'm more than happy to send you a full description of Zak Smith, DCI Greenway.' He spoke into the phone as he powered up the laptop on his desk. 'And I'll send you some mugshots to go with it. But I can't really see that they will be of much use to you. Smith isn't exactly the intellectual type. And it sounds to me as though you already have a prime suspect of your own.'

*

Kathryn switched on the light and closed the door of the storeroom behind her. She had carried a mug of coffee carefully down the path from the kitchen, an insurance policy of warmth against the damp chill of the storeroom, and she glanced around for a suitable place to stand it. 'I suppose it will have to go on here.' She took a sustaining sip from the mug and then placed it down on the top of a tower of sturdy cardboard boxes.

This wasn't exactly how she had planned to spend her Sunday. She had been relishing the prospect of a coastal walk with Ennor, a healthy stretch in the sharp, spring sunshine followed by the pleasure of a relaxing pub lunch. And his early-morning text had been an unexpected blow: another day's unpaid overtime in the office, for reasons he couldn't yet explain.

The sight of DS Parkinson's shiny new Mazda parked up to greet them outside The Zoological Hotel the previous evening had hardly been a propitious omen. But then the solemn expression on Ennor's face as his colleague drove him away had not been particularly encouraging either. Kathryn could only suppose there had been some development in the hunt for Zak Smith, though she couldn't shake off the notion that positive news of Smith's capture would have cheered Ennor up, not drained the colour from his face and the light from his eyes.

She knew better, by now, than to pry. He would explain himself when he could, and at that point she would be there to congratulate or commiserate, whichever the situation demanded. Until then, she might as well keep herself busy.

She tugged on the cuffs of her thick, lambswool jumper, pulling them up in the hope of keeping them clean, and turned her attention to a nearby empty tea chest. 'I suppose we could start by packing the china in this one.' Always supposing that the china would fit into one chest when the items were properly packed. They were going to need copious amounts of packing materials to protect the precious items from breakage, and she wasn't going to procure that too easily on a Sunday.

It was a pity that Nancy hadn't seen fit to preserve most of the original wrappings. But then, of course, Nancy had been under the impression that the items had come back to England for good. Just as Nancy herself had expected to remain at Salvation Hall with them.

Kathryn sighed, and pushed the empty crate up against the wall. Nancy's peevish refusal to give her any help with the packing was probably no more than a reflection of the girl's reluctance to face up to the prospect of her own enforced return to St Felix. It had taken some time for Kathryn to get the measure of the girl's unpredictable, often petulant moods, but now that she understood them they were easier to deal with. And in most cases it didn't take long for the storm to pass. With a fair wind, Nancy's mood would soon improve work could begin in earnest. For now, with one helpmate sulking and the other accompanying Richard to church, Kathryn would have to be content with her own labour and company.

She moved away from the tea chest and stepped into the middle of the room. 'One, two, three...' She counted packing crates quietly under her breath, pointing to each in turn with her finger. Seventeen in total, not all of them empty. She placed a hand on the edge of the crate nearest to her, and bent forward to peer into it. 'Oh, my word. I remember this.' She reached into the crate and pulled out a small tea tin. 'I haven't seen you since the first day I brought Ennor into the storeroom.'

They had barely been acquainted at the time. Police divers had just searched Salvation Hall's ornamental lake in the hunt for the missing gardener, Philip McKeith, and found him in the water, weighted down by a set of iron manacles. The manacles had been one of the items shipped back to England from the Woodlands estate, one of the artefacts that Kathryn had been engaged by Richard Lancefield to examine and advise on. They had been taken from the very storeroom she was standing in, and Ennor had enquired whether there might be a set of keys with which to release the body. The request had sounded almost ludicrous to both of them. And yet the keys had been found in the small tea tin and the manacles had duly been removed. It occurred to her now that neither manacles nor keys had been returned to the Lancefield family. But the idea of asking for their return seemed unthinkable.

She dropped the empty tin back into the chest. She'd had no idea then just how close she and Ennor would become. No idea that their friendship would be forged over murder after murder, as forces beyond either of their comprehension sought to bring the Lancefield family down. No idea that their relationship might endure *beyond* the Lancefield family and its history, beyond Ennor's investigations into the crimes that beset them, into a future that consisted of just the two of them. And she couldn't help wondering, for a moment, whether the events that had taken Ennor away from her today might put that prospect in jeopardy.

It was a possibility that she didn't want to consider. She pulled her mobile phone from the rear pocket of her jeans and swiped at the screen with her thumb. She couldn't disturb him with a call, but a text would let him know she was thinking of him.

Missing you today. Hope all is okay.

She had barely placed the phone down on the top of a nearby packing case before his brief reply came through.

We need to talk.

*

'The guy is from Cornwall and on the run. He's a rural type, hardly likely to show up in London, according to DCI Price. But you never know. And you can't deny the coincidence. I've just received this.' Chris Greenway rotated the computer's screen so that Bob Marwick could see it. 'He's already murdered two people in his attempts to take out Eva McWhinney. And he's confronted her, face to face, and told her that he was paid to get rid of her.'

'Does he know about Obeah?' Marwick leaned forward to examine the picture of Smith more closely. 'He doesn't look the intellectual type.'

Price had said the same. Did you have to be an intellectual to know about witchcraft? 'His sister might know something about it. She used to be the Lancefield's housekeeper, until she blotted her copybook and was dismissed.'

'Could that be a motive for Eva McWhinney's murder? Some sort of petty revenge on the family?'

'She certainly has a motive for wishing the family ill, and there's nothing petty about it. Eva's boyfriend, Marcus Drake, was responsible for the murder of her partner last year. Though why she would take her revenge on Eva rather than him is anybody's guess.' It wouldn't make sense. 'I just want you to keep that image of Smith in mind during the day. Get some copies printed and take them to the dockside restaurants and see if anyone recognises him. He's been on the run for weeks and might be looking pretty dishevelled by now.'

'If he's been on the run, how would he know that Eva McWhinney was in London? Could his sister have known?'

It was a fair question, for which Greenway didn't have a ready answer. 'I suppose she might, if someone told her.' He mulled the question over in his mind. Could there be a connection between her and the brother, and Laurence Payne?'

'The sister wants rid of Eva, arranges for the brother to do the deed, and Payne provides the garland as an embellishment? Why would he do that?'

'Who knows? Maybe he has a grudge of his own against the Lancefields. It doesn't sound as though he has a direct connection himself. Perhaps he resented that. We don't have anyone to back up his explanation of Eva's visit to London because conveniently it was meant to be a secret.' Greenway stretched out a hand to the computer screen. 'I think we should show this to Laurence Payne and see what reaction we get. And take it to the hotel where she was staying, and see if they recognise him. He might have been there at some point.'

'If we do find evidence that Smith was in London, where will that leave DCI Price's case?'

'It isn't just Price's case. Only one of those murders was committed in Cornwall. The other was in Edinburgh. There's a DCI Alyson Grant leading on that one.' *Complicated* didn't even begin to cover it. 'They're in daily contact, though right now it doesn't sound as though they have a lot to talk about. Price hasn't had a sniff of Smith since the night he did a runner, and that was months ago.'

'Why does DCI Price think he wouldn't travel to London?'

'He doesn't think he would have had the resources to make the journey, even if he knew Eva was going to be here.' The more Greenway thought about, the more likely it was that Laurence Payne was the only person who knew where Eva would be, and why. 'Look, I think this whole Smith thing could be a red herring. The most unbelievable of coincidences. But we have to keep an open mind. It's a lead, and one we can't afford to dismiss at this stage. But I don't want it to railroad the investigation at the expense of more realistic theories.'

'Laurence Payne?'

'Or an unknown opportunist. Let's not forget that one while we're clutching at straws. A chance thief, someone with his eyes on her handbag.'

'A chance thief who knew about Obeah?'

Trust Marwick to point out the obvious. 'You're right. That theory is even more unlikely than the idea of Smith knowing that Eva was in London.' Greenway pushed his chair away from the desk and stood up. 'It's pointless sitting here, going round in circles. We both know that Laurence Payne is our only real lead. He knew she would be in London, he spent the evening with her, he walked her along the dockside towards her hotel, just yards from where her body was found. And he had the specialised knowledge to create that garland.'

'And the motive?'

'Could be anything. Jealousy. Resentment.' Greenway scratched thoughtfully at the back of his neck. 'Maybe he took a fancy to her and tried it on, and couldn't take the rejection. Right now, I don't really care about the motive. I'll take opportunity and probability to be going on with. It's time we went over to Canary Wharf to question him further.'

*

Barbara placed a mug of freshly made peppermint tea down on the kitchen table and sat down opposite Nancy. 'There wasn't much of a congregation at St Felicity's this morning. I think Richard was quite disappointed.' She watched with interest as Nancy pored over a large, leather-bound book. 'It still tired him, though. He's gone back to the Dower House to rest, so I've offered to take Samson for his morning walk around the lake. Perhaps you'd like to come with me?'

Nancy smiled, but didn't look up. 'If you don't mind, I'd rather continue with this. I'm still trying to find my distant ancestor, Abigail.' She turned a page in the book. 'Well, I say ancestor. She was the sister of my direct ancestor, Millie. I was hoping to find a mention of her here, in the estate's hospital book. I've already searched the daybook and the annual slave inventories, but without much luck.'

There were several pieces of paper on the table and Barbara reached out a hand to pick one up, a section of hand-drawn family tree. 'Your mother's name is Honeysuckle? Nancy, that's charming.' She ran a finger across the page. 'Your father is Lester, and your grandparents on your mother's side are Angel and Addison.' The finger wandered to a second piece of paper on the table as she spoke. 'Good heavens, you've got all the way back to the eighteenth century. Were you able to do all of this with records from Woodlands?'

'Yes. With Kathryn's help, of course.'

Barbara kept her eyes on the paper. 'I thought you might have been helping Kathryn this morning. Wasn't she planning to make a start on the storeroom?'

'I believe so. But it felt a little cold this morning to be working out there. Kathryn doesn't mind.'

From Nancy's tone of voice, Barbara couldn't help thinking that Kathryn's opinion wouldn't have influenced the girl's decision one way or the other. 'Do *you* mind, Nancy? I mean, that Kathryn is packing up the items that you will ultimately be responsible for?'

Now Nancy looked up. 'Why would I mind? Kathryn will undertake the job with her usual care and consideration. She knows how precious the items are.'

'Indeed.' Barbara sipped again on her tea and tried to size up her companion. She had a brittle quality about her that morning, an untrusting wariness in the eyes at odds with the charming smile on her lips. Not quite aloof, not quite unfriendly but... proud. That was the word for it. There was a pride in Nancy that somehow didn't sit quite right with her role within the family. Was that what Richard had meant, when he said that she could overstep the mark? 'You must be delighted that Richard is going to entrust the family's heritage to you.'

'To be honest, it would have been my preference to have that privilege here, at Salvation Hall.' She lowered her eyes, her disappointment suddenly visible. 'But, of course, it is not my decision to make. And if Richard wishes me to return to St Felix then that is what I must do.'

Barbara felt a sudden pang of sympathy and placed a hand gently on the girl's arm. 'Don't take it to heart, Nancy. Richard is very fond of you, you know. He must be, because the family's heritage is so important to him. He wouldn't just entrust it to anyone.'

The girl's brittle veneer seemed to melt under Barbara's words and she placed her own hand on top of Barbara's. 'Can I speak plainly to you? I know that Richard is fond of me. And I am fond of him. Fond enough to wish I could stay here for the years he has left. I don't just enjoy being his secretary, I enjoy his company. And I have always considered myself a part of the family, because Richard himself refers to our one, big, Woodlands family. But I feel that things are changing. He sent me out to St Felix after Stella's death, and denied me the opportunity to pay my respects at her funeral. And he has chosen Marcus to eventually take over the running of Woodlands.' She pouted. 'Marcus, who doesn't know one end of a plantation from the other.'

'I thought that you and Marcus were friends?'

'Oh, we are. I don't blame Marcus for what is happening to me now. But I cannot help wishing that Richard had given that privilege to me.' She lowered her eyes. 'I feel that history is repeating itself. In the past, it was always the intention that Marcus would marry Lucy, and they would take over the running of Salvation Hall. Now the hope is that Marcus will marry Eva, and they will take over the running of the Woodlands estate.'

'Silly girl, are you disappointed that Marcus is going to be married?'

Nancy stiffened. 'Good heavens, no.' Her voice grew suddenly stronger. 'I am disappointed that, yet again, it would appear that I am to be sidelined.'

9

It didn't take Kathryn long to drive to the shoreline at Marazion. She swung her ageing blue Volvo convertible into the car park and braced herself as it bumped across ruts and potholes, coming to rest in the unmarked parking space next to Ennor's coupe.

Ennor was already out of his car, sitting on the wall that separated the car park from the beach, staring out across the clear, blue water to St Michael's Mount. He had barely seemed to notice the Volvo's approach, and it was only when Kathryn alighted and slammed the door loud enough for him to hear that he turned his head to look at her. 'Sorry to drag you away from all those dusty old torture implements.' His voice had a curious hollow quality. 'But I thought it best that we talked away from Salvation Hall.'

She flicked her key fob at the Volvo to lock the door and stepped forward to sit down on the wall beside him. He looked tired, his usually amiable face drawn by some so-far-undisclosed sorrow, and she shuffled along the wall to be closer to him. 'Whatever it is, it's bad, isn't it?'

'Yes, it's bad.' He took hold of her hand and held it against his chest . 'Did you know that Eva was going to London this weekend?'

It wasn't the opening gambit she expected, and it took her by surprise. 'I didn't realise that Eva *ever* visited London. She told me that she very rarely left Edinburgh, and then usually only to take short rest breaks in Scotland.'

'So you didn't know that she was going to visit Laurence Payne?'

Kathryn flinched. 'Laurence? But Richard forbade it.'

'Forbade it? What the hell does that mean?'

'She was keen to meet with Laurence, to find out more about his connection to the Lancefields, but Richard didn't want her to. Because of his promise to David, that no more attempts would be made to extend the family. You already know about that.' Kathryn frowned. 'So, when Eva pushed the point, Richard expressly asked her to drop any notion of it.'

'And when was this?'

'On Tuesday evening. We had a video call with her, just a chat to catch up and say hello.'

'And she agreed to let the matter drop?'

'Yes. At least, that was what she said.' Kathryn's nerves began to jangle. 'Ennor, what's this all about?'

'Did Laurence Payne know at that point that she was planning to travel to London?'

'Yes, that was the main reason she was disappointed with Richard's dismissal of the idea. Laurence was keen to meet up and she didn't want to let him down.' Kathryn nestled a little closer to Ennor's shoulder. 'Why would she undermine Richard, and go to London anyway?'

'Because she's a grown woman? Why the hell should she do what Richard Lancefield says?' The words came out a little too harshly, and Ennor lowered his head. 'I'm sorry, I didn't mean to snap.'

'Ennor, has something happened to her?'

He didn't answer the question. 'Do you know anything very much about this Laurence Payne?'

'No, not much. Eva told me some time ago that they exchanged Christmas cards each year. Her parents had always exchanged cards with his family, and she continued the practice after they passed away. Then on Tuesday's call she told us that she had spoken to him, to let him know that she had made a connection with David and Richard. She told him about the work I was doing to document the family's history, and in return he said he had a lot of information about his branch of the family and would be happy to share it with her.'

'And on this occasion, Richard said no, even though the information was readily available?'

'Yes. He wouldn't break his promise to David.'

'Did anyone ask David how he felt about it?'

'Nancy suggested that, but it just made Richard cross.'

'Do you have much information on the Payne side of the family?'

'Not much, no.' Kathryn lifted her head away from Ennor's shoulder so that she could turn to look at him. 'I believe that Laurence Payne is descended from Maria Lancefield, the sister of Eva's distant ancestor Charlotte Lancefield. In the early nineteenth century Maria married a man called George Payne. His father, William, owned the St Aldate's plantation on St Felix, adjacent to the Lancefields' Woodlands estate. I know that the Paynes sold their plantation and moved back to England, taking Maria with them. And I know that there was a minor scandal around the marriage, and not long afterwards George Payne took his own life.'

'What was the scandal?'

'There was a suggestion that George Payne was illegitimate, and that the match would bring shame on the Lancefield family.' Kathryn paused to draw in a breath. 'But what does any of this have to do with Eva?'

'Possibly nothing. But you never know with this family.' Ennor sounded uncharacteristically bitter. 'Eva went ahead and travelled to London to meet with Laurence Payne. They met for dinner in a restaurant on the dockside at some place known as West India Quay.'

'Well, I guess that was appropriate.'

'How?'

'West India Quay is at the West India Docks. And the West India Docks were built in the early nineteenth century to receive goods imported from the Caribbean. When the Lancefields had sugar and rum to sell in Europe, it was shipped across the Caribbean from St Felix to London, and it was unloaded at the dedicated West India Docks.' Kathryn's pulse began to quicken. 'Ennor, please tell me what's happened to Eva.'

Slowly, he lifted his arm to wrap it tightly around her shoulders. 'I'm going to need your help, Kathryn. We're going to have to break the news to the family that Eva McWhinney is dead.'

※

DS Marwick gazed out of the window to admire the view. He'd always heard that the residents of Canary Wharf lived in a different London from his own, and now he'd seen the evidence for himself.

The window itself was a case in point, not so much a window to look out of, but a floor-to-ceiling wall of glass that served to separate the lounge of Laurence Payne's apartment from the sprawling, metropolitan landscape outside. From his viewpoint, Marwick could see the whole of London before him: the gentrified docks in the foreground, the muddy Thames meandering its way through acres of towering concrete and glass, the vague but unmistakeable outline of leafy, somnolent suburbs in the distance. It was a far cry from the three-bedroomed semi that he shared with Mrs Marwick in Woodford Green. And yet he couldn't help thinking that he wouldn't swap places with Laurence Payne for all the sugar in Jamaica.

He turned on his heel to face into the room. Though

the view outside was modernity itself, the interior of the apartment was curiously traditional in its furnishings. 'Have you lived here long, Mr Payne?'

Laurence, sitting awkwardly on a plaid-covered high-backed chair, shook his head. 'I've only had this particular apartment for a little over two years. Before that, I had a place in the City itself, just off Eastcheap. But I felt like a change and thought it would be rather fun to have a base close to the docks, where my ancestors conducted their commercial dealings.'

Marwick nodded, and turned his head towards DCI Greenway. The inspector was standing beside a tall, mahogany bookcase and he met Marwick's gaze with a sardonic smile. 'It must be nice to have the choice. We humble police officers don't earn enough for that kind of rent, unfortunately.'

If Laurence understood the jibe, he didn't let it show. 'Yes, I've heard that the rents are nothing short of extortion. I was very lucky to be in a position to buy.'

To buy? With a price tag that must have been north of a million and a half? An involuntary whistle hissed between Bob Marwick's teeth. 'I think we must move in very different circles. Mind you, I don't think I would like to be in the City all of the time. I like to get out in the fresh air at the weekends.'

'Oh, so do I. I usually go back home to Hertfordshire for the weekend, but this weekend was an exception, due to Eva's visit.'

'You have a place in Hertfordshire too?' Greenway began to examine the contents of the bookshelf, his head slightly tilted, his eyes sweeping coolly across the collection of leather-bound volumes as he spoke. 'Is that your primary residence, then?'

'Yes, just outside the village of Ayot St Laurence. It's why the name Laurence is so recurrent in my family. My ancestors bought the property when they returned from the Caribbean. The ladies in the family lived there permanently, while the men spent their working week in London.'

'I suppose they made their money in the sugar trade, like the Lancefields?'

'Yes, that's right.' Laurence made it sound as though everybody's family made their money that way. But then, in the circles he moved in, perhaps they did. 'They eventually sold up, of course, around the end of the eighteenth century and moved back to England.'

'Is that why you're interested in Obeah, Mr Payne?' Greenway continued to examine the contents of the bookcase as he spoke. 'I can see you have a lot of reading material on the subject.'

'To some extent, yes. Although my interest extends beyond Obeah to other areas of the occult.'

Marwick stepped away from the window to sit down, uninvited, on a large, damask-covered sofa beside the bookcase. 'We were wondering if you could tell us something more about the garland that was found around your cousin's neck. You seemed to recognise it straight away.'

'Ah, yes. The omen of ill fortune. It might have been artificial, but it was a very clever imitation of a hex garland that was once used against a plantation owner on the island of St Felix.'

'You sound very certain?'

'That's because the plantation owner in question was the man who bought my ancestors' estate.'

It was sounding more unlikely by the minute. Marwick looked across at his senior officer just as Greenway turned his head, and the two men exchanged a knowing glance.

'Can you tell us what happened to him?' It was Greenway who asked the question.

'Oh, he died. He was, by all accounts, a very cruel man and he was murdered by one of the slaves on the plantation.'

'And would that have had anything to do with the

Lancefield family?'

'You mean, because an imitation of the garland used against him was found around Eva's neck?' Laurence considered the possibility for a moment. 'The Lancefield's estate was next to ours, but I don't know about a specific connection to that incident.'

'Did Eva know about it?'

'Not that I'm aware of. We didn't discuss it yesterday evening.'

'What did you discuss, Mr Payne?'

'Our respective ancestors, Inspector. As I've already explained to Sergeant Marwick, it was the whole point of our meeting. We are descended from siblings who lived at the end of the eighteenth century, as are Richard and David Lancefield, our distant cousins in Cornwall.'

Talking about dead people didn't do much for Bob Marwick, but he guessed it took all sorts. 'Are you married, Mr Payne?'

'Not yet. But I will be, later this year.'

'Does your fiancée live here with you, or is she in Hertfordshire?'

'Neither, I'm afraid. She and her family run a country house hotel in East Yorkshire. We usually spend our weekends together, but this weekend I was here to meet Eva.'

'Did your fiancée know about that?'

'Yes, we talked about it on the phone several times during the week.'

'You must miss her.'

'Of course.'

Marwick's change of tack was seamless. 'Your cousin was a very attractive young woman, wasn't she?'

'Yes, I suppose she was.' Laurence nodded, and then his shoulders stiffened. 'I hope you're not suggesting there was any impropriety in our meeting?'

Impropriety? Was that what they called it in the ivory towers of Canary Wharf? They had a far more basic name for it out in Woodford Green. 'I wasn't suggesting anything, Mr Payne.' Just fishing. 'You were aware of Eva's relationship with Marcus Drake, David Lancefield's stepson? She mentioned it to you yesterday, I believe?'

'Yes.'

'And did she also mention that he had recently avoided a prison sentence for the manslaughter of his late fiancée's lover?'

Evidently not, judging by the speed with which the colour left Laurence Payne's cheeks. 'I can't imagine she would have felt comfortable mentioning that.' His deep, blue eyes darted from Marwick to Greenway, and back again. 'Is that true?'

Greenway replied by moving away from the bookcase to sit down on the sofa beside Marwick. 'Did she mention that she had recently been the target of a murder attempt?'

'Good heavens, no.'

Greenway pulled a photograph of Zak Smith from the inside pocket of his jacket and offered it to Laurence. 'This is the man who attempted to murder her. His name is Zak Smith and his sister, Becca, used to work as the Lancefield's housekeeper. The man Marcus Drake murdered was Becca's partner, and the father of her child.'

Laurence took the photograph and stared at it. 'This all sounds rather sordid, Inspector. And rather beneath my cousin. She was a professional woman, highly regarded in her field and possessed of good manners and refinement.' He looked up at the policeman. 'May I ask what Smith's motive was?'

'I'm afraid we can't disclose the full details to you at this stage.' Greenway pointed at the photograph. 'I take it that Eva didn't mention Smith to you?'

'No. Not at all.' Laurence looked crestfallen. 'Do you suspect this man of murdering her?'

'We're keeping an open mind. The original attempts on her life were several months ago and he's still on the run. You should know that in his attempts to murder Eva, he murdered two other innocent women by mistake.'

'I see.' Laurence almost whispered the words. 'Am I at risk, Chief Inspector, because of my connection to the Lancefield family?'

Greenway and Marwick exchanged another glance. Laurence Payne was certainly at risk, one way or another. But whether there was a risk to his safety, or whether he was at risk of being named their number one suspect for Eva McWhinney's murder, at this stage neither of them could say.

*

Kathryn sat down on the Dower House sofa and bent her head so close to Richard's that they were almost touching. 'Richard, I'm so very, very sorry.'

The old man grasped hold of her hand, curling his gnarled fingers too tightly around her own. 'How on earth do we break the news to Marcus and David?' His voice was weak, a hoarse whisper. 'It will break their hearts.'

'I know. But we're all going to have to be brave, for their sakes. And if it would help, you know that I will break to the news to them.'

'You have been a stalwart friend, Kathryn, and I thank you for the offer.' Richard studied her face with moist, rheumy eyes. 'But it must be me. It was my decision to invite Eva into the family fold, and it is my failure to protect her that has brought about this dreadful outcome.'

'Of course it isn't. Richard, you mustn't take that upon yourself. You made it perfectly plain to Eva that you didn't want her to meet with Laurence Payne. It isn't your fault that she chose to ignore that request.'

'It wasn't a request. I positively forbade her to do so.' There was a hint of bitter disappointment in the old man's voice. 'I hadn't realised that my wishes would be so unimportant to her. Nor that she would dismiss my concern for her welfare.' His lips curled inwards, in a vain attempt to suppress his grief. 'I knew no good would come of it. And I was right.' He blinked away a tear. 'And yet, even I didn't think that Zak Smith would sink this low after promising to leave her alone.' He turned to DCI Price, standing quietly by the fireplace. 'Have they caught the beggar?'

Price shook his head. 'At this stage, there is nothing concrete to suggest that Zak was involved in any way. We only know that Eva was murdered in the early hours of Saturday morning, and her body was discovered shortly afterwards. The London team are pursuing a number of possibilities, and keeping an open mind where Zak Smith is concerned. It goes without saying that we, and DCI Grant up in Edinburgh, will be giving them as much support as they need. It might help you to know that the place where Eva was found benefits from almost wall-to-wall CCTV. The senior officer investigating, DCI Greenway, has requested immediate access to all CCTV footage from the area. In fact,'—Price moved away from the fireplace to perch on the arm of a nearby armchair—'they're struggling to understand why anyone would commit such a crime, given the extent of camera surveillance in the area. It's inevitable that some aspect of the crime will be caught on camera.'

'So, it will be clear if Zak Smith was responsible?'

'I can't guarantee that, but it's highly likely.' Price fixed his eyes on the old man's face. 'I have to ask, Mr Lancefield, why you forbade Eva to meet with Laurence? Kathryn tells me you were honouring your promise to David, to stop searching for any more members of the Lancefield family. But I can't help wondering'—he uttered a soft, self-deprecating laugh—'well, call it my policeman's intuition. I can't help wondering whether you had any cause for concern about Laurence Payne himself?'

The question hung in the air for the moment, and then Richard's brow beetled forward. 'How could I? I know of the Payne connection, but never heard of the man himself until Eva made me aware of his existence.' He tilted his head, thinking. 'Is there some possibility that Payne might have been instrumental in her death?'

'We believe that he was the last person to see her alive.' That was all Price was prepared to say on the matter. The old man would have to draw his own conclusions. 'DCI Greenway has asked if we can help in the identification of Eva's next of kin. I have explained to him that she has no immediate family, so at the moment it is believed to be either yourself or Laurence Payne.'

'As we are descended from the same set of siblings, I think it will be myself as the elder cousin. Though if you are asking who will make the arrangements to bring her home, I suspect that will be Marcus.'

'Marcus is in St Felix.'

'Do you imagine, Chief Inspector, that he will stay in St Felix when he hears the news? The two of them were in contact on a daily basis and growing ever closer. The poor boy had begun to envisage a future with Eva and losing her will be the bitterest of blows.'

Might Marcus, then, have known about the plan to meet with Laurence Payne? It was a question that Price would have to save for later. 'I'm sorry if my next question sounds insensitive, but do you have any idea who would benefit from Eva's death?'

'Ennor, for pity's sake. Richard has just received the most distressing news.'

Richard patted her hand. 'You are the best of friends, Kathryn, but the chief inspector has a very good reason for asking me the question.' He turned his eyes to Price. 'If an examination of the CCTV footage proves that Zak Smith was the culprit, then we will know the motive for the murder was revenge against the family. But if Eva met her death at the hands of an unknown assailant, then your colleagues in London will be looking for a motive for the murder. There has been no mention so far of this being a mugging or, God forbid, some kind of sickening sexual assault. So another possibility is that Eva was murdered for financial gain. Perhaps that was your real reason for asking me who was Eva's next of kin. There is no question that she leaves a significant estate: the three properties in Hemlock Row alone must be worth in the region of three to four million pounds. It is only to be expected that somewhere along the line the police will ask *cui bono*?

10

'Well, this is a pleasant surprise, Sergeant Parkinson. However did you find me?' Becca Smith made no attempt to hide her disdain at the policeman's arrival. 'I wish I'd known you were coming. I'd have organised a housewarming party.' She leaned against the doorframe, blocking the way into the house, arms folded across her chest in defence against the presence of law and order. 'I'm glad you've parked that swanky new car of yours outside. At least that will impress the neighbours.'

Parkinson, halfway up the path, fixed her with a stern eye. 'This isn't a social visit. It's about Zak.'

'Zak? I'm not sure that I know anybody called Zak. Are you sure you've got the right house?'

The sergeant smiled. 'If I'm going to have to jog your memory, you might want to invite me inside.'

'Might I? I wouldn't think so. Out here on the step will do just fine. I've just finished tidying up inside.'

'Tidying up? That doesn't sound like the Becca Smith I've come to know and love.' He walked up to the doorway and craned his neck to look over her shoulder. 'I really do think it would be better if we continued this inside.'

She put up a hand to his chest. 'This place is a new start for me. And I don't have to invite you in if I don't want to. Not unless you have a warrant.'

'Or unless you don't want me to stand out here in the garden and discuss your murdering brother in a very, very loud voice.' He raised his voice to prove the point. 'After all, it looks like a very nice neighbourhood and you're going to have to put in some effort after moving here from that tatty council estate.' He was almost shouting now. 'And now it looks as though your brother has gone too far and committed another murder...'

The booming declaration took the wind out of Becca's sails. She swayed slightly against the doorframe and pushed out a petulant lip. 'You bastard. I don't believe you.' She cast furtive eyes to left and right. 'Why do you have to come round here, shouting out lies like that?'

Parkinson lowered his voice. 'It's not a lie, Becca. It's possible that Zak has killed again.' He put a hand up to the doorframe and leaned closer to her. 'Look, I just want to let you know what's happened.' At least to begin with. 'Why don't we talk inside, so that we can't be overheard?'

For a moment, it looked as though she might refuse. And then she stepped back slowly to let him pass by into the small, dark hallway. 'Down there.' She pointed along the hallway with a reluctant finger. 'The lounge is at the end.' She let the front door swing shut. 'You can sit down anywhere, so long as you don't make a mess.'

It was an invitation of sorts, but there wasn't a great deal of choice. Parkinson glanced around the small, sparsely furnished lounge and plumped for one of two small, grey armchairs on either side of the fireplace. 'You really have turned over a new leaf, haven't you?' Compact or not, the place was spotless, clean and tidy in a way he would never have associated with Becca Smith. 'I'm glad you've found somewhere better than that dump in Penzance.' The unexpected compliment was spontaneous, and he was surprised to realise that he meant it. 'I hope you and Frankie can make a go of it here.'

'We're more likely to do that if you would leave us alone.' She sat down on the other armchair. 'Now, what's all this about Zak? Who is he supposed to have killed this time?'

'Eva McWhinney.'

Becca let out a short, sharp shriek. 'What, again?' She rolled her eyes. 'You let never give up, do you? He promised he wouldn't do that, didn't he? He promised her to her face that he wouldn't make another attempt on her life.'

'So he did. But your brother's promises were always made to be broken, weren't they?'

It was a fact she couldn't deny. Her amusement made way for a scowl and she looked down at her fingers, pretending to examine her fingernails. 'So, Eva really is dead this time?'

'Yes. They found her body yesterday morning, floating face down in a dock out at Canary Wharf.'

Becca winced. 'I'm sorry for the girl, if that's the truth. But I don't see how you can blame Zak. He wouldn't be able to find his way around London, let alone know where to find her. You can't pin that on him, just because you haven't got another suspect.'

'We can't pin that on him, *yet*.' Parkinson bent forward and rested his forearms on his knees. 'We know you're helping him, Becca. Someone has to be giving him the money to stay afloat. He wouldn't have been able to stay on the run for this long unless someone was bankrolling him. Why don't you do yourself a favour and tell us where he's hiding out?'

'I can't tell you where he is, because I don't know.' Becca's eyes flicked up to his face. 'I'm telling you the truth, Sergeant Parkinson. I don't know where he is. And if he was dumb enough to try to turn up here, I wouldn't give him houseroom. I've already told you, this is a new start for me and Frankie, and I don't want anyone –

anyone at all – spoiling that for us.'

*

DCI Greenway, black marker pen in hand, stared hard at the empty whiteboard in his office. He didn't usually find it so difficult to sketch out the beginnings of an investigation but, for once, the complexities around the murder of Eva McWhinney left him unsure where to start.

He lifted the pen and scrawled Eva's name in the middle of the board and then added a long, sweeping arrow upwards and to the left. 'Laurence Payne, distant cousin.' He muttered to himself as he wrote. 'Wealthy. Well-educated. Good-looking…' The pen hovered in mid-air for a moment, and then he added, 'Weird.'

Weird had been Bob Marwick's assessment of the man and Greenway, having taken the time to examine Payne's collection of esoteric books, had to concede that his colleague had a point. Anyone with an interest in titles like *Magick in Theory and Practice* and *Obeah: Witchcraft in the West Indies* was bound to have something of the night about him. Greenway couldn't help wondering what Eva McWhinney had made of her cousin and whether she, like Marwick, had found him weird. Maybe she had regretted setting up the meeting. At this point they only had Payne's word for it that he had walked her to within yards of her hotel. Maybe the CCTV footage they were waiting for would tell a different story.

He swept the marker pen across the whiteboard again, another long arrow upwards and to the right. 'Zak Smith.' Now there was a tale and a half. Already in the frame for two attempts on Eva's life for what might be the flimsiest of motives, and currently on the run for taking out two completely innocent women in the process. According to DCI Price, the man could be anywhere but he was unlikely to make his way to London.

Greenway clipped the top back on the marker pen and rested it underneath his chin. Laurence Payne had betrayed no obvious signs of recognising Zak Smith when Marwick showed him the photograph. And yet the policeman couldn't help thinking that somehow there might be a link between the two of them. What that link was, and how it might have resulted in Eva McWhinney's death, were the two critical factors that evaded him. But Smith had history when it came to attempts on Eva's life, and Payne knew where she was going to be on Friday evening. That, plus he had sufficient knowledge of Obeah to know just what that garland found around her neck represented. It was hinting at a link to either Laurence Payne himself, or to the Lancefield family.

And what about the Lancefield family? Greenway pulled the top from the pen and drew a third sweeping arrow on the board, down and to the left. 'Lancefield family. History. Sugar?' Sugar was brought from the Caribbean to the West India Dock, hundreds of years ago. More to the point, the Payne and Lancefield families brought sugar from the Caribbean into the West India Dock, a practice which had led them both to accumulate significant family fortunes.

He swept a fourth and final flourish of the pen across the board, down and to the right. 'Unknown assailant?' There was still no sign of Eva's handbag, but he didn't think they were looking at robbery as a motive. He didn't know much about jewellery himself – much to Mrs Greenway's obvious chagrin every Christmas, birthday and wedding anniversary – but when Eva's body was fished out of the dock there must have been at least several thousand pounds' worth of gold on her. And much of it would have been easy enough to remove for anyone strong enough to overpower her.

He clipped the top back onto the pen a second time and stepped back from the board to admire his handiwork. It wasn't much to show for a day and half's graft, but then it didn't help that it was the weekend. Getting hold of CCTV footage could be slow at the best of times, and nigh on impossible on a Sunday. The foot soldiers were slowly working their way through the quayside restaurants, asking for sightings of Eva or anyone resembling Zak Smith. Marwick was over at West India Quay, talking to the staff at the restaurant where Laurence and Eva had dinner. And DCI Price was giving up his Sunday to break the news of Eva's death to the Lancefield family, and find out whether it was true that she had kept the details of her meeting with Laurence a secret.

Greenway took a farther step backwards and leaned on the edge of his desk. She must have told someone she was going to London. If not the Lancefields, then a friend, a neighbour, a work colleague.

And that would probably mean someone in Edinburgh, not on Price's patch in Cornwall.

*

'I don't understand why Eva would go against Richard's wishes.' Barbara ran a contemplative finger around the rim of her teacup. 'And neither does he.' She kept her eyes on Nancy's back as she spoke. 'It seems out of character for her. To just take off to London like that, without letting anyone know.'

Nancy, busy washing lunch dishes in the kitchen sink, just muttered under her breath. 'It seems to me that everyone in this family has been beguiled by Eva.' She addressed the pronouncement to the soapy water in the sink, swirling it around with a sweep of her hand. 'Eva was only human, like the rest of us. And surely she had every right to go to London if she chose to. After all, Richard is only a very distant relative to her. It's not as if she were a member of the immediate family and living under Richard's roof.'

'I thought you liked Eva, Nancy?'

'Of course I liked her.' Nancy lifted a handful of cutlery from the sink and rinsed it vigorously under the running tap. 'Just because the men in this family chose to put her on a pedestal doesn't mean that *I* thought any less of Eva.'

The bitterness expressed caught Barbara unawares. She had always felt an undercurrent of friction between the two young women, though if challenged both of them would just laugh it off as good-humoured banter. But this was far more than an undercurrent. This was Nancy's true feelings laid bare. 'Aren't you sorry that she's dead?'

'Of course I'm sorry.' Nancy pulled the plug from the sink and reached for a towel to dry her hands. 'I know how deeply this must have hurt Richard, and how much distress it will cause for David and Marcus. And I hope you know me well enough to know that I will do everything I can to ease their pain.' She dropped the towel onto the worktop and stepped forward to the table to sit down opposite Barbara. 'But I also hope that you and I know each other well enough for me to be honest with you. I liked Eva, and I made every effort to get on with her. But she was not a member of my family, and I had not known her long enough to consider her a firm friend. So you should not be surprised if my reaction to her death is proportionate to my relationship with her.'

Well, that was blunt. 'Did you pretend to like her, because it was what Richard and David wanted?'

'No. I liked her because she was Eva. She was a decent person, hard-working and kind. At least, that was the opinion I formed in the short time I knew her.' Nancy softened her tone. 'I didn't have to pretend to like her. But I didn't consider her worthy of worship. Because I didn't consider her a replacement for Lucy.'

'You think that the Lancefield men were projecting their feelings for Lucy onto Eva.'

'Of course. What other explanation can there be for the way they all behaved towards her?'

The answers to that question were plentiful: regard, genuine affection, even love… Perhaps those possibilities might never have occurred to Nancy. Or perhaps they occurred to her, but her own petty jealousies made it difficult for her to accept them.

Barbara reached out for the teapot and topped up the cup in front of her. 'Did you know that Eva was going to London, Nancy? Did she mention it to you?'

'No, why would she? You know I was there on the call on Tuesday evening, when she discussed the possibility with Richard and Kathryn. Richard made his feelings quite plain.' Nancy pouted. 'To be honest, Barbara, I was most disappointed that he was against it. I have taken some time myself to look at the Payne connection and it is one of the most interesting stories within the family.'

'Is it? Does Kathryn know that you've been looking at it?'

'Yes, I mentioned it to her earlier this week. I knew we were going to discuss it on the call, and I wanted to be prepared.' Nancy lowered her voice a little. 'There was a question of legitimacy, you know. Of a member of the Lancefield family marrying a man who turned out to be illegitimate.'

'You astonish me, Nancy.' Barbara's eyes lit with a faint smile. 'I would have thought that was a regular occurrence in the eighteenth and nineteenth centuries, given how difficult it was to obtain a divorce. It was hardly a scandal.'

Nancy bridled. 'Richard, I'm sure, would consider it a scandal. In fact, I wondered whether it was his reason for not wanting to pursue the Payne connection to the family. Because Laurence was descended from an illegitimate line.'

'I wouldn't have thought so. After all, Laurence is still descended from the Lancefield's bloodline.' Barbara picked up a teaspoon and stirred her tea. 'I hope you're not planning to cause trouble over this. It's bad enough that Eva has been murdered. Richard is devastated, and David and Marcus will be heartbroken. The last thing they need is you making waves about the family connection that led to Eva's death.'

'I wasn't thinking of making waves. I was just thinking that Laurence must have been the last person to see Eva alive. Surely that in itself is enough to persuade Richard that he needs to at least speak to the man?'

'And if it isn't?'

Nancy's lips curved into an enigmatic smile. 'Then perhaps one of us should reach out to Laurence Payne and ask him just exactly what Eva was doing in London when Richard had forbidden it?'

11

It was quiet in The Lancefield Arms.

'I suppose now you're going to tell me that I should have ordered something a little stronger than coffee?' When Ennor had suggested a walk down into the village, Kathryn had hoped it was simply to clear their heads. But now she wasn't so sure. 'You know I don't normally hit the hard stuff in the middle of the afternoon. But I could always make an exception.'

'Maybe you should wait to hear what I have to say. And then you can decide.' He picked up his cup and sipped on his coffee. 'I hardly dare ask this question, but what do you know about Obeah?'

'Obeah? Eva's been murdered, Zak Smith is still on the run, and you're asking for another history lesson?'

'I'm serious, Kathryn. It's important.'

She studied his face, the tense folds of his brow and the anxiety in the soft, brown eyes. Whatever it was, it *was* serious. 'Well, I'm not an expert, but it's a kind of Creole witchcraft. The slaves who were transported to the Caribbean from Africa brought certain beliefs and practices with them, and Obeah grew from those.'

'Was it harmless?'

'For the most part. Each plantation had an Obeah man or woman, and a slave might save up to pay for a spell to be cast. It was claimed that Obeah could help you to attract a partner or bring you luck.'

'So it wasn't used to kill people?'

'Kill people?' Kathryn rolled her eyes. 'I hope you're not going to tell me that Eva was cursed.'

'Kathryn, was it ever used to kill people?'

He wasn't joking then. 'An Obeah man or woman could be asked to place a curse or a hex, or to bring bad fortune on someone. There is very little evidence to suggest that such curses worked, of course.' But there was more to it than that. 'For the most part, plantation owners tolerated Obeah because it was considered fairly harmless and it kept the slave population content that they could practice their own beliefs. But Obeah practitioners were also knowledgeable in herbs. And they were often skilled in using botanical poisons.' She didn't like the direction the conversation was taking. 'I thought Eva drowned?'

Ennor didn't answer her. 'Has the Lancefield family ever been associated with Obeah?'

'Woodlands had a succession of Obeah men and women. It was common practice, and the Lancefields tolerated it just as other plantation owners did. The details of them all are recorded in the Woodlands estate daybook.'

'But nothing specific? Nothing out of the ordinary where the family was concerned?'

'No, not at Woodlands. But…' She hesitated again. 'I have seen something in the records which might be relevant. The plantation next to Woodlands, St Aldate's, changed hands during Benedict Lancefield's lifetime and was sold to a man called Edward Mason. Mason proved to be a cruel master, so cruel that a number of slaves dared to approach Benedict Lancefield and ask for help. Benedict sent them away, refusing to interfere between slaves and master, and Mason sought to make an example of those slaves who had dared to question his authority. Within a matter of days, Mason was found dead in his plantation house. He had been poisoned with an unknown substance and his body bore the trappings of Obeah; a garland had been hung around his neck, a piece of thin rope decorated with flowers, long bird-feathers and …'

'A monkey's skull. And probably a bottle with a cockroach in it.'

Kathryn sucked in a sharp breath. 'How on earth did you know?'

Another question not answered. 'Was that the end of the story?'

'No. An investigation into the death was held and Benedict Lancefield played a leading role. The Obeah man on the St Aldate's plantation was found guilty of Mason's murder and hanged.' She placed a hand on Ennor's arm. 'Ennor, how did you know about the garland?'

'A replica of it was found around Eva's neck when they took her body out of the water.'

'It was around her neck?' Kathryn shivered. 'How did you know it was an Obeah hex?'

'Laurence Payne identified it. According to DCI Greenway, Payne is an expert in Obeah.' Ennor frowned. 'Can you think of any reason why he might be?'

'Not why he should be an expert in it, no. But I can certainly give you a reason why he might have been familiar with that particular hex.' Kathryn looked Ennor squarely in the eyes. 'Don't you remember what I told you this morning? The St Aldate's plantation originally belonged to the Payne family. And it was Laurence's direct ancestor, William Payne, who sold the plantation to Edward Mason.'

*

'How did you get on at Vincenzo's?' Given his propensity to moan at doing all the legwork, Chris Greenway had been surprised when Marwick volunteered to go over to the restaurant. 'Were they helpful?'

'Couldn't have been more so.' Marwick sat down on the chair at the other side of Greenway's desk. 'The manager I spoke to was on duty on Friday evening and he remembered Eva and Laurence. Laurence booked the table, and arrived early for the meeting. They met in the bar for a drink before dinner, enjoyed a three-course meal with wine, and then returned to the bar for more drinks.' The sergeant pulled his notebook from his pocket and flipped it open. 'The manager said that as far as he can remember, they looked at ease in each other's company. And, better than that,' Marwick grinned, 'he let me see that for myself.'

Greenway straightened in his seat. 'You've seen CCTV footage?'

'Yep. He said it might take a few days to get the footage downloaded for us to view here at the station and asked if I wanted to take an initial look at the images today. He has access to the camera files from the computer in his office.'

The inspector whistled softly. 'So, what did you see?'

'The two of them in the restaurant having dinner, and then leaving the restaurant at eleven fifty-six. They turned left, towards the floating footbridge. There were a few seconds when they were out of shot, and then a security camera higher up on the outside wall of the restaurant picked them up again just a few yards away from the bridge. They stood and chatted for a few minutes, and then Laurence took hold of Eva's hand and pecked her on the cheek before turning away and walking off along the footbridge.'

'And Eva?'

'She stood for a moment to wave him off and then set off walking towards her hotel. And this is where it gets interesting. She doesn't walk very far before she moves out of shot. And just as we lose her, a man walks into view from the direction of Vincenzo's. He's smartly dressed in a suit, walking briskly with his hands in his trouser pockets. I couldn't make him out in detail, the camera wasn't close enough. But he appeared to have grey or white-blond hair.'

'So, now we have a possible witness?' If not a suspect. 'He might have seen Eva walking down the side of the hotel.' Or perhaps even something more suspicious. Greenway picked up his pen and rapped it thoughtfully on the desk. 'If we want to see where Eva went after that, and whether this man continued to follow her, we'll need the footage from the street cameras and the hotels.' And that was going to take anything from hours to days. 'Could we ask the manager at Vincenzo's if we could examine that footage again?'

'Looking for what?'

'The man following Eva. I want to know if he was in the restaurant and followed her from there.'

'He might be a completely innocent bystander.'

'And he might be an opportunistic killer. He would have seen Laurence walk away across the bridge, leaving Eva unaccompanied.' Greenway twirled his pen around between his fingers. 'The only thing we can be sure of at the moment, based on your description of him, is that he wasn't Zak Smith.' The inspector thought for a moment and then pushed his chair back away from the desk and rose to his feet. 'What do we need to focus on to complete the picture of where Eva went?' He stepped over to the whiteboard and picked up a marker pen. 'CCTV images from the Canary Wharf Estate from eleven fifty-six.' He scribbled on the whiteboard as he spoke. 'Also from the Excelsior Hotel. Images from…' He turned, annoyed, to look at Marwick. 'What the hell is that vibrating noise? Is that your phone?'

Marwick's cheeks flushed pink and he fished the phone from his jacket pocket. 'Bob Marwick.' He pressed it to his ear, turning his eyes down to avoid the inspector's admonishing gaze. 'Right.' His face began to run a gamut of emotions. 'My God, you're joking?' He lifted his head to stare at Greenway, his eyes wide. 'And you can definitely see that on the footage?' He raised his eyes upwards. 'I can't thank you enough for doing that. And I'm sorry you had to see it. We'll be with you within the hour.' He pressed at the phone with his thumb to end the call. 'That was the manager of Vincenzo's. After I left, he decided to take a look at some more of the footage. It troubled him that Eva's body was found so close to the restaurant.'

'And he saw something?'

'He saw "*the* thing".' Marwick gave a disbelieving shake of the head. 'The poor bloke saw that blond man half-dragging Eva back along the quayside. He said it looked as though she was drunk, or drugged.'

'So how the hell did she end up in the water?'

'The bastard put her in there.'

Greenway froze. He stared at Marwick with unseeing eyes, trying to fathom whether this latest turn of events was fact or fiction. And then he spoke, quietly and with deliberation. 'He put her in there?'

'He lifted her up over the railings, lowered her body down the other side by her arms, and then he slowly let go so that she slid into the water.'

'And all of that was captured on CCTV? What the bloody hell was he thinking of? He must have known that we would see the footage of that eventually?'

'I don't think there's any question of that. According to the manager at Vincenzo's, after the bastard had dropped her into the water he turned round and waved directly into the CCTV camera.'

*

Richard sat down on the large Liberty sofa and looked around him. It was the first time in many months that he had entered Lucy's suite of rooms, and for the life of him he couldn't fathom why the news of Eva's death had prompted him to venture in there now.

The sitting room was just as it had been on the day of his granddaughter's death: the sleek Italian console tables, with their highly polished glass tops; the oversized television set; the marble fireplace against the innermost wall. The mantel above the fire still bore an impressive collection of family photographs, most of them in elegant silver frames, and the sight of them brought an unbidden lump to his throat. Images of himself and his darling Alice, and of David and his first wife Susanna, flanked a striking picture of Lucy and Marcus taken at Lucy's final birthday party.

He fixed his eyes on the print, remembering the occasion. Two young people, their whole lives ahead of them, the future of the Lancefield family secured. At least, that's how it had seemed before Lucy so cruelly lost her life.

And that's how it seemed again, now.

He had never intended Eva to be a replacement for Lucy. In any case, the cool and sophisticated Eva had been a very different creature from the wild and vibrant Lucy, despite their physical resemblance. Each girl had their own place in his heart. But now that place was empty again, an aching cavity that might never be filled.

'Marcus and David will be home soon, Lucy. They are coming home to face our new loss. With a fair wind, they will be back in England by the morning.' He spoke the words quietly, addressing them to the picture on the mantelpiece. 'Eva has been taken from us, just as you were taken from us. Murdered by an unknown hand.' He blew the breath out slowly. 'She was never you, my dear. But her presence in our lives brought us all hope, hope that the void you left could be filled. She was a surrogate daughter for your father, and a comfort and companion for Marcus. And I won't deny that it was a blessing on the family when Marcus grew fond of her.' And now that blessing had become a curse. A curse that seemed to follow the Lancefield family at every touch and turn. A curse that had led so many to lose their lives.

He felt the sting of a tear at the back of his eye and he brushed at his face with the cuff of his shirt. 'I think the time has come to clear out your room, my dear. It has quite become a shrine to your memory, but Eva's untimely death has made me realise that it's time for us all to move on.' He would have to speak to Barbara and Kathryn. It wouldn't do for Nancy to undertake this particular task. 'We will see that your belongings are donated where they will do most good, and hang some of your photographs in the library.' The rest could go into storage in the attic. 'I will have to speak to your father about your jewellery.'

The old man looked down at his hands. 'I do so wish you could talk to me, Lucy. I wish that you could tell me just what happened to you on that fateful evening back in September. Marcus has sworn to me so many times that he didn't take your life, and I desperately want to believe him. And yet my own heart finds it impossible to believe that you died by Philip's hand.'

Philip was far too gentle a soul to harm a girl he loved. But the truth would never be known.

Richard braced his hands on the sofa and levered himself to his feet. He had stayed too long in Lucy's domain, meandered too close to his memories. He turned his eyes around the room, quickly taking in the bookshelves laden with books, the writing desk with its diaries and journals, the entrance to the small dressing room that led to Lucy's bedroom. And for the first time he realised that the room still smelled of Lucy: that faint, rose-tinted fragrance that had always hung about her.

He tilted his head back towards the mantelpiece, ready to make his goodbyes, and as he did so his eyes lighted on a small, framed print hanging to the left of the fireplace: a colourful period portrait of two young women in exquisite silk gowns.

Elizabeth Murray and Dido Belle.

The old man's body stiffened. The room must be emptied, and emptied with haste.

12

The car park on the shoreline at Marazion was almost empty, save for Tom Parkinson's Mazda.

'We only just got here in time. They're closing the coffee bar early.' He folded himself into the car, still grasping two cardboard cups. 'I think this one is yours.'

DCI Price, seated in the passenger seat, took the cup from him. 'I'm not surprised they're closing up. The rain's coming in.' And that was an understatement. Heavy black clouds were rolling towards them from the west, blotting out the watery sun and spraying the air with a thick mist of precipitation. 'So, how did it go over in Truro?'

'I think it's fair to say that Becca wasn't too pleased to see me.' Parkinson balanced his cup on the lower rim of the Mazda's steering wheel as he spoke. 'To be honest, I almost felt sorry for her. I think she really wants to make a fresh start, but this thing with Zak is never going to leave her alone.'

'It would leave her alone if she did the right thing and turned him in.'

'You're still convinced that she's covering for him, aren't you?'

'Aren't you? Nobody else is going to cover for him.' Price sipped his coffee. 'Did you learn anything?'

'Not directly from Becca. She's still a little angry ball of venom.' Parkinson grinned. 'But there were two mobile phones in the living room. One on the coffee table next to the sofa, for anyone to see. And one secreted behind a potted plant on the top of a bookcase.'

'And she doesn't know that you saw them both?'

'No. She'd gone upstairs to check on Frankie so I took the opportunity to scout around. I don't think there's any question that she's helping him, boss. I think that she knows where he is, and somehow she's keeping him in cash.'

'Did you ask her?'

'Of course I did. She just got angry.' Parkinson chuckled at the thought. 'Really angry. Angry enough to look as guilty as hell.'

'We still don't have any evidence of that, though, do we?'

'No. Not without taking both of those phones.' He turned his head to look out of the window. The clouds were almost above them. 'I just didn't have time to scan the phone on the bookcase for a number. If I had…'

It was pointless fretting over a missed opportunity. Price, of all people, knew the futility of that. 'What about persuading Amber Kimbrall to lean on her? I know they're not speaking to each other, but it has to be worth a try. I think Amber would agree, if we asked her to do it for the Lancefields. The family have been good to her. And she wants to see Zak brought to justice, just as much as we do.'

'I could try. But I don't share your conviction that she'll do it. What reason could she give for trying to build a bridge, other than asking about Zak? And then it will look like she's interested in him again. He might take that as a green light to seek her out, and she's already risked her life once to turn him in. There's no guarantee he wouldn't take it out on her the next time.'

It was a fair point. Smith had already raised his hand to

Amber once, and with two – and possibly three – murders under his belt there was no telling what he might do next. 'How did Becca take the news that Eva McWhinney had been murdered?'

'It took the wind out of her sails. But she's loyal to Zak, she wouldn't believe he had anything to do with it.' Parkinson ran his tongue thoughtfully around his teeth. 'To be honest, boss, I'm struggling to see it myself. I mean, I know he's already had two attempts to murder Eva, but how the hell would he have known where she would be? Even the Lancefields didn't know that she was going to London.'

'The London team are exploring the possibility of a link between Smith and Eva's cousin.'

Parkinson whistled. 'They're looking at the cousin as a suspect?'

'At the moment, it's the only thing they've got. He knew exactly where Eva would be, and when. And he knew about the thing that was hanging around her neck. Either he put it there, or Smith put it there.' Either way, it could only have been done by someone who understood the significance. 'Kathryn reckons that there is a tenuous link between that garland and the Lancefield family.' He was beginning to feel a familiar prickle of unease. 'It has to be Smith, Tom. There can't be any other explanation.' He let out a sigh. 'Maybe we've been looking in the wrong place for him all this time. Maybe the reason we haven't found him is because he's three hundred miles away in London.'

*

Matthew Foster was a slim, fair-haired young man with an anxious smile. In DCI Greenway's considered opinion he looked too young to be managing a busy restaurant like Vincenzo's, but then Greenway knew next to nothing about the hospitality trade. And in any case, the only thing that mattered here was that Foster had not only taken it upon himself to trawl through the restaurant's CCTV footage, but had immediately alerted the police to what he'd discovered.

Now, in the confined and clammy space that Foster called his office, Greenway and Marwick could only wait with bated breath as the manager deftly navigated his way around the computer on his desk.

'This is the file here.' He clicked at the computer's keyboard with a firm, decisive touch. 'Just bear with me while I fast-forward to the right timeframe.'

Bear with him? Greenway could hardly stand the suspense. 'You haven't shown this to anyone else, have you? Only we need to keep the footage secure. It's not the sort of thing we would want leaking out onto social media.'

'No one has seen it, apart from me. I didn't want to upset the rest of the staff.' Foster leaned back in his seat to afford the policemen a better view of the action. 'This is it. If you watch the left-hand side of the screen, in a couple of seconds you'll see the man appear.'

Greenway craned his neck over the young man's shoulder, silently watching the drama on the screen unfold. The quayside was empty until two shadowy figures emerged from the alleyway at the side of the restaurant. At first sight they might have been a courting couple, making their way home after an evening's drinking, more than a little worse for wear.

The man was slim and well-dressed in a sharp suit; his left arm was fixed firmly around the young woman's waist, while her right was draped loosely around his neck. They were walking slowly towards the water's edge, their progress halting, the man struggling under the weight of his companion. If you could call it walking.

'She's unconscious.' It was Marwick who spoke. 'Her feet are dragging on the cobblestones.'

The woman certainly appeared to be unconscious. On closer inspection, the man was carrying her rather than supporting her. Greenway had seen some cruel spectacles in his time, but the sight of Eva McWhinney's lifeless body being slowly manoeuvred to a watery grave would probably haunt his sleep for months. 'Poor kid, she didn't stand a chance. Can you pause the film? I want to take a closer look.' His eyes were still transfixed on the screen. 'The garland is already around her neck.' He bent forward until his face was just a matter of inches from the image. 'Is that the same man who was following her two hours earlier?'

'Yes.' Foster paused the video. 'At least, he looks the same to me. You can't miss that hair. Or the beard.'

There was no denying that. The man had a head of close-cropped, white-blond hair that appeared almost luminous under the moonlight, and a flush of honey-coloured fuzz around the lower half of his face. 'Well, we know for sure now that it's not Zak Smith.' Greenway tapped Matthew Foster gently on the shoulder. 'Can we see what comes next?'

Foster clicked at his keyboard and the video resumed. Greenway watched in disgust as the man hoisted Eva's body up onto the wire railings that separated the pavement from the dock, turning her over until her chest was against the other side of the railings, and lowering her slowly down into the water. He watched as her body slipped away from him, and then he turned to face the CCTV camera.

'Oh, for pity's sake, that's not a beard. He's wearing some sort of mask.' It was Marwick who spoke. 'How the hell can we identify him with that in the way?' The sergeant's voice was full of anguish. 'The only thing we have to go on is the hair.'

'Well, it's better than nothing.' Greenway pointed at the small, digital display at the top of the computer screen. 'Does that say one fifty-three? Two hours after he was seen following Eva in the direction of her hotel?' The policeman drew in a breath. 'Then what the hell was he doing for those two hours between appearances?'

'I would have thought that was obvious.' Marwick turned to the inspector. 'Amongst other things, he must have been killing her.'

*

Barbara relaxed back into the soft folds of the Dower House sofa and patted her knees with her plump, warm hands. 'Come on, boy. You know you want to.'

Samson took a tentative step forward and then checked himself, turning his head towards Richard's armchair. His master smiled and lifted his hand to signal his approval. 'Go on, old boy.' The dog didn't need any further encouragement. He padded towards Barbara's legs, bent back on his haunches, then launched himself shakily into her lap.

'Oh dear, that was a struggle, wasn't it?' Barbara stroked the fur behind his ear as he circled awkwardly, searching for a comfortable position. 'I think you're getting arthritis.' She looked up at Richard. 'Are you taking him with you to St Felix?'

Richard's lips curled. 'You're fishing, Barbara. I am considering my return. I do not recall saying that I had made firm plans.'

'No. But we both know that you will, at some point. I can't imagine that Eva's death will prevent that. Delay it, perhaps. But not prevent it.' The dog had settled and Barbara gently ruffled his ear as she spoke. 'I suppose it's a question of what's best for Samson: whether the journey and change of climate will be too much for him, compared with the pain of being separated from you. If you leave him here with us, he may just pine.'

'Leave him here "with us"? My dear Barbara, is that the answer to my question?'

'It might be. Let's just say that Eva's death has put things sharply into perspective. David has already lost Lucy and Stella, and now he's lost Eva. I can't imagine how he is going to cope with another bout of grief, but at least I can be there to help him rebuild, especially if you decide to return to St Felix. So, yes, I am more than happy to accept your invitation to move to Salvation Hall. I think I would prefer to be at Holly Cottage, if that is still a possibility.'

'My dear, it's a certainty. Although I hope you won't delay your move until the place has been upgraded. There are more than enough rooms in the main house for you to choose from.' For a moment Richard could hardly hide his delight. And then his eyes clouded. 'Of course, there are difficult times ahead. At least until we resolve the matter of poor Eva's death.' He turned his head away, to stare into the fire. 'I spoke to David earlier. He and Marcus have secured flights back to Gatwick tonight, and will pick up a connecting flight to Newquay in the morning. I've asked Nancy to drive over to the airport first thing, to collect them and bring them home.'

'Don't they want to stay in London to see Eva?'

'Inspector Price has advised against it. He's asked them to come straight back to Salvation Hall, and leave him to liaise with DCI Greenway. The police investigation is at a very sensitive stage.' Richard rubbed at his brow with a bony finger. 'There will be time enough to say goodbye to Eva when we bring her home. Always assuming there is nothing to prevent us from bringing her back to Salvation Hall. It is only now that I realise how little we really knew of her. Did she leave a will? Were there people in her life, in her career or her neighbourhood, who were close to her in some way and may have expectations about the disposal of her estate?'

It wasn't something Barbara had considered. It wasn't the sort of thing you *would* consider about a fit and healthy young woman in the prime of life. 'Are you suggesting that one of us should go up to Edinburgh and make enquiries?' Barbara puffed out a breath. 'Heavens, Richard, how do we go about that? I suppose it will be straightforward enough to make enquiries of her colleagues at the hospital, but the houses in Hemlock Row – do we know if anyone had a key? We would need to gain access to number three in order to search through Eva's personal papers. Do we even know if she had a regular solicitor?'

'I can answer none of those questions. I suppose it's possible that Marcus may know something.' Richard let out a sigh. 'I fear that I am going to have to call upon your kindness again, Barbara, and ask if you would represent us in Edinburgh. I cannot ask it of David and Marcus. And I feel it should be a member of the family. It would not be fair for me to ask Kathryn, although I'm sure she would rise to the challenge as she always does.'

'You wouldn't consider asking Nancy?'

The question hung in the air for a moment and then Richard bristled. 'I said a member of the family, Barbara.'

'I know. But you're always telling me that the residents of the Lancefield's estates are all one big, blended family.' She sensed his irritation, and moved in for the kill. 'Tell me, Richard, has Eva's death changed your thinking about Nancy returning to Woodlands? You know, she and I had a long chat earlier today and she opened up to me a little. She confided that she feels sidelined and disappointed that you are putting the estate in Marcus's hands. But I can't help wondering if things may be different now that Eva has gone.'

Richard grumbled under his breath. 'I do not wish to discuss it.'

'Perhaps not. But sometimes those things we avoid most fervently are the very things that we should be discussing.' Barbara leaned forward towards him. 'Nancy also confided to me that she wants to stay in England because she wants to be with you. Why don't you at least tell her that you are thinking of moving back to St Felix, to put her mind at rest?'

'There are things you do not know about Nancy, Barbara. More than that I do not wish to say.'

'And does your wish to avoid discussing this outweigh my right to know the truth? If I am to give up my home and my life in Liverpool to move down here and support the Lancefield family, don't I at least have a right to know of any secrets in the family's closet that might lead me to wish that I hadn't been so hasty?'

13

'I managed to sneak an hour alone in the library this afternoon. I still might not have the full story for you, but it will give you an idea.' Kathryn placed a handful of papers down on the table, a collection of hastily written notes. 'At least it's relatively quiet in here, so we won't be overheard.'

Ennor could barely resist a smile. The bar at The Zoological Hotel was almost empty, as was usual on a Sunday evening, and he guessed that the elderly American couple occupying the corner table by the window probably couldn't have cared less about the distant, dusty history of the Lancefield family. But he didn't want to spoil her fun. 'Go on, then, shock me. I could do with a bit of light relief.'

She pouted at him, the hazel eyes mildly reproving. 'Unless I'm mistaken, you thought that this piece of history'—she tapped the papers with a firm finger—'might be relevant to Eva's murder.'

'I know. I'm sorry.' He tried to look sheepish, and wasn't sure that he pulled it off. 'Laurence Payne has claimed that his ancestors were familiar with Obeah. But I thought that Obeah was practised by the slave population, not by the plantation owners?'

'And you would be right. I've already told you there was a rumour that Maria Lancefield's husband, George Payne, was illegitimate.' She gave Ennor time to consider the implications. 'Now I've found documentary evidence of the rumour amongst letters that went between Maria, her brother Benedict back in St Felix, and her sister Charlotte in Edinburgh.'

'The same Charlotte that married James McWhinney? Eva's direct ancestor?'

Kathryn's eyes lit with amusement. 'Well, what a diligent pupil you've turned out to be. You've actually remembered something.' She picked up a page of handwritten notes. 'George Payne was the son of William and Beatrice Payne, who owned the St Aldate's Plantation. By all accounts, Beatrice was a sickly woman who struggled with the Caribbean climate, and failed to produce an heir. In desperation, William made a proposal to her that he father a child with his Creole mistress, Abigail. It was intended to be a sort of surrogacy, and Abigail understood that any child would be raised as Beatrice's child and given legitimacy. She was content to give up the child to secure its future and position, not least as that would also guarantee a secure future for herself.'

'So that child was George Payne, Maria Lancefield's husband?'

'That is the inference from the letters I've seen. Beatrice wasn't happy with the arrangement, but didn't have much choice if she wanted to keep her marriage. When Abigail fell pregnant, both women absented themselves to another part of the island, supposedly for Beatrice's health, and stayed there in seclusion until the child was born. When they returned, the child was passed off as Beatrice's son.'

'Then the child wasn't black?'

'Obviously not. But then, Abigail was referred to in the letters as "Creole". That just means she was born in one of the colonies. She might easily have been fair skinned herself.'

'I still have a lot to learn.' Ennor folded his arms. 'Did George Payne know the circumstances of his birth? And that he was technically illegitimate?'

'Not initially. He was raised as William and Beatrice's son. And clearly the Lancefields had no idea, as Benedict gave his permission for George's betrothal to Maria. The marriage took place in 1805, the same year that William Payne inherited his family's estate in Hertfordshire. He decided to sell up and return to England, to set up in business as a sugar merchant, using his contacts and knowledge of the industry. That was when he sold St Aldate's to Edward Mason.'

'The guy who was poisoned?'

'Yes. Everything seemed to go smoothly for the Paynes at first, but a little over a year after they moved back to England, Benedict Lancefield received an anonymous letter, advising him that his sister had been duped into marrying an illegitimate Creole with a wicked reputation. Benedict was furious and immediately wrote to William Payne, demanding to know the truth. William held fast to the lie that George was his son, but then Benedict received a letter from Charlotte advising him that George Payne had been involved in a scandal in London. Something to do with a young woman of easy virtue.'

'*Cherchez la femme?*'

'You may scoff, but the outcome was terrible. Maria, by now pregnant and utterly humiliated, wrote letters to Charlotte, and to her sisters-in-law, Benedict's wife Eugenie and Richard's wife Leonora, pleading for help. They were all sympathetic, but unable to offer any practical advice. Divorce was out of the question. In desperation, Maria wrote to Benedict asking for leave to separate from her husband and return to St Felix. But before she received a reply, George took his own life. His parents were heartbroken and Maria opted to stay with them in England. But she lost her standing in society. The Paynes legally adopted her child, to ensure its future, but the drama cost her the Lancefield connection in any real sense.'

Ennor thought for a moment. 'It's a sad tale, I'll grant you that. But it doesn't tell me why the family would be knowledgeable about Obeah.'

Kathryn put the page of notes back down on the table. 'I would suspect it was because of George's natural mother, Abigail. But at this point I don't have any proof.' There was a glass of Chablis on the table in front of her, and she picked it up and sipped it. 'Of course, if the answer to the question is important there is one person who might be able to help, if you were in a position to ask him. And that would be Laurence Payne himself.'

*

'I'm sorry to disturb you again today. But we've identified a suspect for Eva's murder, and we need to follow up as quickly as we can.' DS Marwick followed Laurence Payne into his sitting room, refusing an invitation to sit with a shake of the head. 'I won't keep you. I'd just like you to take a look at this.' He held out a piece of paper. 'I'd like to know if you recognise the man.'

Laurence took the paper and stared at it. 'It isn't a very good photograph, is it? It's quite blurred.' He squinted at the image. 'But yes, I think I recognise him.'

'You've seen him before?'

'Yes. He was in Vincenzo's on Friday evening.' Laurence tipped the picture away from him, towards the light of a nearby table lamp. 'You couldn't miss that hair, could you? White blond.' He pursed his lips. 'If I remember rightly, he was drinking alone at the bar when we arrived, and I have a vague recollection of him being taken to a table behind us in the restaurant, just after we had ordered our meal.'

'Did anyone join him?'

'I don't think so.'

'Can you remember when he left?'

'Oh, definitely before we did. We went back to the bar for another drink after our meal, and he wasn't there then.' Laurence offered the photograph back to the policeman. 'Is this a still from the restaurant's CCTV footage?'

'Yes.' It had been a struggle to print it from Matthew Foster's computer, but somehow they had managed. 'We think this man followed Eva as she walked on her own back to the hotel.' Marwick folded the piece of paper and tucked it back into his pocket. 'Did the man speak to you at all? Or to Eva?'

'No. The only reason I remember him is because of the hair. It makes a statement, doesn't it? Of course, he wasn't wearing a mask when I saw him. But I can't recall much about his face, just the hair and his suit.' Laurence looked suddenly troubled. 'You say you think he followed Eva? You don't think...' His voice trailed away. 'I mean...'

'Did he kill her?' Marwick hesitated, weighing up the pros and cons of telling Laurence Payne the truth, and decided upon a small deflection. 'We have evidence that this man put Eva's body in the water. We're still awaiting confirmation of her cause of death. She may have been murdered some time before that, in which case we have to keep an open mind about the person responsible for her death.'

'I see.' Laurence swayed slightly, and then took a step backwards to perch on the sofa's arm. 'Was this person responsible for putting the Obeah garland around Eva's neck?'

'Again, we can confirm that it was around her neck when she went into the water. But we cannot confirm at this stage that he put it there.' Marwick fixed his eyes on Laurence's face. The man was beginning to look anxious.

'We haven't discounted the possibility that he was working in conjunction with a third party.'

The colour faded from Laurence's chiselled cheeks. 'I thought her murder was opportunistic? That she was murdered by some passerby with a grudge against humanity.'

'Did you?' The sergeant adopted his best poker face. 'The garland around her neck had a clear connection to your family's history. What explanation could you give for that, if this was just a random killing?' The sergeant glanced around as he waited for Laurence to reply, and for the first time he noticed that a small, half-filled suitcase was resting on a chair beside the mahogany bookcase. He turned his eyes back to Laurence. 'Are you going away, Mr Payne?'

Laurence blushed. 'I wasn't aware that travel was a crime, Sergeant Marwick. Is there any reason why I shouldn't make a trip?'

Apart from the fact that he was a key witness in a murder case, possibly even a suspect? Marwick gave a noncommittal smile. 'None at all. But it would be helpful if you could tell me where you're going. We may need to speak to you again, and I wouldn't like to think that we couldn't get hold of you.'

'I'm going home to Hertfordshire to spend a couple of days with my fiancée. To make up for not being there this weekend.'

'Ah.' Marwick nodded, unconvinced. 'Are you leaving tonight?'

'In the morning. I'll be taking an early tube across town to Paddington. My train leaves just after seven.'

'Then I won't detain you any further this evening. We'll be in touch as soon as we have any further news about the investigation.'

Outside in the hallway, Marwick muttered under his breath. 'A train just after seven? Very likely. But if you're heading for Hertfordshire it wouldn't make much sense to be catching it from Paddington.'

*

Nancy lifted a log from the basket on the hearth and dropped it carefully into the grate. It collapsed into the smouldering mess of ashes with a hiss, sending a shower of tiny sparks up into the chimney. She gave a tiny murmur of satisfaction, brushing the dust from her hands, and watched for a moment as most of the quivering sparks floated gently back down into the grate.

Lighting a fire in the library had been a tiny act of rebellion: the library was customarily Kathryn's domain, and it was Kathryn's call whether the fire would be lit or not. But Kathryn was out with Inspector Price, and Richard and Barbara were secreted in the Dower House, no doubt talking about things which clearly didn't involve Nancy.

She had already manoeuvred the sofa to be closer to the fire and she sank onto it with a sigh, curling her bare feet up onto the seat and pulling a soft, woollen blanket over her knees. There was a cardboard box on the cushion beside her and she dipped a hand into it to pull out a scrap of paper, a dog-eared, handwritten bill of sale. The document was fragile, the paper so thin in places it was almost transparent, and she opened it up carefully and placed it down on the blanket, smoothing it out with her fingers.

'The fourteenth of May, 1777.' She whispered the words to herself as she took in the details. 'Received from Mr William Payne: forty-five pounds for the lady's maid, Abigail Woodlands.'

Nancy's face softened into a smile. 'Well, Abigail, I have finally found you.'

Born in 1760, the girl must only have been seventeen when her ownership passed from Benedict Lancefield to his neighbour at the St Aldate's plantation. No wonder there were so few references to her in the Woodlands estate daybooks. At least she didn't travel far, and perhaps she may still have had contact with her sister, Nancy's own direct ancestor Millie.

Nancy nestled back into the sofa's cushions with a frown. Why would Benedict Lancefield have sold the girl and not recorded it in the daybook? To be a lady's maid was a privileged position; house servants at Woodlands were treated kindly and looked upon as valued members of the household. She glanced back in the direction of the cardboard box. Perhaps the answer to that question lay in the handful of private family letters that Nancy had yet to read.

It was lucky, she supposed, that she had come upon this particular box of so-far-unexplored treasures. Not that Kathryn would have hidden anything from Nancy – she was far too honourable for that. But finding the information first afforded Nancy the opportunity to dig a little deeper and draw her own conclusions. Kathryn might not have hidden the information but she might have been inclined to dismiss its obvious importance.

It's obvious importance to Nancy.

Things being important to Nancy didn't seem to figure too much in the Lancefield family's plans at the moment. Why else would Richard be planning to banish her back to St Felix? It was all well and good to make her custodian of the family's heritage, but why did it feel to her like a consolation prize?

The thought unquestionably irked her, and she tipped her head back to stare up at the ceiling. Since the day of Lucy's death, Richard had been hellbent on turning up distant members of the family to replace her, a venture which only served to bring even more pain for the family. Dennis Speed had been the first to die. Inviting him to connect with the family had exposed the truth of his own son's illegitimacy, a long-kept secret that Jason Speed tried to bury by murdering his father. And now, Eva McWhinney was lying on a mortuary slab, her brief tenure within the family brought to an abrupt end by her determination to bring Laurence Payne into the fold. Only cousin Barbara remained: warm, funny, understanding Barbara. Nancy liked Barbara; liked her down-to-earth honesty and her tendency to speak her mind whether Richard appreciated it or not. It was a pity, Nancy mused, that the house wasn't full of Barbaras. Had that been the case, then Nancy might not be facing the prospect of returning to St Felix to be buried alive with the rest of the family's heritage.

She turned her eyes back down to the document on her knee, and caressed it slowly with a gentle finger. Perhaps, she considered with a pang of excitement, it wasn't going to be so easy for Richard to banish her back to the Caribbean after all.

*

The mobile phone atop the chest of drawers let out a loud buzz and began to skitter across the polished surface.

Becca's stomach churned. *Not now. Please not now.*

She could hardly bring herself to look at the offending phone. She knew the pleading was in vain, that whoever was calling had no intention of hanging up. And she knew that if she didn't answer, there would be call after call after call until she did.

The remote control for the television was resting in her lap and she picked it up and flicked it at the screen to mute the sound, swearing under her breath. 'Alright, for pity's sake, I'm coming.' She pushed herself up out of the chair and stepped across the room to sweep up the phone with an impatient hand. The number on the screen caught her eye before she answered, and for a fleeting moment she was caught off guard. The number displayed wasn't the number she expected.

She swiped at the screen, silent as the call connected, and waited for the caller to speak.

For a few taut seconds there was only silence. And then a familiar voice: 'Becs, is that you?' The voice at the end of the line was angry. 'What the hell took you so long? I thought for a minute then, you weren't going to answer.'

'I didn't recognise the number. How many new mobile phones have you had since you went on the run?'

Zak Smith chuckled as he answered the question. 'I dunno. I've lost count. It's handy to keep changing numbers. It helps me to keep one step ahead of the pigs.' He sniffed loudly. 'What's your new place like, then? Did Robin help you to move all your stuff in?'

She stiffened at the question. 'It's lovely, thank you. We're settling in well. It's the new start that we need.'

'Well, that's grand. I'm looking forward to seeing it for myself.'

Becca felt her face begin to burn. 'You won't be seeing it. I've told you, it's a new start for me and Frankie.' Her pulse began to quicken. 'You're not coming here, Zak. You have to promise me.'

'You don't mean that, Becs. I'm your favourite brother, remember?'

Once upon a time, maybe.

She couldn't lose courage now. She'd made up her mind. 'I know you are. That's why I've been sending you the money. It's why I helped you to get away.' That, and to make sure that there was no risk of him coming back. 'Where are you now? Are you still in Weston?'

'Weston? Nah, I left there a few days ago.' For all his bravado he sounded weary. 'Sis, I need a bed for the night.'

Panic gripped her stomach. 'You're not back in Cornwall?'

'You don't sound very pleased about it.'

'Zak, you can't come here. I didn't want to say anything, because I didn't want to worry you. But the police have been here. Sergeant Parkinson… he came this afternoon, poking around, asking questions about you.'

'So much for your new start then. You've already had the police round, you might as well let me stay.'

'He came to tell me that Eva McWhinney has been murdered. In London.' She paused, waiting to see how he would react, but there was only silence at the end of the line. 'The police think it was you.'

'Do they?' He sniffed loudly. 'I'm not really bothered what they think. It's what you think that counts.' He lowered his voice and growled down the line. 'Do you think it was me, Becs?'

'Please tell me that it wasn't.' Her voice was beginning to quaver. 'You promised that you wouldn't hurt her. You promised her to her face.'

'And a very pretty face it was, too.' He was beginning to sound impatient. 'I need somewhere to sleep tonight. I'll be gone in the morning.'

'Zak, did you kill her?'

'I think Frankie would be pleased to see her Uncle Zak.'

'Leave Frankie out of it.'

'How can I do that, when she's in the house?'

A solitary tear of panic began to roll down Becca's cheek. 'The police are watching the house. If they see you…'

'Police? I can't see any police.'

Becca's stomach somersaulted, and her eyes darted towards the window at the front of the living room. The street outside was in darkness. 'You're not here?'

'No?' Her brother laughed, a hollow cough. 'You've landed on your feet with that house. Everything shiny and new, and a nice back garden for little Frankie to play in.' He sniffed again. 'You could probably do with a new lock on the back door, though. It's too flimsy to be secure. You wouldn't want to risk a break-in, now, would you?' He was breathing heavily down the line. 'Come on, sis, I'm frozen out here. I haven't had anything to eat or drink for hours. Can't you just open up and let me in, so that we can put the kettle on? Or am I going to have to prove my point about that flimsy lock?'

14

Early-morning calls from DCI Greenway were in danger of becoming an unwelcome habit, and today's could hardly have been more disappointing.

'You're absolutely certain that it wasn't Smith?' Despite his own reservations, Price could hardly contain his frustration. 'You could see the man clearly enough to be sure?'

'He was clean cut with short, white-blond hair. But you don't have to take my word for it. We've produced some stills from the CCTV footage. I'll email a couple of them over to you after this call. Of course, we won't discount Smith completely from the enquiry, just in case there is some connection.' Chris Greenway clicked his teeth. 'We're pretty certain that she was already dead when she went into the water, by the way. We should get the autopsy report today to confirm that. In the meantime, DS Marwick is going to focus on piecing together the sequence of events. We know this man was in the restaurant on Friday evening at the same time as Eva and Laurence, and that he appeared to follow them as they walked along the quayside. We think that he continued to follow Eva after she'd said goodbye to Laurence at the footbridge, and probably overpowered her somewhere between the quayside and the entrance to her hotel. Her handbag, shawl and shoes were found in an alleyway not too far from her hotel, so it's likely that he dragged her there.'

'But I thought there was a two-hour time lag between her leaving Laurence and the CCTV footage that showed her being lowered into the water?'

'There was. Whoever he is, he's a cool bugger. We think he dragged her into the alleyway, murdered her, and then stayed there with the body until he thought it was safe to break cover and take her to the quayside. That takes a certain degree of sang froid, doesn't it?'

Unquestionably. The sort of sang froid that might be displayed by a man who had already killed more than once and overcome his aversion to the smell of death. 'So, you think you can piece that together from the various sets of CCTV footage, when you get them?'

'That's the hope.'

'And what about the motive? Was everything you would expect still in her handbag – purse, mobile phone, hotel key?'

'Ah, yes: motive. We're still working on that. The contents of the bag suggest it wasn't robbery. So, we're still looking at Laurence Payne and hoping the motive will become clear as we work through the evidence. Our working hypothesis is that he engaged the killer to dispose of his cousin. We can't see any other explanation for that bit of rubbish that was strung around her neck. Only Payne could have known what it meant.' The inspector sniffed loudly down the phone line. 'I don't suppose you've managed to find anything out on the Lancefield side that might help us?'

'I can tell you that Laurence Payne's line of the family was most likely illegitimate, and that they were cast out of the family because of some sort of scandal. The Lancefields had a habit of casting out family members who didn't fall in with their own very particular view of the world.' Now wasn't the time to remind DCI Greenway that the present-day descendants of those castaways had a tendency to end up dead once the family connection was rekindled. 'As to Obeah, we think that the Payne family's knowledge of it is linked to the illegitimacy; there's some Creole blood in there if you go back far enough.' Price screwed up his face. 'Though I don't totally understand the relevance of that. The whole thing sounds too farfetched to me.' He thought for a moment and then said, 'Have you considered the possibility that Payne might not have been working with the killer, and that someone else is involved? Someone who might have used that Obeah garland to point the finger in Payne's direction to throw attention away from other possibilities?'

'Such as who?'

Well, that was the question, wasn't it? Price tipped his head back and focused his eyes on the ceiling. 'Anyone might have known about Laurence Payne's connections with Obeah and the esoteric. He's written a book on the subject, which is available online, and he has his own website promoting what he calls his consulting skills.' All it had taken to turn up the information was a simple internet search. 'There's even a photograph of that damn garland on his website.'

Impervious to his failure to conduct such an obvious check, Greenway simply cackled. 'Click here to order your own personal Obeah garland? And you thought that our theories were farfetched?' He blew out a breath. 'Listen, pal, there's another reason I needed to give you a call this morning. We think it's possible that you might soon be able to make your own assessment of Payne. Bob Marwick paid him a visit yesterday evening and discovered that he was planning a trip away. He claimed he was planning to return to his home in Hertfordshire for a few days, but let slip that he was travelling from Paddington.'

Price felt his heart sink. 'You think he's coming down

to the West Country?'

'We know he is. We had him tailed this morning and he boarded the three minutes past eight from Paddington to Penzance. Our guess is that he's heading for the Lancefields, but we don't know why. It's possible that he was invited, but…'

Price sat bolt upright in his seat. 'I don't believe he was invited. I was with a friend of the family yesterday evening, someone very close to them. If he'd been invited, she would know. And she would have told me.' At least, he hoped that she would. 'Do you want me to pick him up from the station? If he left around eight, he'll probably arrive in Penzance sometime between one and two o'clock. If you think there's a risk to the family…'

'I can't say with any certainty that there is. But if I were you, I might want to make them aware that he was making the journey.'

'Are you treating him as a person of interest?'

'Let's just say that we're keeping a very open mind. We know Payne wasn't directly responsible for Eva's body going into the water. But at this stage, although we suspect him, we can't say for certain that the blond man who put her in the dock was responsible for her death. The only thing we know for definite is that he wanted to be seen doing it.'

It took a few moments for the words to register. Then Price bent forward and placed his mobile phone down on the desk in front of him. 'Say that again.' He spoke the words directly into the mouthpiece. 'He *wanted* to be seen?'

'Without a doubt. After her body slid into the water, he turned around and waved at the CCTV camera before walking off along the quayside. He wanted us to know that he did it, and that he knew the CCTV cameras would pick it up. What other explanation would you have for it?'

*

Marcus Drake was barely recognisable. Slumped in the armchair by the library fireplace, his once-handsome face was gaunt with grief, his skin sallow, his lips pinched and bloodless.

For a moment Kathryn wavered in the doorway, her hand still on the door, the possibility of retreat more tempting than she might care to admit. And then Marcus turned his head to look at her through unseeing, pain-filled eyes.

'Please don't go, Kathryn. I need to talk.'

She let go of the door and stepped forward into the room. 'Marcus, don't you think you should sleep?' She sat down on the sofa. 'You must be exhausted.' And not just from the overnight flight to Gatwick and the onward journey to Salvation Hall. 'There will be plenty of time for talking when you've had some rest.'

'I can't think about sleeping. I keep asking myself why it happened. How it could possibly have happened.' There was a hollow, bitter edge to his voice. 'I loved Lucy, and I lost her. And Eva was my second chance. I thought that we had a future together. And now she's gone.' He blinked back a tear. 'I don't understand... any of it. How anyone could hurt her. How this could happen to me twice. What the hell I'm supposed to do now.'

'Sometimes there isn't anything to be done. Sometimes we just have to roll with the grief. Give ourselves time to come to terms with it.'

'When it keeps on happening? First Lucy, then my mother, and now Eva?' He stared blankly into Kathryn's eyes. 'I want to go to London to see her. Will you talk to Inspector Price for me? Can you make him understand? I don't think I can believe it's really happened until I see her for myself.'

'I can try, but it wasn't Ennor's decision for you to come straight to Penwithen. DCI Greenway is leading the investigation in London and he was concerned that your presence might complicate things.' There was no easy way to say it. 'Ennor has told him about Zak Smith's earlier attempts on Eva's life. But DCI Greenway doesn't buy the theory that Zak might have been responsible for her death. At this stage he wants to keep the two cases separate.'

'Does Inspector Price think that Smith might have travelled to London to kill her?'

'He didn't say that. Only that the possibility would have to be considered.'

'So, who does this DCI Greenway think was responsible?'

'At the moment, he only seems to have one viable suspect.' She watched Marcus's face as she spoke. 'Laurence Payne.'

The name had an immediate effect. 'Is that why she went to London? To meet with Laurence Payne?' Marcus stiffened. 'Why the hell didn't Richard tell me that when he broke the news of her death?'

'He told you that she had travelled to London, but he didn't tell you why?'

'No.' The omission clearly puzzled him. 'I knew that she wanted to meet with Laurence, she made no secret of that. And she was disappointed that Richard didn't approve of the idea.' The corner of his mouth began to twitch, puzzlement making way for frustration. Or perhaps even disappointment. 'And why didn't *she* tell me? We spoke every day on the phone. Every day.' He blinked. 'We spoke on Friday evening and she told me that she had just got home from the hospital. But it must have been a lie.' His mouth twisted as he considered the implications of the tiny act of betrayal. 'She lied to me.'

'Put it like that, she lied to all of us. But I don't believe there was any malicious intention behind it. How could there be? She already knew Laurence, and she had every right to meet with him if she chose to. Is it possible that she chose not to tell any of us that she was going to London because she didn't want to anger Richard?'

'But why lie to *me*? If she didn't want Richard to know,

couldn't she trust me to keep her secret?'

It could only be the grief talking. 'Would it really have made any difference? Would telling you that she was meeting Laurence have made any difference to what happened to her? Would you have prevented her from going? *Could* you have prevented her?'

'She might still be alive.'

'No, Marcus. That isn't your burden to bear.' Kathryn breathed out a sigh. 'Torturing yourself isn't going to bring Eva back.' She leaned back against the sofa's cushions. 'Ennor is planning to come over to Salvation Hall later this morning. He's hoping to have more information on how the investigation is progressing.'

'I take it they've already questioned Laurence Payne?'

'Yes.'

'And he has confirmed that the meeting went ahead?'

'He and Eva had dinner together on Friday evening.'

'And she was found dead the following morning.'

'Yes.'

'So they've arrested Laurence?'

'Arrested him? No, I don't think so.'

'But you said that he was the only viable suspect.'

'As far as I know. But they would need grounds to make an arrest. Suspicion alone isn't enough.'

'Has Richard made any attempt to speak to Laurence? To ask him what happened when he met with Eva?'

'Not that I'm aware of.'

'I see.' Marcus tilted his head back. 'Does that make any sense to you, Kathryn? Because it doesn't make any sense to me.' He narrowed his eyes. 'For months now, Richard has been obsessed with the idea of raking up distant members of the family. And when Eva presents him with a distant cousin he doesn't have to search for, suddenly he doesn't want to know. So much so, that when Eva is murdered and that cousin might be able to shed some light on what happened to her, Richard doesn't even bother to pick up the phone and ask?' Marcus shook his head. 'What is he hiding, Kathryn? What is it that Richard knows about Laurence Payne that he doesn't want to confront?'

*

'And you're saying that Zak's in the frame for that?' Amber Kimbrall, busy sprucing up the bar at The Lancefield Arms, kept her eyes on the polished counter top as she spoke. 'I wouldn't have thought he had the gumption to get himself on a train to London, never mind find Eva McWhinney while he was about it.' There was a duster in her right hand and she lifted it to her lips and tentatively licked it. 'Anyway, what does it have to do with me?' She dropped her hand to the counter and rubbed viciously at an invisible stain. 'I've already told DCI Price that I don't know where he is. And what's more,' she fixed DS Parkinson with a defiant stare, 'I don't want to know.'

Parkinson pulled a stool away from the bar and sat down on it. The news of Eva's death had been bound to unsettle her but Amber was a feisty piece, quick to react, and he was beginning to learn that, with the right words of encouragement, she was just as quick to calm down. 'Right now, it doesn't have anything to do with you. And we don't have any evidence to put him in the frame. But we know that you want to see Zak behind bars as much as we do.'

'I've already had this conversation with Inspector Price.'

'I know. But that was before we knew Eva had been murdered.' Parkinson gave her a moment to think about it. 'She was a decent person, Amber. You know that. And you know how much she meant to the Lancefields.'

Amber pushed out her lips and dropped the duster onto the bar. 'Zak said he wouldn't hurt her.'

'And if I remember rightly, you said that Zak was a

lying toerag who couldn't be trusted.' The sergeant risked a smile. 'And that was when you were fond of him.'

'Well, I don't suppose I can deny that, can I? He's capable of anything if his back is up against the wall, and I should know.' She leaned forward and folded her arms on the bar, dropping her head close to the policeman's and enveloping him in the familiar musky perfume. 'I'm scared, Sergeant Parkinson. And that's the truth.' The anger had blown out of her voice. 'It isn't that I don't want to help, but I'm scared that he'll come looking for me.'

In Parkinson's opinion, there was every chance that one day Smith was going to come looking for her anyway, if they didn't catch him. But now wasn't the time to point it out. 'The detectives investigating Eva's murder don't think that Zak was responsible. But Inspector Price isn't convinced. He knows what Zak is capable of. Just as you do.' He gave her a moment to think about it. 'We don't want you to reach out to Zak. But we're as convinced as we can be that Becca has been helping him to stay on the run. I paid her a visit in Truro yesterday, and I know for a fact that she's running two mobile phones. We have a hunch that one of those phones is her hotline to her brother.'

'And what does that have to do with me?'

'When I spoke to her yesterday, it seemed pretty obvious that she was lonely. She might have landed on her feet with a new job and a new place to live, but she doesn't have any friends in Truro. Not that she was pleased to see me as a familiar face. She made that pretty clear. But I asked her if she'd heard from you, and I could tell that it upset her.'

Amber raised her head. 'I hope you're not asking me to be disingenuous, Sergeant Parkinson, and pretend to be her friend. I don't have any contact with Becca now because she chewed me out for not covering for her murdering scumbag of a brother. She's not exactly somebody that I want back on my Christmas card list.'

'The two of you go back a long way, don't you? All the way back to school days?'

'That just means we went to the same school. It doesn't mean we hold the same values.' She tapped the bar top with a long, polished fingernail. 'Becca's not the only one who's made changes to her life. The Lancefields have been very good to me, and I'm the first to admit that I regret how I've behaved towards them in the past. I might not like how they made their money, but David and Richard are true gents and I'm very happy working for them. I don't want to do anything that's going to jeopardise that.'

'I don't see how helping to catch Stella Lancefield's killer would jeopardise your relationship with them. You've already tried to do that once.' He studied his watch. 'Look, I've got to get going. The boss has another job lined up for me, and I know you need to get the bar ready to open up. But won't you at least think about it? All we're asking you to do is pay her a visit. Take her some flowers, wish her well, see if she'll open up a bit.'

'And the mobile phones?'

Parkinson smiled to himself. There was no question that Amber Kimbrall was bright. 'If you can get any information at all on why she has that second phone…' He whistled through his teeth. 'The Lancefields will probably sign the pub over to you as a thankyou gift.'

Her face broke into a coy smile. 'Don't push your luck, Sergeant Parkinson. I don't think they would go that far. Though I might be tempted to put in for a pay rise.' She blew out the longest of sighs. 'So, when do you want me to go?'

'This afternoon.'

Amber stared at him. 'But she'll be at work.'

'She's taking the day off.'

'And how do you know that?' She narrowed her eyes, and then widened them again. 'You haven't got her under surveillance when the poor girl is trying to make a fresh start?' Incredulous, she shook her head. 'It's the last time,

Sergeant Parkinson, do you hear me? I'll do it for David and Richard, and I'll do it once. But that's it. And if Zak Smith comes looking for me after I've done it, and I don't live to tell the tale, you'd better hide. Because you'll be the first person I come back to haunt.'

15

Ennor Price ran his tongue around his teeth, but his mouth was still dry. Facing the loved ones of a murder victim wasn't any kind of novelty to a seasoned detective chief inspector. But facing those same loved ones for the second time in a matter of months? It had to be up there, didn't it? Top of the list of nightmare scenarios?

David Lancefield and Marcus Drake, united in grief, were sitting side by side on the library sofa. David, grey and solemn, his body slumped against the sofa's arm, was watching Price intently with mournful, melancholy eyes. But Marcus? The younger man, his jaw rigid beneath a deeply furrowed brow, bristled angry, defiant energy from every pore and sinew.

'I hardly know where to begin.' Price spoke with a slow and measured deliberation. 'I know you need answers and right now there are very few answers I can give you.' He was standing behind the armchair to the left of the fireplace, his hands on the back of it, and he flexed his fingers into the firm damask upholstery. 'I spoke with DCI Greenway, the senior investigating officer, first thing this morning, and they are concentrating their search on an individual seen following Eva as she made her way back to her hotel on Friday night.' It wouldn't do to say too much at this stage. 'Everything that can be done at the moment is being done.'

'Who is questioning Becca Smith?' It was Marcus who spoke, his voice low and brittle. 'Are you dealing with that?'

'We don't believe that any member of the Smith family was involved in Eva's murder.'

'How do you know that? How do you know that the man who followed Eva wasn't just an innocent passerby?'

'I'm sorry, Marcus, I can't share that information with you.' Price swallowed hard. He wanted to say, I know you think I'm to blame for this. I know you think Eva is dead because I failed to catch Zak Smith. But the words escaped him. 'I hope that I can trust you not to try to take the law into your own hands. I have to caution you very strongly to stay away from the Smith family while you're back in England.'

David lifted his head and put a restraining hand on Marcus's arm. 'The inspector is quite right, Marcus. We must give the police the time and space to conduct their investigation. It wouldn't do to muddy the waters by interfering.' He turned back to Price. 'When will we be able to bring Eva home, Inspector?'

The awkward questions were coming thick and fast. 'May I sit?' Price rounded the armchair slowly and sat down. 'There are certain protocols which have to be followed. We have to determine Eva's technical next of kin, and confirm whether or not she left any specific instructions to be followed in the event of her death. Are either of you aware of a will, or whether she had appointed an executor or a power of attorney to act on her behalf?'

'She was a young woman, Inspector, only in her thirties. I would be surprised if such a thought had ever occurred to her.'

And Price would be more than surprised if it hadn't. Eva McWhinney was an educated woman possessed of an impressive heritage and a substantial estate, but as far as he could see she had no natural heirs. And she didn't strike him as the sort of woman to abandon that heritage and property to fate. He turned to look at Marcus. 'You and she had grown quite close, I understand. Did she discuss her financial affairs with you?'

Apparently not, if the angry flush that flared in the young man's pale cheeks was anything to go by. 'What the hell does this have to do with the fact that she was murdered? Eva was a member of the family and we want to bring her home.'

'I understand that.' Except, of course, that for Eva McWhinney home was Hemlock Row and Edinburgh, and not Salvation Hall. Price thought for a moment and then said, 'DCI Greenway is planning to ask DCI Grant in Edinburgh to arrange for Eva's neighbours, friends and colleagues to be questioned. It's primarily to establish whether any of them knew that she planned to travel to London to meet with Laurence, but it's possible that one of them might also know something of her personal affairs.'

David leaned towards the policeman. 'Our cousin Barbara is also on standby to travel to Edinburgh, to act on the family's behalf. Would it help if we put her in touch with DCI Grant?'

Price welcomed the suggestion with a smile. 'I think DCI Grant would be very grateful to have a direct contact in the family. With your permission, I'll ask DCI Grant to make contact with her.' He furrowed his brow. 'I'm still finding it difficult to accept that Eva didn't advise anyone in the family that she planned to meet with Laurence. Did she really not make any reference to it at all?'

It was Marcus who answered. 'What possible reason could we have for lying to you about that?' His eyes were glowering now. 'For what it's worth, Inspector Price, I wish to God that I had never heard the name Laurence Payne.' He threw up his hands in despair. 'What kind of a man is he, anyway? Who leaves a young woman to walk about London on her own late at night? Why the hell didn't he walk her back to the door of the hotel and make sure that she was safe?'

It was a question that Price had asked himself more than once over the last twenty-four hours, and he still didn't have the answer. But then, at some point that afternoon, both he and Marcus might have the opportunity to ask Laurence Payne that question for themselves.

*

'I don't believe him, Barbara. He claims to have been so close to Eva and yet he didn't know she was planning to travel to London, let alone meet with Laurence Payne?' Nancy let the attic door swing shut behind her. 'Does that sound likely to you?'

Barbara, momentarily astonished by the vast, dusty room in which she found herself, was reluctant to answer the question. 'I'm not sure what you're suggesting, Nancy.' She only knew that she would prefer the girl to stop talking about it. She dragged her eyes away from the expanse of packing crates and dust-sheet-covered furniture to look at her companion. 'Are you saying that Marcus is lying?'

Nancy answered the question with a shrug, and dropped the clipboard she was holding onto the top of a packing crate. 'That, or that he wasn't quite as close to her as he liked to think.'

Of the two possibilities, Barbara was inclined to favour the latter. 'I suppose, if you think about it, they had only known each other for a few months. And for most of that time Marcus has been out in St Felix.'

'And yet he still thinks it's his decision what happens to Eva when the police release her body.' Nancy turned to a small table beside the door and picked up what appeared to be a pile of old clothing. 'You may wish to wear one of these over your clothing, Barbara. They are old shirts of Richard's. It's very dusty up here.' She tossed a faded blue shirt in Barbara's direction before continuing her tirade. 'Do you know, it took me almost ninety minutes to drive them back from Newlyn Airport this morning, and they spent the entire journey discussing what kind of funeral service they should arrange, and where Eva should be buried. Marcus wants to have a service here at St Felicity's, and for Eva to be buried in the churchyard. In the churchyard, if you please, so that she will lie in the same ground as Lucy.' Nancy sucked in a breath. 'But David does not agree and says she had a life before she met the Lancefield family, and that her friends and colleagues in Edinburgh must be sought out and consulted.'

'Well, that seems a very reasonable approach to me.' Barbara held the shirt up in front of her and examined it. 'Does Richard know that you have purloined his cast-off shirts?'

Nancy ignored the question. 'David seems more concerned about who will administer Eva's affairs.'

'Does he?' Barbara slipped the shabby shirt over her dress. 'Perhaps I should speak to him about that. Richard has asked me if I will travel to Edinburgh to deal with it.'

'*You?*' Nancy stared bleakly at the woman for a moment. And then she bowed her head. 'I mean no disrespect, Barbara. But surely David would have been a more appropriate choice? He was also supposedly close to her, while you had barely met the woman.'

The conversation was veering into choppy waters. Barbara ran her hands down the front of the shirt, smoothing the fabric. 'You were quite right to bring something for us to wear.' She stared along the length of the attic. 'You know, I've never been up here before. When Kathryn said it was going to be a challenge packing everything up, I had no idea that it would include furniture.' She walked over to what appeared to be a bookcase beside the wall and lifted the corner of the dustsheet covering it. 'This is a beautiful piece. It should be down in the house, where it can be seen. What's it doing locked away up here?'

Nancy bristled, her flow of venom stemmed by Barbara's clear refusal to be drawn. 'The Lancefields have always kept a house in London, but after Alice, Richard's wife, died he decided to rent it out instead of using it. The furniture was shipped back to Salvation Hall for storing.' She moved away from Barbara and stepped towards another shrouded shape in the middle of the floor. 'This is my favourite piece.' She peeled back the dustsheet. 'Isn't it beautiful?'

'Oh, it's a spinet.' Entranced by the finding, Barbara stepped closer to examine it, and ran a hand gently across the polished walnut top. 'Do you know anything about it?'

'I know everything about it.' Nancy lifted the lid to reveal a set of carved ebony and ivory keys. 'It was made in the early eighteenth century by a very famous London cabinet maker called Thomas Barton. I believe the piece was commissioned for the family and shipped out to St Felix for the ladies to play during their leisure time.' She depressed a key and a sweet, solitary note echoed through the attic space. 'Alice only visited St Felix once, and she fell in love with the spinet. But she didn't fall in love with St Felix, so she had this piece shipped back to London for her own personal use.'

'Well, I suppose, in a sense, she brought it home.'

'Very nearly. Thomas Barton's workshop was in Bishopsgate and the family's London house is in Wilkes Street.'

'You say that as if I should know where Wilkes Street is.'

'It's in Spitalfields, close to the City.' The girl's smile softened. 'You still have a lot to learn about the family, Barbara.'

While you already know so much about it? Barbara kept the thought to herself. 'Is the spinet one of the pieces to be shipped back? I didn't see it on the inventory. But that's no reason for it stay here, if you would like it to go back?'

'I see that you understand.' Nancy's eyes clouded. 'Of course I would like it to go back. It should never have been removed from Woodlands in the first place.' An angry note had crept into her voice. 'My grandmother used to play this instrument, Barbara. But when Alice decided that it should be returned, she had no say in the matter.'

'Is your grandmother still alive?'

'No, she left us last year.' The girl's lower lip began to tremble. And then she checked herself. 'But there is no time for maudlin memories today. We have work to do.' She lowered the lid of the spinet and replaced the dust sheet. 'Now, where did I put the inventory?' She retraced her steps to the attic door. 'Ah, here it is. I have no idea what was in Richard's mind when he decided which items were staying and which were going.' She lifted the clipboard from the top of the packing crate and examined it. 'There are the boxes of documents, obviously, and several crates of china to be paired up with those out in the garden storeroom. And he has listed a dining table and six chairs, a walnut dresser and a set of bedroom furniture.' She clicked her teeth. 'There is no method here. I have no idea what he intends me to do with these things when they arrive back in St Felix, and now is not the time to ask him.' There was a small wooden chair beside the packing crate and Nancy sat down on it. 'I know we have to keep moving forward with our plans, Barbara, but how can we, in the light of Eva's murder? We are all at sixes and sevens. It might not touch you or I, or Kathryn. But Richard and David are grieving again and cannot be disturbed, and Marcus is full of anger that his latest attempt to marry into the Lancefield family has been derailed. How are we supposed to proceed when those who need to guide us are distracted by this latest calamity?'

Marcus's latest attempt to marry into the family?

'Surely you don't think that Marcus only cared for Eva because of her connection to the family?'

Nancy lifted her eyes from the inventory with a slow deliberation. 'Surely, Barbara, after everything that has been said, you are not naive enough to think there was any other reason?'

*

'He's on his way to Penzance?' The news of Laurence Payne's imminent arrival had taken Kathryn by surprise. 'There's no wonder you wanted to have this conversation where we couldn't be overheard. If he's heading for Salvation Hall, I don't think Richard will be very pleased.'

'We can head him off at the pass if you want us to.' Ennor turned in his seat to look at her. 'We don't know for certain that he's planning to present himself to the family, but we can't think of any other reason he would make the journey. I've asked Tom to be at Penzance station when the train arrives.' They were sitting at a corner table in the lounge bar at The Lancefield Arms, and Ennor picked up a beer mat and twisted it around in his fingers. 'DCI Greenway wants us to intercept him, anyway. He's decided that Laurence is his prime suspect, even though he knows it was another man who put Eva's body in the water. They think he might have arranged the killing, because he's the only person who knew where she was going to be on Friday evening.'

'I can't bear to think about it. I still can't quite believe that she's gone.' Kathryn followed Ennor's gaze out of the window to stare at nothing in particular. 'Do you agree with their theory?'

'You know me. I can't accept that Smith isn't involved

somewhere along the line.' Ennor dropped the beer mat onto the table. 'But he couldn't possibly have known where Eva would be unless someone told him. And so far we haven't been able to find a single person who knew that she would be in London to meet with Laurence, except for Laurence himself. Unless someone in the Lancefield family is lying.'

'Or unless Eva had told one of her colleagues or friends in Edinburgh that she was making the journey. Everyone seems to forget that she had a life outside of the family.'

'You wouldn't think so, to hear the way that Marcus talks about her. I'm beginning to wonder if the two of them were as close as he makes out. If they were, I don't think she would have hidden the trip from him.'

'But you only have to look at him to see how distressed he is by her death, and to know that she mattered to him a great deal.'

'Maybe. Or maybe not. Maybe he's that distressed because Richard was right, and it *was* dangerous for her to go to London. And he knows now that he should have tried to stop her.'

'But that would mean that he's lying. That he knew about the trip and hasn't admitted it.' Kathryn's eyes darkened as she considered the implications. 'In which case, Marcus would also have known just where Eva could be found on Friday evening.'

At least he didn't have to spell it out for her. 'So now you know the other reason I didn't want to have this conversation at Salvation Hall. If Marcus is lying and, let's be honest here, it wouldn't be the first time, he could have told a third party where she could be found.'

Kathryn sighed. 'I don't know what you want me to say. Why on earth would Marcus want to hurt a girl he was so fond of? He told me this morning that he thought they had a future together.'

'And was Eva of the same mind?'

'Yes. At least...' Kathryn faltered, suddenly uncertain. 'She never gave me any reason to think she wasn't. They always looked at ease with each other.'

'And when did you last see them together?' He studied her face as she considered the question. 'He's been out in St Felix for weeks now. They may have spoken on the phone or by video call, but you only have Marcus's word for it that those conversations were as intimate as he suggests. Eva might have just considered it a strong friendship.'

'They were more than friends, Ennor. I saw them together. They were affectionate.'

'You and I are affectionate.'

'And we're more than friends.'

'Are we?' A wry smile played around Ennor's lips. 'Are we really, Kathryn?'

A deep blush made its way into her cheeks. 'I know what you want me to say. You want me to say that we can't be more than friends because we're not lovers. But I don't agree with you. I think that our relationship is past the point of friendship now.' A sudden doubt crossed her face. 'Or have I got that wrong?'

Ennor took hold of her hand and squeezed it. 'No, you haven't got that wrong.' He spoke softly. 'Were Marcus and Eva lovers?'

'Good heavens, I have no idea. I suppose I just assumed that they were, from the way Marcus spoke about her.'

'And the way in which she spoke about him?'

Possibly not. Kathryn stared down at the hand holding hers. 'What does any of this prove?'

'It proves that if Marcus *is* lying, whatever the reason, Laurence Payne might not be the only person who knew where Eva was going to be on Friday. Either way, I need your help. I think we need to establish just what Laurence hopes to achieve by coming down to Cornwall. I don't want Richard and David upset by his visit if they don't want him at Salvation Hall, and I don't want Marcus confronting him with dubious accusations. Kathryn, will you come with me to the station, and meet him from the train?'

16

DCI Greenway stared down into the rippling, murky waters of the West India Dock. 'What sort of a scumbag puts a lovely young woman into this cesspool?' He still couldn't fathom the cruelty of it, the wanton waste of a life full of promise. By all accounts, Eva McWhinney had been a talented and dedicated cardiologist: a saver of lives. And now her own life had been forfeit, for a reason that no one could fathom.

Certainly not for a cheap thrill. There had been too much deliberation in the execution of the crime. This was no random murder committed by a passing, mindless opportunist. This had been planned by someone who knew where to find her, when to strike, and what to do with the body. Someone callous enough to sit with her corpse until he considered it safe to consign her remains to the water. Someone egotistical enough to want the CCTV cameras to pick up his image.

Someone arrogant enough to think he could get away with it.

Greenway looked over his shoulder at DS Marwick, standing just a few feet behind him. 'Why did he want to be seen? Was he taunting us, or was there something more subtle at play?'

Marwick, hands deep in the pockets of his raincoat, considered the question. 'If he was committing the crime on behalf of a third party, he could have been drawing attention away from the person who wanted her dead.'

'Laurence Payne wants her dead, our mystery blond man is hired for the job, and a condition of the trade is that the killer has to be seen to draw attention away from Payne?'

'Do we have any evidence yet that Payne wanted her dead?'

Greenway grumbled. 'Just trying out a theory, Bob.' He rolled his shoulders back and turned to face the sergeant. 'Eva and Laurence were in the restaurant behind you.' He pointed towards Vincenzo's. 'They were seen by the blond man, who followed them out of the building when they left.' He lifted a hand and pointed along the quayside. 'He followed them at a distance to the floating footbridge, and then what? We saw him following Eva, so he must have hung back while they said their goodbyes. Then he must have caught up with her as she walked along the side of the hotel.' Greenway tilted his head in Marwick's direction. 'Are we any further forward with the CCTV footage for the hotel's external cameras?'

'Tomorrow, at the latest.'

'So we're not going to be able to confirm that theory until it arrives.' Greenway turned up the collar of his coat and began to walk slowly along the quayside. 'Eva would have gone left beyond the bridge, and headed towards Hertsmere Road to return to the Excelsior. We can only hope to God that there are no blind spots in the camera footage.'

The inspector halted. The buildings to his left had made way for a broad plaza and he stared along its length. Six enormous, raised beds filled the space, vast concrete caverns overflowing with miniature trees and shrubs. 'Every one of those things provides a hiding place. She could have been pulled to the ground between them.' He glanced up, sweeping his eyes around the surrounding walls. There are cameras, alright, but I doubt they'll cover everything.'

'But he couldn't have killed her here.' Marwick, following in his wake, sounded unconvinced. 'This plaza is too public. It would have been too risky.'

'Then it had to be in the alleyway behind Vincenzo's.' Greenway set off walking along the plaza, beckoning for Marwick to follow him. 'It's the only place he could have taken her without being seen.'

The alleyway in question was a secluded passage that ran from the end of the plaza along the back of the quayside restaurants, and it took little more than a minute for them to reach it. Accessed by a descending ramp and sunk below pavement level, the alleyway was bounded by a firm, steel handrail that ran the length of the retaining wall. Greenway stopped beside it, gripping the cold metal with both hands. He peered down into the cold, deserted space and shivered. 'This was it. It has to be.' They had searched here on the day that Eva's body had been discovered and found nothing of value to the investigation. But that didn't mean that nothing had happened there. 'Entry to the passage is easy, it's just an opening in the retaining wall. He could have overpowered her, dragged her down the concrete ramp, and murdered her without being seen. You would have to peer over the handrail to see anything going on down there, and who's going to bother to do that late at night?'

'They wouldn't see anything, even if they looked. There are no lights on the back of the building. And no CCTV cameras.'

'And so he could have hidden down there indefinitely with the body until he was ready, and then half-carried her back to the waterfront when the coast was clear.' Greenway turned to Marwick. 'What's this used for?'

'It isn't. When we ran our initial enquiries, we were told

that the doors down there were always kept locked and bolted for security.'

Greenway let go of the railings. 'I want this roping off now. If Eva was down there, there could be dirt or dust on her shoes or bag to prove it. We should have conducted a more thorough search. If she was down there, the killer must have come back to collect the bag, shawl and shoes to dispose of them in the alleyway near the station, where we found them.' He spun on his heel and set off back towards the dock, striding out with angry purpose. 'I want that bloody CCTV footage, and I want it yesterday. If Eva was seized as she walked through this plaza it will be on film. And so will the bastard who abducted her.'

*

'Why on earth is Laurence coming here?' Richard had been resting in the Dower House sitting room when Kathryn broke the news. 'Do we know if he has any other connections in the area, apart from his tenuous connection to us?'

Now that was a curious choice of word – tenuous. 'Are you suggesting that this particular Laurence Payne isn't the one related to your family? Because I'm quite satisfied that I have identified a direct link from your ancestor Benedict to his sister Maria, and from her down a direct line to a descendant named Laurence Payne. And that has been validated further by Eva's existing connection to a distant cousin of the same name. There is no scope for doubt in my opinion, Richard. His connection to the family is as solid as Eva's.' Kathryn watched the old man's face closely as she spoke. 'Of course, I'd be happy to reconsider if you have further information on the connection that hasn't so far been shared with me.'

Richard growled softly. 'I am not seeking to question the veracity of your work, Kathryn. My choice of word was a clumsy one.' He pursed his thin lips inwards for a moment, thinking. 'Inspector Price has no clear information on the purpose of Laurence's journey to Penzance?'

'I'm afraid not. Ennor has sent Sergeant Parkinson to the station to meet the train, with the intention of asking Laurence where he's heading. And he would like me to go to the station, so that if he's heading for Salvation Hall I can meet with him first on behalf of the family.' She turned her head to stare into the fireplace. 'It's only natural for Ennor to be worried about the situation, given what happened when Jason and Emma turned up here unannounced.' Let alone what happened to Eva when she was invited. 'But for what it's worth, I think it's important to remember that Laurence might be coming here to share information about Eva, not to take advantage of the family.'

'Then why not contact us by telephone? Why not call to share that information, instead of travelling all the way from London?'

'I don't know, Richard. Perhaps he felt calling would be too impersonal. Has it occurred to you that Eva might have told him about your reluctance for their meeting to take place?'

'Then surely common sense would tell him that he wouldn't be welcome here.' There was an unfamiliar bitterness in the old man's voice. 'Is this man suspected of harming Eva? Do the police consider him a suspect for her murder?'

'I was hoping you wouldn't ask me that.' Kathryn looked down at her hands. 'Ennor says that the London investigation team suspect him of being involved in her murder somehow, though not necessarily of committing the murder himself.'

'And what does Inspector Price think?'

'He is keeping an open mind.'

A perceptive smile crossed Richard's face. 'He still

suspects that Zak Smith is involved.' The idea seemed to please him. 'Kathryn, you have always given me wise counsel. What do you advise?'

'I think that I should meet with Laurence. And afterwards'—she lifted her eyes to look at the old man—'I think that *you* should meet with him. You didn't seek him out, he's coming to you. So, I don't believe that you would be breaking your word to David by speaking to him.' Any more than she believed that his promise to David was the reason Richard was so very reluctant to meet with Payne in the first place. She let out a sigh. 'Richard, it's an opportunity to hear about Eva's last few hours. Laurence may be able to tell you just why she was so determined to meet with him behind your back. And that might bring you, and David and Marcus, some peace.'

'Are you suggesting that I should permit him to visit us here, at Salvation Hall?'

'Why not?' She still couldn't understand his reluctance. 'If nothing else, I would like to meet with him to discuss the family's history. I've been examining the last few documents relating to Maria Lancefield and George Payne, but there are some parts of the story I don't know. I've seen a letter from Benedict to his brother Richard in England, telling him that he had given his consent for Maria's marriage to George Payne. But there is a part of the story that I don't have all the details for.'

'You may not have all the details, but I think that you have already deduced the relevant facts.' Richard fixed her with a steely gaze. 'And I hope that, having deduced those facts, you will continue to keep them to yourself.'

'Of course, if that's what you want.' It would be pointless trying to tell him that the facts wouldn't always stay buried. 'Are you content, then, for me to meet with him on your behalf? And to extend an invitation to supper, if it seems appropriate?'

'Very well. But'—the old man leaned forward in his seat—'I do not think he should come to Salvation Hall. If we are to meet with him, then let it be at The Zoological Hotel. I will travel out to Penzance for the event, and David and Barbara can join us. I do not want to risk Marcus venting his spleen on the man who did not protect Eva when she was vulnerable.'

'And Nancy?'

The old man narrowed humourless eyes. 'Do not test me, Kathryn. I have always appreciated your challenges, and value your friendship too much to want it to founder. But you would be well advised to remember that some lines are simply not meant to be crossed.'

*

Amber Kimbrall was about to give up when the front door finally opened to reveal a pale and anxious face. She took a step back, hugging the bouquet of roses and tulips to her coat with a smile of nervous anticipation. 'For a minute, I thought you weren't going to answer.' She lowered her head and peered over the top of the flowers, hoping to hide her surprise. 'Aren't you going to let me in? I've come all the way from Penwithen.'

Becca scowled through the gap between door and frame. 'What do you want?' She snapped the words out in a harsh whisper. 'What the hell are you doing here?'

'I wanted to know that you were alright.' And that was the truth of it. Whether DS Parkinson's cajoling had led Amber to Becca's front door was really neither here nor there. 'I know there's been a gulf between us, Becs, but I don't want it to be like this. I've been worried about you, moving away and starting again.' And judging by the wraith-like vision in front of her, the worry had been justified. 'I just wanted to see for myself that you were settled.'

'I'm fine.' Becca cast a furtive glance down the hallway behind her. 'So now you've seen for yourself, you can be on your way.' She refocused her eyes somewhere over Amber's shoulder. 'I don't need your concern.'

'Come on, Becs, don't be like that. I know you're angry with me, but what harm could it do letting me in for a minute?'

'It's not convenient.'

'Well, I don't really care about convenient. It's not convenient for me, either. I'm short-staffed at the pub on a Monday.' Amber stepped forward, propelled by a sudden surge of courage, and pushed on the door with a determined hand.

To her surprise, both door and Becca gave way. 'You can come in for a few minutes, but you can't stay. Frankie's not well, she's got a tummy bug.' Becca let go of the door and turned on her heel to walk down the short, narrow hallway. 'I had to keep her home from nursery so she didn't pass it on to the other kids.'

Amber followed her into the small, neat lounge. 'Is a few minutes long enough for a coffee? I came on the bus, and there isn't anywhere for me to get a drink before I head back to Penwithen.' She sniffed, and held out the flowers. 'Please take these. I can't take them back with me.'

Becca screwed up her face. 'I haven't got a vase yet. They'll have to go in a bucket.' She stretched out an ungracious hand to take the bouquet. 'How did you know where I live?'

'People talk. You know how it is.'

'Really? People talk? Is that honestly the best you can do?'

Amber's cheeks dimpled in reply as Becca made her way into the kitchen, but behind the coy smile her trepidation was growing. She had expected to find Becca both buoyant and defiant, energised by the move to Truro and most likely spoiling for a fight with the friend she felt had betrayed her. It had been a shock to see the reality. 'Your new place is lovely, Becs. You must be pleased.' She hovered by the sofa as she spoke, reluctant to sit in case no other opportunity came to search the room. 'It's a nice street too. Did I see a park on the corner? That'll be lovely for Frankie.'

'I know.' Becca's voice rang out from the kitchen. 'That was one of the reasons I chose the place.'

'I don't blame you.' Amber tried to sound relaxed, but in truth her sense of dread was growing. It had been no great surprise that Becca didn't want to invite her into the house, but the reason behind the decision was more elusive. It wasn't because she was angry or bitter or resentful; all the obvious things that Amber would expect from the Becca she knew so well.

It was because she was afraid.

Amber took a step towards the rear of the room, moving closer to a tall, cherrywood chest of drawers against the wall. Two mobile phones lay side by side on the top of the chest: one she knew to be Becca's smartphone; the other a small, grey, unremarkable device like the one she'd seen elderly customers use in The Lancefield Arms. The sort of phone a young woman like Becca might only keep as a spare. She flicked her eyes to the right just as Becca emerged through the kitchen doorway, mugs of coffee in hand.

For a fleeting second their eyes locked, and then Becca's drifted to the mobile phones. 'I put extra milk in the coffee, to cool it down.' She extended one hand towards Amber without looking at her. 'What time is your bus back to Penwithen?'

Amber's hand trembled as she took hold of the mug. 'I can't remember.' Rooted to the spot, frozen with the guilt of discovery, she sipped on the coffee. 'Have you heard about Eva McWhinney?'

Becca stiffened. 'You haven't come here to see me at all, have you? You've come to see if I know where Zak is.' Her voice was quivering with anger. 'I've already told Sergeant Parkinson, Zak couldn't have done it. He's too dim to make his own way to London.'

The tension between the girls was palpable now, as if both knew that a choice would have to be made: a brave choice, a choice with unpredictable consequences.

A choice they would have to make together.

'I don't need to ask the obvious question, do I?' Amber nodded towards the phones. 'I'm worried for you, Becs. He can't be trusted. You saw what he did to me, and I thought he loved me. But it didn't stop him, did it? And it won't stop him from hurting you, if you get in his way.'

'I don't know where he is.'

'Stop lying. I'm trying to help you.' Amber lowered her voice to a whisper. 'I'm trying to give you a way out.'

Becca's lower lip began to quiver. 'But he'll hurt me. He'll hurt me if I…' She could barely get the words out. 'If I give him away.'

'Then let me help you.' Amber took a step closer. 'Just tell me where he is.'

'He might hurt Frankie.'

'Hurt Frankie? How could he do that? He'd have to be here, to…' Amber's stomach somersaulted, and her eyes widened. She shook her head, her mouth suddenly too dry to speak, her eyes full of a million questions. And then she whispered the only question that mattered. 'Where?'

Becca held her gaze for a moment and then slowly, fearfully, lifted frightened eyes up towards the ceiling.

17

It was warm in DCI Greenway's office. Or perhaps he was just beginning to feel the heat.

'I've finally managed to speak to DCI Grant in Edinburgh.' The woman had been annoyingly elusive. 'She did get the message I left for her this morning, and she's already managed to touch base with a couple of Eva's colleagues at the Edinburgh Royal Infirmary.' He ran a finger around the collar of his shirt. 'Eva McWhinney was a very affluent young woman. She didn't just own her own home, she owned two adjacent properties and rented them out. And we're not talking back-to-back terraces. We're talking spacious, Georgian properties in the centre of Edinburgh's New Town.' He rested an elbow casually on the desk. 'And according to one of the colleagues Grant spoke to, she changed her will in the last few weeks.'

Bob Marwick whistled softly. 'Since her acquaintanceship with the Lancefields?'

'I'm wondering if it was because of it. Both of the colleagues questioned had become quite close friends of Eva's over the last few years, and one of them acted as a witness for the will.'

'Does it give us a motive for the murder?'

'I wish I could say yes. But Grant hasn't been able to

procure any details of the bequests yet. The colleague in question doesn't know what was in it, she just witnessed Eva's signature. She was able to provide DCI Grant with the name of Eva's solicitor, and Grant is following that up today.'

'Do we conclude, then, that there could be a financial motive for the murder?'

'We can't discount it. Both Payne and the Lancefields were so distantly related to her that neither would have inherited via the laws of intestacy if there hadn't been a will. I suppose it's possible that Payne might have deluded himself that she had left him a legacy. She might even have told him that she'd included him in her will. But he hardly needs the money, does he?'

'Do you think we should check on that, just to be on the safe side? After all, he'd recently discovered that he wasn't her only known relative. And just because he looks wealthy, it doesn't mean that he is. We only have his word for it. That Canary Wharf apartment could be rented, just as the family home in Hertfordshire could be a figment of his imagination.'

'You might as well follow it up. There doesn't seem to be much else we can do until DCI Price picks him up in Penzance.' Greenway sniffed. 'I still can't make sense of that garland. If Payne was behind the murder, why leave that thing as a calling card? It would lead us straight to him.'

'Maybe that was the idea.'

'What, give the impression that someone else was trying to pin the murder on him, when he was behind it all the time? He doesn't strike me as being that cunning.' Greenway folded his hands behind his head and stared up at the ceiling. 'There was something else. The colleague told DCI Grant that she was worried about Eva. That Eva had written letters to the family to be stored with her will, personal letters only to be opened by the recipients. The colleague said that ever since Eva had returned from her first visit to Cornwall, she seemed to be looking over her shoulder.'

'I take it this colleague didn't know about Smith's attempts on Eva's life?'

'No. But Eva couldn't have been afraid to meet with Laurence Payne, could she? Or she wouldn't have gone through with it.' Greenway frowned. 'I think Grant feels bad about the way things have panned out. She said that talking to Eva's colleagues confirmed for her that Eva was afraid, even though she didn't admit it to the police. And she wishes now that she'd reached out to the girl again. Because, if you think about it, Eva wouldn't have had any peace until Smith was under lock and key.'

It was a sobering thought. Marwick scratched at his forehead. 'Price let Smith wriggle off the hook, didn't he? And now we're trusting him to keep an eye on Laurence Payne.'

'I know. I had that conversation with DCI Grant. I asked her outright what she thought of Price and the way he'd screwed up, and she didn't seem to think that he'd screwed up at all. In fact, she thought he'd been brave to go out on a limb and try to flush Smith out into the open.'

'Even though an innocent bystander died as a result?'

Greenway lowered his eyes to the sergeant. 'How can you predict that sort of outcome? As Grant said to me, how could they have been certain that Smith wouldn't have travelled back to Edinburgh to take another shot at Eva on her home turf, if he'd been that determined to finish her off?' The inspector picked up a pen and tapped it on the desk with a laugh. 'And that was before Grant's best question of all.'

'Which was?'

'How did we know that Laurence Payne wasn't heading to Cornwall not to visit the Lancefields, but because that was where he would find Zak Smith?'

*

'There's no need to introduce yourself, Kathryn. Eva told me all about you.' Laurence rose to his feet and pointed to a chair, inviting her to sit. 'I'm delighted to meet you. Though I have to admit, neither the circumstances nor the location are what I would have hoped for.'

It was hardly surprising. Kathryn cast a glance around the ramshackle coffee bar as she took her seat. 'I hope you haven't been inconvenienced by the interruption to your plans. But Eva's death has left everyone down here very twitchy. And when the local police heard that you were on your way to Cornwall…'

'They decided that I must be up to no good?' He seemed to take the suggestion in his stride. 'See those two men?' He pointed to a table at the other side of the café. 'The one on the left is my minder. His name is Sergeant Parkinson and he was sent to meet me from the train. He was at pains to reassure me that I was free to come and go as I pleased, as long as I wasn't planning to visit the Lancefield family.'

'Did he explain why?'

'Oh, yes. He told me that the family had endured a number of traumatic losses over the last few months, including the loss of their cousin Eva McWhinney.' Laurence lowered his head towards Kathryn. 'When I challenged him about his right to stop an innocent man from going about his business, he calmly suggested that an innocent man wouldn't have told the police he was going to Hertfordshire for a few days and then boarded a train for Cornwall.'

'Well, at least he was direct.' Kathryn held Laurence's gaze. 'And have you come here to see the family? Because if you have, I would have to ask why you didn't just call them first to introduce yourself, and ask if it would be convenient.'

'I thought that calling would give Richard an opportunity to refuse to meet with me. That if I just turned up here, it would be harder for him to do that. Of course, I didn't reckon on a welcoming party from the police.' Laurence chewed on his lip. 'Kathryn, can I speak openly to you? I haven't come here to cause trouble. I want the family to know that I'm heartbroken by Eva's death. And that I feel, to some extent, responsible. If I had thought for one moment that she would be in danger, I would never have agreed to meet with her.' He put a hand up to his ear and tugged on it, nervously. 'She made it clear that Richard didn't want her to meet with me and I did wonder, when she suggested it, whether it would cause more trouble than it was worth. But like Eva, I'm the end of my particular line of the family. And I think my own lack of connection drove me to go through with it.'

'So, it was her idea for you to meet?'

'Absolutely. She seemed almost lit up by the notion, and I must admit I was carried away by her enthusiasm. It was infectious.' His face straightened. 'We had a delightful evening, we hit it off straight away. She shared lots of information with me about her line of the family, and I gave her as much information as I could about mine. And she was thrilled by the idea of sharing it all with Richard. It mattered to her.' He cast a glance towards DS Parkinson. 'Most people wouldn't understand it, I suppose. The detectives I met in London looked at me as though I was a madman for being interested in the family's history.' He looked back at Kathryn. 'I suppose you know what that feels like too?'

In reply, Kathryn raised an eyebrow and nodded across the room. 'See that rather serious-looking man sitting with your police minder? That's Detective Chief Inspector Price, who brought me here to meet with you. He and I are very good friends. And he chides me on a daily basis for spending my time with dusty old books and papers. But, very occasionally, he can see the importance of it. Especially if he thinks it might have a bearing on a case.' She looked back at Laurence. 'Are you still determined to meet with Richard?'

'If he would agree to it. I would like to talk to him about my last few hours with Eva. I don't expect anything from the family, only to be heard and acknowledged, rather than summarily dismissed. And I would like to reassure Richard that I had nothing to do with Eva's death.'

'Have you been accused of that?'

'Not openly. But I know I must be high up on DCI Greenway's list of suspects. I'd be a fool to think otherwise. After all, he must have had me followed to Paddington station this morning, or he wouldn't have known I was heading for Penzance.'

'Wouldn't you also like to hear for yourself why Richard didn't want Eva to meet with you?'

'Perhaps.' Laurence tilted his head. 'If you had spent most of your life alone and without a family, Kathryn, wouldn't you be excited if someone talked to you of distant cousins and family connections?'

'That would depend on the particular family. The Lancefields are by no means perfect.'

'Well, that's lucky.' His cheeks dimpled disarmingly, and he lowered his head farther until it was almost touching hers. 'Because neither am I.'

The playful gesture caught Kathryn unawares, and a blush swept into her cheeks. 'Do you have a place to stay, Laurence?'

'No. I was hoping for a recommendation when I arrived.'

Or perhaps an invitation to stay at Salvation Hall? Kathryn kept the thought to herself. 'The family has an account with The Zoological Hotel, here in Penzance. I stay there myself. Would you be prepared to stay there this evening, and have supper with Richard and David? The food is excellent.'

'With Richard and David? Kathryn, I would be overwhelmed.' He could barely hide his delight. 'Is it far from here? Could we walk?'

'I don't think that will be necessary.' She pointed towards a scowling Ennor Price. 'I think one of those nice policemen could probably be persuaded to give us a lift.'

*

Zak Smith folded his arms and leaned back against the kitchen worktop. 'I say the police put her up to it.' He was standing close to Becca and he nudged her arm roughly with a sharp elbow. 'I hope you kept your mouth shut.'

'I'm not stupid.' His sister buckled slightly under the weight of his assault. 'And don't push me like that when I'm doing the dishes. You'll make me break something.' Her hands were deep in the washing up bowl and she pulled out a plate to rinse it under the tap. 'Amber was just being Amber. She was sorry that we'd fallen out and she wanted to make it up.

'If Amber was being Amber, she was just being a nosy bitch.' Zak sniffed loudly. 'I bet she came here to ask about Eva McWhinney, didn't she?'

Becca's stomach tightened. 'Are you surprised?' Her own voice sounded strangely confident to her. Funny how fear could sometimes give you courage. 'She knows you murdered Eva.'

'She *thinks* I murdered Eva. The important question is, do *you* think I murdered Eva?'

'Why is that important? You don't care what I think. Becca pulled another plate from the soapy water and set about rinsing it. 'All I know is that I want you to move on. I told you the police were watching the house. Sooner or later they'll work out that you're here, whether Amber tells them or not.'

'Let them think what they like. He pushed himself away from the worktop. 'I'm going out for a few hours, but I'll be back later.'

'Where are you going?'

'None of your business.' He strode past her, into the lounge. 'If you go out, leave the back door unlocked so I can get back in.'

'Are you going out on that motorbike?' Becca stepped away from the sink to lean on the doorframe, hands still dripping. 'If it's stolen, the police will be looking for it. They might see the number plate.'

'Will you give it a rest?' His anger was growing. 'Of course the bloody thing is stolen. I've been on the run for three months. Where the hell would I get seven grand to buy a motorbike?'

'Where did you steal it from?'

'Outside a house in Exeter.' His full lips curled into a sneer. 'It was begging to be pinched.'

'Exeter? I don't understand. You were staying in Weston-super-Mare.'

'I know I was. Until the end of last week. Then I had a little trip to make.' He sniggered under his breath. 'I took the train to Exeter yesterday, pinched the bike and rode it over here last night to visit my favourite little sister.'

'It's not a visit. You said you just needed a bed for the night.' Becca wiped her hands down her jeans, drying them roughly on the stiff denim. 'Zak, you have to find somewhere else to stay. It isn't just that the police keep coming back here to check on the place. I have to go back to work or I'll lose my job. And Frankie needs to go back to her nursery. It's not fair on her.'

'She can't go back yet. You can't trust a kid to keep her mouth shut. If she tells somebody she's seen her Uncle Zak, I might not get away.' He picked up his leather jacket from the back of the sofa and slipped an arm into it. 'I'll be gone tomorrow and I'll need a couple of hours' head start. She can go back then.' He turned to Becca and wagged an admonishing finger at her. 'You keep your nose clean and your head down. I'll be back before bedtime.' He pushed past her a second time, heading for the back door. 'Make sure there's something for me to eat when I get back. '

'Why can't you tell me where you're going?'

'What you don't know, you can't spill to the police.' He pulled the back door open and swaggered out into the garden without a backward glance, letting the door slam shut behind him.

Becca stepped forward into the lounge and sat down on the sofa, wrapping her arms around herself in a hopeless search for comfort. He was spiralling out of control, this Zak that she didn't recognise. No longer a brother, but a menace.

No longer a fly-by-night poacher, but a cold-blooded killer.

Geraldine Morton, Stella Drake Lancefield and probably Eva McWhinney: he'd murdered three women, now, and God knew why. All that Becca knew was that she was afraid. Afraid for herself, afraid for Frankie… even afraid for what Zak might do next, and what the consequences of that unknown action might be.

She'd helped him to stay on the run. She'd kept his secrets, sent him money, hoped beyond reason that he might at some point see sense and come home to give himself up. But the killings had brought out his dark side, a menacing evil that she couldn't have dreamed lay within him.

Without her support he might never have lasted this long on the run. Without her silence, he wouldn't be on the run for very much longer. There was only one path open to her now.

Amber had opened the door. All Becca had to do was find the courage to walk through it.

18

'Kathryn tells me that you've travelled to Cornwall to reassure Richard Lancefield that you had nothing to do with Eva's death.' DCI Price settled back in his seat. 'Is that true?'

Laurence answered the question with a tilt of the head. 'Kathryn tells me that an attempt had already been made on Eva's life, here in Cornwall, some weeks before she agreed to meet with me. Is that true?'

The inspector smiled. 'Touché.' They were sitting at a small corner table in the bar at The Zoological Hotel, and the room was reassuringly deserted. 'As we're alone, I can speak freely to you. I'm assuming that DCI Greenway has told you about Zak Smith? After his attempt on her life failed, Smith promised Eva that he wouldn't try again. Unfortunately, Smith is a habitual liar. And I've been foolish enough to think that he would be too preoccupied with keeping out of sight to try again.'

'DCI Greenway has shown me photographs of both Zak Smith and the man they believe murdered Eva. They're not the same man.'

'We can't be sure. The man who put Eva's body into the dock, the man in the CCTV footage, was wearing a mask.' It still angered Price to think of it. That Greenway had failed to mention that *minor detail* in any of their conversations. 'I take it that your meeting with Eva went well?'

'It went very well. We hit it off straight away.'

'And you spent the evening talking about the family's history?'

'Yes.'

'Did you talk about Obeah at all?'

Laurence stiffened, caught off guard. And then he laughed. 'Kathryn also mentioned that you can be quite interested in the family's history if you think it's relevant to an investigation.' He licked his lips. 'So, what relevance would Obeah have to your search for Zak Smith, or his original attempt on Eva's life?'

Was Payne trying to suggest that the investigation into Eva's murder was nothing to do with Price? If so, he was in for a disappointment. 'Eva was the intended victim when Geraldine Morton and Stella Lancefield were murdered, and it matters very much to me what happened to her.' He gave Laurence a moment to think about it. 'The two of you spent most of Friday evening discussing the family's history, and I'm given to understand that your particular line of the family has links to the practice of Obeah. That they were responsible for the sale of a property on St Felix to a less-than-compassionate plantation owner called Edward Mason who treated his slaves harshly, and as a result was murdered by an Obeah man.' Price raised an eyebrow. 'And whose body was adorned with a garland very similar to the one that was found around Eva's neck.'

'My word, Inspector, you *are* interested in the subject.'

'Not as interested as you, if my sources are to be relied upon.' Price leaned forward. 'Do you think that garland was used to throw suspicion on you?'

'What other explanation could there be?'

'I don't know.' At least, he hadn't come up with one

yet. 'Tell me, did Eva already know about the murder that took place on your family's plantation?'

'You mean, prior to our meeting? Yes, she did. She told me that she'd seen it mentioned in correspondence between her ancestor, Charlotte McWhinney, and my ancestor Maria Payne. The two women were sisters.'

'And did she know that your ancestors were knowledgeable in Obeah?'

'I can't say that it came into the conversation.'

'Obeah was practised by the slave population, wasn't it? Not by the plantation owners.'

'I won't be offended if you ask the question directly, Inspector Price. What you really want to know is, am I descended from one of the plantation slaves?' A flicker of amusement lit Laurence's eyes. 'And the answer is yes. My direct ancestor William Payne took a slave woman as his mistress because his wife was unable to produce an heir. It's believed that the woman was fair of skin, as many native-born women were. It's highly likely that she herself was the illegitimate offspring of a plantation owner or manager. She bore a son to William Payne and that son, George, married Maria Lancefield. So from a legal perspective, the entire line descended from an illegitimate son.'

'And the slave woman in question practised Obeah?'

'I have no idea. But if she did, I don't believe it would have anything to do with my family's interest in the subject. That came from quite a different quarter. That came from Darby.'

'Darby?'

'Yes. He was William Payne's manservant. The Paynes brought him to England when they returned. He had a very strong interest in the black arts and that interest was shared with George Payne. There *is* an old family scandal there. After the family moved to England they set up home in Hertfordshire. The ladies stayed there all the time, but George and William took rooms in the City to be closer to their business interests during the week, and Darby went with them to run the household. The story goes that William was quite a liberal master and gave his servant free rein to follow his own interests. At some point, Darby became a member of a rather notorious esoteric sect in London, and he introduced George Payne to the same group. George became embroiled in a scandal involving another member of the sect…'

'A young woman.'

Laurence smiled. 'Ah, you've heard the tale?'

'Not all of it. I've heard that the Lancefield family received an anonymous letter, telling them that Maria's husband was illegitimate. And I've heard that George became involved with a young woman of dubious background. But I still don't see how these things are linked by Obeah.'

'Because of Darby, Chief Inspector. Darby is the answer to everything. Darby's own knowledge of Obeah was his passport into the esoteric sect. He introduced George Payne to the group and to the young woman you have mentioned. And it is more than likely that he wrote the anonymous letter to the Lancefields, alerting them to the scandal.'

'But why would he do that?'

'Because he wanted to cause trouble for both the Paynes and the Lancefields. You see, both were instrumental in the death of the Obeah man who murdered Edward Mason. The Paynes sold the plantation to the cruel master that he murdered, and Benedict Lancefield was the magistrate who passed the death sentence on him for committing the murder.' Laurence leaned forward with a smile. 'And William Payne's manservant, Darby, was the Obeah man's younger brother.'

*

'I don't understand why Richard hasn't discussed the arrangements with me yet. He isn't giving me very much time to prepare a room and arrange a supper.' Nancy slipped the precious book into a dust cover and placed it gently into the cardboard box on the desk. 'That's the estate daybook for 1817, by the way.'

Kathryn ticked off the item from the inventory in front of her. 'What volumes do you still have there?' She waved her pen in the direction of a small stack of books on the desk beside the box.

Nancy picked up another dust cover. '1818 to 1825.' She slipped the next book into it as she spoke. 'I won't be able to engage the outside caterers now, so I suppose I will have to rustle something up. I picked up lamb cutlets from the butchers when I walked down into Penwithen this afternoon, that will have to do. And I think I have enough vegetables to serve everyone. But it will have to be a cold dessert. There are some slices of truffle torte in the freezer. If I take them out by six they should defrost in time.' She glanced up at the clock on the mantelpiece. 'What time are we expecting Laurence to arrive?'

'We're not.' Kathryn kept her eyes on the checklist in front of her. 'He's staying at The Zoological this evening.'

'He's not coming to Salvation Hall?' The book still in her hand, Nancy waved it in Kathryn's direction with a hiss. 'Why on earth not? Is he not welcome, as a member of the family?'

'Of course he's welcome.' The girl's reaction to the news had not been unexpected, and Kathryn had her script prepared. 'Richard was thinking of you. Laurence wasn't invited, and Richard knew there wouldn't be enough time to engage the outside caterers for a formal dinner. You have enough to do now, helping me to catalogue everything.' Kathryn paused, to let the suggestion sink in. 'And, of course, there is Marcus to consider.' She lowered her voice, hoping that a hint of conspiracy might pacify Nancy. 'Richard is concerned about Marcus meeting

Laurence so soon after Eva's death. It's hit him very hard and Richard is worried that he is looking for someone to blame.'

The subtle manoeuvre appeared to work. 'You are always so pragmatic, Kathryn.' Nancy pushed out her lips and lowered the volume for 1818 into the box. 'Surely Laurence will not be left to dine alone this evening, after taking the trouble to travel here? Will you be dining with him?'

'No, I was planning to work on here this evening. And lamb cutlet for supper sounds very tempting, if you can spare one.' Kathryn put down her pen and reclined back in the captain's chair. 'I'm hoping that Laurence will come to Salvation Hall tomorrow, when the dust has settled and Marcus has been primed to be on his best behaviour. He's quite charming, you know. And handsome.' She swivelled the chair gently. 'And very knowledgeable about his branch of the family's history.' She knew that snippet of information would pique Nancy's interest. 'He knows all about the slave revolt on the St Aldate's estate, and the history of the Payne line of the family after they returned to England.'

'And what did he make of Eva?'

'He liked her very much. And he's obviously been deeply affected by her death.'

'When he hardly knew her?' Nancy puffed out a breath. 'Perhaps he's affected not so much by her death, but by the way it has rebounded on him.'

What would be the point in pleading his case, when Nancy was so hellbent on causing trouble? However much she wished it false, Kathryn had to admit that Richard had a point – Nancy *was* becoming a loose cannon. 'Wouldn't you like to speak to Laurence about the family's history, Nancy?'

'Of course I would. And not least because I have finally discovered what happened to Abigail.' A hint of triumph had crept into the girl's voice. 'I've found a bill of sale that proves she was sold to William Payne, Laurence's ancestor from St Aldate's. She was a lady's maid, Kathryn. Just a girl of seventeen. Can you imagine how she must have felt, being sold away from her family at Woodlands?'

'I can't imagine how it would feel to be *sold*, like a piece of property. But St Aldate's was adjacent to Woodlands, and as a lady's maid she would have held a privileged position in the household. I would imagine she still had plenty of opportunity to see her family at Woodlands.'

'Perhaps.' Nancy smiled. 'But you don't appear to be too surprised by the information. I can't help wondering if you were already aware of Abigail's fate?'

Of course she was aware of it. Truth be told, it would be a relief to admit it. Just as it would be a relief to admit that Richard wanted to keep the information from Nancy. As to why, Kathryn was beginning to wonder now, how she had managed to sleepwalk into the role of unwilling referee in a distasteful game of bluff between Richard and Nancy. With each passing day, Richard appeared to grow more determined to deny Nancy her rightful recognition as his granddaughter. And Nancy, for her part, was growing ever more determined to turn up evidence of a link between her own bloodline and that of the Lancefields. If she had already worked out that Abigail had been William Payne's mistress, the mistress who bore him a son, she would know that any link to the Lancefields by that line was tenuous in the extreme.

But it was still a link. And she was beginning to show every sign that she already knew the secret.

If that was true, how far would Nancy be prepared to push things in attempt to be recognised by Richard as his granddaughter?

*

Amber Kimbrall looked tired. She ushered DS Parkinson into the small private room at the rear of The Lancefield Arms and closed the door gently behind her. 'Take a seat, Sergeant.' She pointed towards a pair of club chairs beside a small, wood-burning stove.

Parkinson sat down and looked around him. There was no question that Amber was making herself at home and putting her stamp on the place; it was warm and cosy, comfortable without being too gentrified. But this evening its cosiness didn't seem to be giving her comfort. 'You look all-in, Amber.'

'Well, it's been one of those days, hasn't it?' She sat down next to him. 'I didn't particularly like being at Becca's, looking over my shoulder in case Zak turned up.' She was holding a mobile phone tightly in her left hand. 'It was a relief to get back to the safety of the pub. I don't mind admitting it.'

She was nervous. Parkinson could almost feel the unease that was stiffening her shoulders and tightening her jaw. 'What made you think he would turn up, Amber? Did Becca tell you he was coming?'

'I didn't say that, did I?' She snapped out the words. 'I just said I was worried about it.'

That, and something else. The policeman studied her face, but the shutters were down: the usually warm eyes cast down towards the phone in her hand; the cheerful, pretty face drawn by some so-far-undisclosed anxiety. 'I knew we should have stayed close by while you were there.' She had asked the police to stay away, to make her visit look more authentic. 'Did something happen? Did Becca turn nasty on you?'

'Becca?' Amber lifted her head, bemused. 'No. It was right for you stay away. She wasn't exactly fooled; she knew I'd come to ask questions. And she wasn't pleased to see me. It was all I could do to persuade her to make me a coffee.' She forced a smile in Parkinson's direction. 'She's landed on her feet with that house, hasn't she? I couldn't understand how she could afford it, but she said she used some of the money Richard Lancefield gave her to pay the deposit and she's buying on a shared ownership basis. The wages from her cleaning job will pay the monthly rent and mortgage.'

If he didn't know better, he would say the landlady was playing for time. 'Are you waiting for something, Amber?'

'Waiting for something?'

He pointed at the phone in her hand. 'A call? A text?'

'Oh, this?' She lifted the hand with the phone. 'It's not important. I'm just waiting to hear from a friend.'

'And this friend makes you nervous?'

'No, of course not.' Her cheeks flushed pink with the lie. And then the phone vibrated.

For several seconds, Tom Parkinson held her gaze, their eyes locked in a momentary stand-off. And then he pointed again at the phone. 'Aren't you going to read it?'

Lips trembling, Amber lifted the phone to her face and ran her eyes across the screen. And then her shoulders relaxed. 'Oh, thank God, she's safe. She's made it to her mother's with Frankie.'

'Safe?' Parkinson blurted out the word. 'What the hell does that mean?' He stretched out a hand and snatched the phone from her fingers. *We're at my mum's, you can tell him now.* Tell who? Tell them what? Jesus, Amber, is this from Becca? I thought we were on the same page.'

A single tear escaped from Amber's left eye to trickle slowly down her cheek. 'I'm sorry, Sergeant Parkinson. She begged me for time to get Frankie out of the house before I told you.'

'Told me what?' Parkinson pushed himself to his feet. 'He's there, isn't he? He's at Becca's house?'

Amber rose to stand beside the policeman. 'He's gone out. She doesn't know where he's gone. Look, I brought you this.' She dug a hand into the back pocket of her jeans and pulled out a scrap of paper. 'The first number is the mobile that Becca's been using to contact him, and the other is the phone number she could reach him on.'

He took the paper from her and stared at it with unseeing eyes. 'How long has he been in Cornwall?'

'He only arrived yesterday evening. He stayed at Becca's last night, and he's supposed to be coming back tonight.'

'And you've known this all afternoon?' He reached into his jacket for his mobile phone. 'Why the bloody hell didn't you tell me?'

The girl was crying freely now. 'I was scared for her, alright? She said he was threatening Frankie. I tried to get her to leave with me, but he had Frankie upstairs.'

'You mean he knew you were there?'

'Yes, so I had to leave without them. Becca asked me to give her time to throw him off the scent and get Frankie to her mother's. We wanted to set it up so that he was on his own, there for you to find. But he went out a couple of hours ago.'

The policeman barely heard her words. He punched angrily at the keypad of his phone and pressed it to his ear. 'Shit. It's going to voicemail.' He lowered his hand and punched another number into the screen. The call was answered immediately. 'Danny, it's Tom Parkinson. I've got a lead on Zak Smith and I can't get hold of Ennor. I need backup to Becca Smith's place in Truro. We can't afford to lose him again. I'm going over there right now. Buckley has the address, he's been staking the place out.' A voice, indistinct, crackled at the end of the line. 'I've no idea how the bloody hell they missed him. Can you keep trying Ennor for me?'

He ended the call and turned disappointed eyes to Amber. 'Why couldn't you trust me? We could have worked out the best way to play it so that Becca and Frankie didn't get hurt.'

The trembling girl sank back onto her chair. 'I was scared. And so was Becca.'

'I know. But if he gets away again, you'll have even

more reason to be scared. Because next time, he'll have another score to settle with you.'

19

'Why am I calling you, and not DCI Greenway?' DCI Grant chuckled down the phone line. 'If I was feeling mischievous, I'd say it was because he's an arrogant little shit and he got right up my nose the last time I spoke to him. But I'm feeling generous, so I'll play the professional card.' She cleared her throat and adopted a playful tone. 'I appreciate that you're at home and off duty, DCI Price, but I have significant information regarding Eva McWhinney and the Lancefields, and I want to share that with the senior officer who is closest to them geographically and therefore able to head off any repercussions as quickly as possible.'

'I'm almost touched, DCI Grant.' Price grinned to himself. 'Is this information that DCI Greenway requested?'

'It is. But I reserve the right to seek advice from you, as someone who knows the family personally, before I share it with him.'

'Alyson, you're a pal.'

'No, I'm not. Don't use that word; Greenway keeps

calling me pal, and I can't say I find it endearing.' A faint rustle of paper made its way down the phoneline. 'I've spoken to Eva's solicitor about the will she made a couple of weeks ago. The changes to her original will were quite significant and I'd like to know what you make of them.' She sniffed loudly. 'Apart from a few personal bequests of jewellery to friends, along with financial compensation for her nominated executors, Eva's original will left her entire estate to a medical charity, a cause that I'm told was very close to her heart. And that estate was quite significant in value: the three properties in Hemlock Row, three hundred and twenty thousand in cash savings and investments, plus a healthy pension pot that will release a cash fund as she died before retirement age.'

'And the new will?'

'Makes changes relating to specific items. The bequests of jewellery haven't changed, nor the payment to her executors. But the new will now bequeaths all the furnishings in the house, and most of her remaining personal possessions, to David Lancefield, for him to use or dispose of as he wishes.'

'To David? Not to Marcus?'

'According to the solicitor, Eva confided that she had grown very fond of David and was planning to support him when he took over running the Lancefield estates. She was well aware that he was a very wealthy man in his own right, and didn't need to benefit financially from her estate. But many of the items in the house are antique and some of them have connections to the Lancefield family. The solicitor said Eva didn't want to be prescriptive. She just wanted to make sure that David Lancefield could pick and choose any items that he would want to safeguard for the family, with the freedom to dispose of the rest.'

Price lifted his elbows from the desk and rolled back in his seat, his mobile phone still tucked into the crook of his neck. 'Was there any mention at all of Marcus in the will?'

'And then some. All of the cash still goes to her

nominated charity, that's both the savings and investments and the pension pot. But the Hemlock Row properties will be folded into a trust, with her solicitor's firm as trustees and executors. The properties are to be rented out, and the rents paid to a nominated beneficiary for his lifetime. After his death, the trust will be dissolved and the properties will be handed to the charity.'

Price felt his pulse quicken. 'And the beneficiary?'

'Marcus Drake.' DCI Grant snuffled another laugh down the phoneline. 'I asked the solicitor for an estimate of the rental value. He thinks it will be just shy of five thousand pounds a month, per property, before the deduction of management fees and overheads. Marcus stands to receive a passive income of somewhere between thirteen and fourteen thousand pounds a month for the rest of his life.' Grant clicked her teeth. 'Always assuming that he didn't have anything to do with her death.'

Price, rendered momentarily speechless by the information, stared up at the ceiling as he considered the implications. Did Marcus know about the bequest? He couldn't have done. When questioned earlier in the day, he had claimed to know nothing of Eva's financial affairs. As far as he knew, she hadn't even made a will.

Unless he was lying.

'Are you still with us, Ennor, or have you passed out with the shock?' Alyson Grant asked the question quietly. 'I wouldn't be surprised if you had. Marcus didn't appear to have a motive the last time someone tried to kill her. But he certainly has one now.'

'Was there any mention of Laurence Payne in the will?' Price roused himself and bent forward again, to lean on his desk. 'Anything at all?'

'No. Just three friends who inherit some jewellery, David and Marcus. Oh, and she left four letters – one for a friend and colleague, and one each for Richard, David and Marcus, to be handed over at the reading of her will.'

'There's to be a formal reading?'

'Yes. The solicitor said she was quite particular about it. It's to be held in his office, in Edinburgh.' Grant hesitated, and then said, 'There's something else, Ennor. The girl was scared.' The inspector had the grace to sound uncomfortable. 'Her solicitor asked her why she was making a new will so soon after her previous one; the original was only written eighteen months ago. She told him about David and Richard Lancefield, and her pleasure at finding some distant family. And she told him that she had begun a relationship with Marcus, that it had brought something new into her life apart from work, and was developing very quickly. They were already talking about a long-term commitment. That was why she was changing her will in his favour.'

'Did she tell the solicitor why she was scared?'

'Yes. She said she didn't believe Smith when he said he wouldn't make any further attempts on her life. She said she was afraid she would spend the rest of her life looking over her shoulder, because he might never be brought to justice.'

'But she wasn't afraid to go to London.'

'She didn't expect him to be in London. And he wasn't. It wasn't Smith who killed her.'

'But what if it was?' Price felt his heart sink. 'If it was, then that's on me.'

'No, it's on both of us. I've told you before, we stand side by side on this one.' Grant gave him a moment to think about it, and then said, 'I'd better call DCI Greenway. Do you have anything you want me to share with him?'

'Yes. You can tell him that I spoke to Marcus Drake this morning and he denied all knowledge of Eva's financial affairs, which suggests that he didn't know about the bequest.'

'Do you believe him?'

'At the time, I did. But now I'm not so sure.' Price, suddenly uneasy, drew in a breath. 'Which is why I'm going to drive over there now, and ask him the question again.'

*

Laurence took a photograph from his wallet and held it out across the table. 'This is my fiancée, Jennet. We plan to marry later this year. The date is set for the twelfth of May.'

Richard Lancefield took the picture with a shaking hand and held it up to his eyes. The girl was pretty, a fresh-faced brunette with rosebud lips and open, smiling eyes. 'She looks charming.' He handed the photograph to David. 'Where did you meet?'

'At a mutual friend's birthday party two years ago. That picture was taken last month. We spent the weekend in Norfolk.' He waited for David to return the snapshot and then secreted it back in his wallet. 'She lives in Yorkshire and I divide my time between London and Hertfordshire, so we often have to meet halfway. Busy lives, you know?'

'Indeed.' They were sitting in the dining room at The Zoological Hotel, and Richard glanced around him as he spoke. 'But not too busy to come to Cornwall.' His tone was dry. 'I understand from Kathryn that you were on your way to see us?'

'I wanted to speak to you about Eva. I realised that she must have meant a great deal to you both, and I was the last person to see her alive. I wanted to tell you about my meeting with her, and how keen she was to surprise you with more information about the family.'

'And to ask me why I was so keen for that meeting not to go ahead?'

'Not if it displeases you to discuss it.' Laurence stiffened, and turned his attention to David. 'Eva was in very good spirits when we met, and we had a delightful evening. She spoke very warmly of you both, and of the other members of your household. And she told me of the family's losses. I can only say how sorry I was to hear what happened to your wife.'

David forced a smile. 'We are somewhat ill-fated as a family, Laurence. One might almost suggest that you would be well advised to have as little as possible to do with us.' He let out a sigh. 'Eva probably also told you that I lost my daughter last year. Losing Lucy was a terrible blow, and to lose Stella so soon afterwards was heartbreaking. I can only say that Eva's appearance in our lives went some way towards filling the void.' There was a bottle of burgundy on the table and David put out a hand to retrieve it. 'You must excuse my father's brittle demeanour, by the way. I'm afraid he grows more cantankerous with each passing day.' David topped up Richard's glass as he spoke. 'He took a little persuading to go ahead with this evening's meeting.' The jibe was delivered softly. 'But I'm sure with a little encouragement, and a little decent wine, we can soften him up.'

Richard met the rebuke with a pursing of his thin lips, and then his brow relaxed. 'You must forgive me, Laurence. David is quite right. I cannot claim to be mellowing with age. But we have endured so many losses in the last few months, so many blows in our simple search for happiness. I know that we must begin to look forward, even as painful events conspire to overtake us. But before we do, may I ask you what you think happened to Eva?'

Laurence frowned at the question. 'At first, I thought it was a simple mugging. She was wearing a lot of expensive jewellery and carrying a clutch bag that would have been easy to snatch. But when I heard that attempts had already been made on her life, both in Edinburgh and here in Cornwall... well, that put a different spin on things.' He hung his head. 'Of course, I will never forgive myself for not walking her all the way back to the hotel's door. And then there is the garland. I still don't know how that can be explained; whether it was hung around her neck to point the finger at me, or whether there was some other intention behind it.'

'Garland?' David, bewildered, stared at his father as he repeated the word. 'What garland?'

'I didn't tell you about the garland because I didn't want to add to your distress. I wanted to break the news to you gently, when you had come to terms with the loss. But, as Laurence has brought it into the conversation, perhaps we should discuss it now.' Richard lifted his wine glass and sipped from it. 'Whoever murdered Eva hung an Obeah garland around her neck. I have been advised that Laurence's branch of the family'—he tipped his head towards his cousin—'have continued their interest in the subject of Obeah since their return to England, and that Laurence himself is something of an expert. Inspector Price is of the opinion that Eva's killer was trying to shift the attention to Laurence, and away from himself. Which suggests that her killer was familiar with the family and its history.' He fixed his gaze on Laurence. 'Would that be a fair summary of the situation?'

'I would say so.' Laurence stared down into his own empty glass. 'Does the subject of Obeah make you uncomfortable, Richard?'

'I would say that the very mention of Obeah should make any sensible person uncomfortable. It is a beastly practice that should never have been allowed to develop.'

'Is that why you were reluctant for Eva to meet with me? Because you knew that I still had an interest in the subject?'

'No. The reason for that was, and remains, a private matter. I can only say that it was not a reflection on you personally.' Richard sighed, and put down his glass. 'I believe I have done you a disservice, Laurence, and it would be inhospitable of me not to welcome you into the family's circle. A man as old as myself is apt to make mistakes, but I hope I still have the sense to realise when I have done so and seek to make amends. You would be welcome to join us tomorrow at Salvation Hall. I know that Kathryn would never forgive me if I denied her the opportunity to quiz you on the family's history. And though you will find the house in mourning for Eva, you will also find that we deal with our grief through industry. Kathryn is busy packing up a collection of items which we will shortly send back to St Felix. I would be pleased to give you a tour of the house tomorrow, and show you those items while the opportunity exists.'

'It would be a pleasure to meet with Kathryn again. And to meet the rest of the household.' It was an olive branch of sorts, and Laurence seemed grateful for it. 'Tell me, will I have an opportunity to meet with Marcus? I heard so much about him from Eva, at the very least I would like to offer him my condolences.'

*

Price sat down on the small, grey armchair and put his head in his hands. 'We've lost him again.' It had taken him nearly forty hair-raising minutes to drive from Penzance to the outskirts of Truro, foot to the floor, blue light flashing. 'How the bloody hell did this happen?'

'We were just too late.' Parkinson hovered beside the chair. 'I still can't believe that Amber didn't tell me straight away.' He looked up sharply as a uniformed officer stepped into the small living room of Becca Smith's house, and shook his head. The officer looked from Parkinson to Price and back again, and then gave a nod of understanding as he backed silently out of the room. 'She gave me some tale about Becca wanting to get Frankie to her mother's before she made the call.'

That sounded like just the sort of thing that Amber Kimbrall would do – think about the child's safety before she thought about the police investigation. But she couldn't really be blamed for that. It was a matter of human instinct. 'Do we have any idea at all about his movements?'

'We think he was here until mid-afternoon, and he left without telling Becca where he was going. According to Amber, he stole a motorbike from a house in Exeter yesterday. A Kawasaki, she thought. So he has transport.'

'And you didn't think about just staking the place out and waiting for him to come back?'

'I panicked, boss. I thought he might already have come back. That we'd find him here.'

'What about Becca?'

'We're bringing her in for questioning.'

Price grunted. 'I don't suppose there's any point in asking how Buckley and Webster missed him? They've been staking this place out all weekend.' But not twenty-four hours a day, because Price couldn't get the excess overtime budget signed off. He puffed up his cheeks. 'What the hell is Smith playing at, Tom? Why has he come back to Cornwall? Why steal a motorbike in Exeter and ride it back to where every policeman is looking for him? Surely he would go in the opposite direction?' Unless there was something drawing him back. The inspector stood up and walked to the window. A small crowd of curious neighbours had gathered in the street to watch the proceedings, their inquisitive faces illuminated by the sickly amber glow of a nearby streetlight. 'Get that lot dispersed, will you? I want this place sealed up and cordoned off. And I want every inch of it searched.'

'Consider it done.' Parkinson made for the door. 'Boss?' He turned to look at Price. 'Don't blame Amber. She was scared witless.'

'I know she was. We asked too much of her.' Again.

Price watched as the door swung shut, and then took his mobile phone from his pocket and dialled a familiar number The call went straight to voicemail and he cursed quietly to himself. 'Kathryn? It's Ennor. I need to speak to you urgently. We've had confirmation that Zak Smith is back in the county.' He swallowed, his stomach churning. 'I don't know how to tell you this, but we've lost him again, and we have no idea where he's headed. Can you let everyone at Salvation Hall know I want them to stay safe within the confines of the house? I'll be over there in about an hour, but I'll make arrangements for a uniformed presence. It might be there before me.' He thought for a moment. 'If Richard and David are still at The Zoological with Laurence, can you ask them to stay there until they hear from me? I'll arrange for an escort back to Salvation Hall.' He laughed softly. 'I'm probably being paranoid. Smith's probably on his way back to Exeter by now. I just don't want to take any risks. Can you call me as soon as you pick this message up?'

He ended the call and leaned back in the armchair. Sooner or later he was going to have to break the news to Alyson Grant. And to his superior officer. And right now he couldn't decide which was worse. Letting down the DCI who had steadfastly fought his corner, or putting the final nail in the coffin of his career.

20

'Kathryn? You left your phone in the kitchen and I think someone has been trying to call you.' Barbara breezed into the library, mobile phone in hand. 'I didn't like to answer it in case it was private.' She handed the phone to Kathryn. 'I hope it wasn't urgent.'

Kathryn swiped at the screen with her thumb. 'It was only Ennor. He was probably just calling to make sure that everything was okay. He knew how unsettled everyone was by Laurence's visit.' She placed the phone down on the desk. 'He's left a message. I'll listen to it before I leave.' She stretched out her arms with a yawn, and rolled her neck around to relieve the growing tension in her shoulders. 'It's been quite a day, hasn't it?'

Barbara sat down on the sofa and picked up a nearby cushion, wrapping her arms around it for comfort. 'Truthfully? I'm not sure how much more I can take.' There was a weariness in her voice. 'I always thought of myself as resilient. But the things that befall this family… one could almost believe they were cursed.'

How many times had Kathryn heard that suggestion? Soon she would begin to believe it herself. 'Have you spoken to Marcus or Nancy this evening?'

'Not Marcus. At least, not since he went up to his room after supper. Nancy and I watched a film together, and that finished about an hour ago. I've been in my room since then, reading, but I thought I just heard Nancy leave the house. She was planning to take Samson for a final walk before bedtime, so I've come back downstairs to make some cocoa for her return. Would you like some?'

Kathryn held up a hand. 'I'll pass, thanks. I'm just waiting for a call from David or Richard to tell me that they're on their way back to Salvation Hall, and then I'll be on my way. I promised to have a nightcap with Laurence.' She swivelled the captain's chair, the better to speak to Barbara. 'He's quite charming, you know. And very knowledgeable.'

'And handsome?'

Kathryn giggled. 'Very handsome, and disarmingly mysterious. But don't tell Ennor that I said so.' She put a hand up to her face. 'My word, I'm starting to blush.'

'Why, Kathryn, I do believe that you're human after all. And just when we all thought that you were a paragon of professional virtue.' Barbara rested her head wearily against the back of the sofa. 'Do you think Eva would have considered him handsome?' She asked the question quietly. 'Could she have taken a shine to him?'

'I suppose so. But didn't she tell us that he was due to marry in the summer?'

'Yes. But people can have their heads turned, can't they?' Barbara rolled inquisitive eyes towards Kathryn. 'Do you think Richard will invite him to Salvation Hall?'

'I sincerely hope so. There is so much that I want to ask him about the Payne line of the family. According to Ennor, he knows all about the slave revolt that happened at St Aldate's. I'm hoping that he might have more information about how the Lancefields were involved. And how they came to know about George Payne's illegitimacy and indiscretions.' Kathryn thought for a moment. 'I suppose I could always ask him about that this evening, when I get back to the hotel.'

'It might be a good idea.' Barbara put a hand up to her throat and ran a finger thoughtfully around her gold necklace. 'Has Nancy spoken to you about Abigail?'

'Abigail?' Kathryn winced. 'The ancestor she couldn't trace?'

'The lady's maid who was sold to Wiliam Payne.' Barbara's lips curved. 'The missing link.'

'Oh, Barbara.' Kathryn's heart sank. 'How much do you know?'

'Probably about as much as you. Abigail is a very distant ancestor to Nancy. Though as she isn't in the direct line of ascent, I wouldn't necessarily consider her an ancestor at all.' Barbara licked her lips. 'As I understand it, Nancy believes that Abigail was sold to William Payne in order to become his mistress and bear him a child. She is convinced that the child was George Payne, and that as George Payne married Maria Lancefield and had a child of his own by her, it proves a blood link between Nancy's family and the Lancefields.'

'And Nancy told you all of this herself?'

'This evening, while we were watching the film.' Barbara's eyes clouded. 'Kathryn, do you have any idea why Nancy is so hell bent on proving there is a biological link between herself and the Lancefields?'

'Yes, I'm afraid I do.'

Barbara sighed. 'And so do I. At least, I think I do. Richard hasn't told me in so many words. But he's dropped enough hints. I feel that he wants me to know, but doesn't have the courage to spell it out.' She folded her arms across her chest and rocked gently against the sofa's cushions. 'If Richard does invite Laurence to visit Salvation Hall tomorrow, are we going to have to keep Nancy away from him?'

A soft laugh escaped from Kathryn's lips. 'What do you think we've been doing this evening?'

'Keeping Marcus away from him?'

The absurdity of the situation was unavoidable. 'Perhaps we should speak to Richard together in the morning.' Kathryn stood up and pulled her cardigan from the back of the chair. 'Things are bad enough without all the secrets and lies.' She wrapped the cardigan around her shoulders and sat down again. 'You do realise that David doesn't know about Nancy?'

'I had concluded as much. But he's going to find out sooner or later, isn't he?' Barbara lifted a hand and rubbed at her forehead. 'Kathryn, why is Richard so reluctant to acknowledge the truth? He seems to be so genuinely fond of the girl, that I can't understand it. Why not just acknowledge her and give her the role she deserves within the family? He's trusting her with the family's heritage. Why not trust her with the estate? Is he really so patriarchal that he doesn't think a woman capable of taking on the role?'

Kathryn closed her eyes. There was unquestionably some sort of prejudice at the root of Richard's reluctance. To discover that it went no further than simple patriarchy or chauvinism would be more than she could possibly hope for.

*

Marcus heard the barking first: short, urgent snaps of canine panic.

Sitting alone at the kitchen table, he froze, his head tilted, but for what seemed like minutes there was only a deafening hush. And then there was another bark, and another, and another: a persistent call of doggy alarm.

He scrambled to his feet and made for the door, pulling it open to lean against the doorframe. He listened again, ears straining against the stillness of the night, but hearing nothing more. 'Nancy? Are you out there?' There was no reply. 'Nancy? Is everything okay?' She had taken the dog for his final walk of the day. It should have been ten minutes of routine exercise before the household settled down for the night. 'Nancy, you're worrying me. Is everything alright?'

Again, no reply. And then a scream rent the air, a shrill cry of terror that shattered the silence and left him breathless.

He launched himself out into the moonlight to stride quickly across the terrace, barely feeling the cold, nighttime air that was nipping at his shoulders. He thought the scream had come from the potting shed, or perhaps the garden storeroom, and as he reached the edge of the terrace he veered left towards the walled garden. 'Nancy? Samson? Where are you?' He ducked his head as he reached the wall, passing through the open doorway without missing a beat. Somewhere in the distance behind him, he thought he could hear Barbara calling his name.

For a moment he stood in silence, his ears pricked for any audible evidence of girl or dog, his eyes adjusting to the darkness. 'Nancy, is that you?' He could just make out what seemed to be a human shape leaning against the outer wall of the storeroom. 'Are you hurt? Can you see me?' He stepped forward towards her. 'What the hell has happened?'

She was bent forward, her head low, her long, dark curls hanging loose across her shoulders. One hand was holding tightly to Samson's lead, and the other was clinging to his collar. And she was shaking.

'In the potting shed.' She looked up through the curls as she whispered the words. 'Samson was scratting at the door and I didn't know why. He wouldn't come away, so I opened the door to let him in.' The words were coming in fits and starts. 'I thought something might have got trapped in there... a bird, or maybe a fox. But it's... it's a man. And I think he's dead.'

'Dead?' Marcus blinked at the word. 'In the potting shed?' He stepped forward and pushed cautiously on the door. 'Did you go in there?' He didn't wait for an answer. He ran a hand down the inside of the doorframe, feeling for the light switch, and flicked it on with nervous fingers.

'Marcus, be careful. You mustn't touch anything. We need to call the police.'

'The police?' There wasn't time to think about that now. 'He might not be dead. We might be able to help him.' The man was lying face down in the middle of the floor, blood congealing on the back of his head, and Marcus stepped forward, bending down low to take a better look. 'I can't tell if he's breathing, and I don't want to move him in case I make things worse.'

'Marcus?' Barbara's voice echoed behind him from the open doorway. 'What's going on? I heard the scream.'

'Samson found him.' Marcus sank to his knees beside the body. 'I think he might be dead.'

'Dead? But what's he doing in here? I don't understand?' She was beside Marcus now, staring down at the prone, lifeless form. 'What on earth is a complete stranger doing in here?'

'He isn't a stranger.' Marcus sucked in a deep breath of courage, and took hold of the corpse's black leather jacket. He heaved the body up and over, turning the man awkwardly onto his side, and stared vacantly down at the faded jeans and the heavy brown boots. And then he ran his eyes reluctantly upwards, to the shock of short, white-blond hair above the collar of the jacket.

For a moment, he fought back the urge to heave the contents of his stomach over the top of the helpless corpse. And then he turned to Barbara with wild, bewildered eyes. 'It isn't a stranger, Barbara. It's Zak Smith.'

21

Price rested a hip against the potting bench and folded his arms across his chest. Early- morning sunlight was creeping into his eyeline from a nearby window and he moved his head back a little to avoid the glare. 'It doesn't take much imagination to still see him there, does it?' He had arrived at Salvation Hall late the previous evening simply hoping to speak to Marcus. Never for one moment had he expected to stumble upon a crime scene, let alone one that included Zak Smith's body.

'I can't say it's something I'll find easy to forget.' DS Parkinson, leaning against the wall by the door, scratched at his ear. 'It's all getting a bit much, isn't it?'

And then some. 'I could hardly believe the coincidence. I'd even put in a request for two officers to come down here, knowing that Smith was on the loose, so I already had backup.' Price could only laugh at his own naivety. He hadn't expected the officers to be needed, he was really just trying to cover all bases. 'I did think twice before I called you out last night, by the way. There didn't seem much point in us both losing sleep. But I knew you'd only give me earache this morning if you woke up to the news and realised that you hadn't been invited to the party.'

'You know me too well.' Parkinson turned his eyes around the potting shed as he spoke. 'What the hell was he doing in here?'

'What the hell was he doing at Salvation Hall at all?' Price pulled in his lips and pressed down hard, thinking. 'There are only two possibilities: he'd broken into the estate again to act against the family, or he came to meet someone. If it was the former, then his killer must have stumbled across him unexpectedly; if it was the latter, then…'

'Either way, we're going to be looking at the family again, aren't we?'

Price didn't answer. He couldn't bring himself to answer. He straightened his back and moved away from the bench. 'Time of death was estimated at between four and six o'clock yesterday afternoon. The cause was a fatal blow to the back of the head.' The weapon, a garden spade, had already been taken away for examination. He took a single step forward, running his eyes along the potting bench to a neat row of gardening tools lined up against the abutting wall. 'It was the same MO used to kill Philip McKeith last September.' Perhaps that *was* the answer. 'Is it too obvious to say that the motive was revenge?'

'For killing Eva?'

'Not just Eva. For killing Stella too.'

'Marcus Drake or David Lancefield?'

'Probably. I couldn't see Laurence Payne in the frame for this, even if we follow up on DCI Greenway's cockeyed notion that Payne could have paid Smith to murder Eva. He didn't arrive in Penzance until just after lunchtime, and he was with me and Kathryn at The Zoological between four and six o'clock.' The inspector pointed to the line of tools. 'There's a gap there, where the spade must have stood.' The previous night it had been found on the floor beside the body. 'But there's nothing obvious to the naked eye, is there? Smith was in here, he encountered someone – either by arrangement or by accident – and a conversation probably ensued. And then at some point, the killer picked up the spade and whacked him on the back of the head with it.'

'Dr Frinton said the blow hit him from behind, and almost straight. He had his back to his assailant and was probably kneeling.' Parkinson frowned. 'Why would he be kneeling?'

'I doubt it was an act of submission. More likely he had dropped something.'

'But you would bend, wouldn't you, to pick something up?'

'That might depend on what you've dropped.' Price puckered his brow. 'If you dropped a bank note or a card, you'd probably bend to pick it up. But I know that if I drop coins I tend to drop to one knee while I gather them up.' Not that there had been anything like coins found under the body. 'I think we're done here. It's time to let the experts back in.' He jerked his head towards the door and watched as Parkinson took the hint and opened it. 'He'd been here between four and six hours by the time they found him.' Price followed Parkinson out into the morning sunlight, letting the door swing shut behind him. 'Did you get any sleep last night?'

'About four hours.'

'I'll try not to be jealous.' It had been one of those nights when sleep had refused to come, and he'd lain awake tormented, trying against the odds to make sense of this most peculiar twist of fate. 'You know we're going to have to talk to Becca Smith?' Price turned right, towards the house, and began to walk slowly along the path. 'And search her house again. We need to recover anything that Smith brought with him.'

Parkinson grunted. 'I suppose by *we* you mean *me*.' He cast a passing glance through the window of the garden storeroom as he passed it. 'Do they still have all that slavery paraphernalia in there?'

'Not for much longer. It's all being shipped back to St Felix.' Price wasn't sure he could admit to Tom that he'd agreed to help Kathryn with the packing. 'Could you do a couple of other things for me this morning? We need to let Amber know that she can stop looking over her shoulder. And DCI Greenway needs to know that we've found his missing blond assailant.'

'How do you think he's going to take it, when he finds out that it was Zak all along?'

'I don't think it will trouble him too much. If I've got the measure of Greenway, he'll just be glad that someone else is dealing with the problem.' They had reached the garden wall and Price ducked his head to pass through the doorway. 'If Becca won't let you search the house, get a warrant. I'm going to stay here and question the family. Call me if you need me.' He watched as Parkinson strode off towards the front of the house.

And then he shivered.

Questioning the family for the second time in less than a few months? He could hardly bear to think about it. He was passing close to the terrace now, the scene of Stella Lancefield's murder, and his stomach lurched. This had to be the end of it. He couldn't take any more involvement with the Lancefield family. When this crime was solved, it would be time to walk away.

If only he could be sure that Kathryn would walk away with him.

*

'I am delighted, of course, that the scoundrel has turned up. Though I would have preferred it not to be in our potting shed. And certainly not as a corpse.' Richard Lancefield picked up a knife from the table and dug it into the butter dish. 'There is no question that Inspector Price will have his eyes on the family again.'

'I suppose he will want to speak to all of us.' Barbara pushed her breakfast plate away. 'Do you want me to stay here in the Dower House this morning?'

'Only if it pleases you. The main house will be overrun with police officers again. It's almost a relief to be able to skulk away in here without having to watch the proceedings. But at least now we know who murdered poor Eva.' The old man waved the knife towards Barbara. 'It was Smith after all, sporting that ridiculous head of bleached hair. No wonder poor Marcus received such a shock when he bent down to the body.'

Had he received a shock? Barbara tried to recall the moment she had looked through the potting shed's doorway. Marcus had been on his knees, his back to her, his head bent over the corpse. But his eyes, when he had turned to look at her, had been full of fear. Perhaps that was what shock did to you. 'I'm still trying to fathom how Smith managed to get in there without being heard.'

'Why should anyone hear him? The potting shed is at a distance from the house on the other side of a seven-foot wall.' Richard scraped the butter knife across the toast on his plate with a shake of the head. 'There's no question that we need to install security cameras now. I only regret that we didn't do it after poor Stella was murdered.'

Would anything be gained by pointing out the irony of his suggestion: that on this occasion it was the intruder who was murdered? 'Could he have come here with an accomplice, Richard? Someone unknown, who argued with him and lashed out?'

'It would be highly convenient to think so. But I regret it is most unlikely. Yet again, I fear we must look amongst ourselves for the killer.' The old man's shoulders drooped, weighed down by the thought. 'The fool obviously came here hoping to cause trouble, and was apprehended in the process. We can only hope that whoever dispatched him was meticulous in their handling of it.'

Barbara blinked. 'Are you saying that you condone his

murder?'

'Not at all. Murder is the most heinous of crimes. If, indeed, it was murder.' Richard put down his knife. 'For murder there would have to be premeditation. There is always the possibility of manslaughter.'

'I hardly think he could have been hit on the head with a spade by accident.'

'There may be an argument for self-defence.'

'When he was hit on the *back* of the head?'

'It might be possible.'

'Richard, this isn't like Marcus and Philip. When Marcus hit Philip on the back of the head, he claimed he was trying to rescue Lucy. He thought Lucy was still alive. But there was no third party in the potting shed, was there?'

'Do you know that to be a fact?'

'Do I…?' Barbara gasped. 'You do understand that a crime has been committed, and that justice has to be served?'

'Of course I understand it. But justice takes many forms and Smith was a threat to society. He murdered Geraldine Morton, a completely innocent young woman. He murdered my daughter-in-law. And now it would appear that he murdered our cousin, Eva. The police will be quietly relieved that he has been found, whatever the circumstances. And the justice system will be saved a great deal of additional expense in prosecuting the man for his crimes and incarcerating him for what would most likely have been a whole-life tariff.'

'If I have the measure of DCI Price, he won't turn a blind eye to what happened here. Much as it pains me to say it, Zak is as much a victim as Geraldine, Stella or Eva.'

'I don't expect the inspector to turn a blind eye. But even if he is certain of his man, I think he may struggle to build a case.'

'And if he doesn't struggle?'

'Then, wherever his sights settle, we will meet him head

on with the best possible legal defence, as we did when Marcus was charged with Philip's murder.' Richard picked up his toast and examined it. 'In the meantime, we must continue with our plans. David will stay at Salvation Hall now. He does not intend to return to St Felix for the foreseeable future. The heritage items will still go back to Woodlands, though.'

'And Nancy with them?'

'With the inspector's permission, once she has been cleared of any involvement.' Richard nodded to himself. 'And we must assume the same of Marcus.'

'And what about you, Richard?'

'Me?' The question seemed to puzzle him. 'I see no reason to alter my own plans. Of course, no one will travel until we have attended to Eva's funeral. David plans to contact DCI Greenway today, to ask when her body will be released, though we still need to speak to her solicitor before any firm arrangements can be made. We've been advised that she left a will, so I must call the man today and let him know that you will be representing the family.' He lifted a sheepish eye to Barbara. 'Assuming, my dear, that you are still willing to travel to Edinburgh? It would be an enormous help, while David and I support the police with their investigation.'

'You don't think that Marcus would wish to deal with Eva's affairs?'

'Marcus will defer to me.' Richard dropped the cold, uneaten toast onto his plate and pushed it away. 'In any case, I think he may be rather preoccupied for the next few days. I suspect that Inspector Price is going to be rather keen for him to remain at Salvation Hall.'

*

'Tell me, Kathryn, have you ever decided upon a course of action that seemed like a good idea at the time, only to realise the folly of it just a little too late to stop?' Laurence Payne stared out of the car's window at the passing Cornish scenery as he spoke. 'I think I must have been full of foolish bravado when I caught the train for Penzance.'

Kathryn took her eyes from the road for a fleeting moment, to offer him what she hoped was a reassuring smile. 'Your supper with Richard and David went well, didn't it? You don't have any reason to think you won't be warmly welcomed at Salvation Hall?' They were approaching a junction and she slowed the Volvo and flicked on the indicator. 'I know Richard is very keen for your visit to go ahead, and we'll be there in another five minutes or so. But if you've changed your mind, you only have to say.' She glanced to the right, checking for traffic, and then guided the car smoothly to the left. 'What is it that's making you uncomfortable?'

'Apart from the fact that we'll be walking into the middle of a murder investigation?' Laurence puffed out his lips. 'Do I have to remind you that I was a suspect for Eva's murder? After all, that's why DCI Greenway arranged for me to be tailed to Paddington yesterday morning, and why he contacted your DCI Price to ask him to head me off at the pass when I reached Penzance.'

'Well, they can hardly think that now, can they?' She had shared the news of Zak Smith's death with him before they'd even sat down to breakfast, and his whole body had quivered with unmistakeable relief. 'And they can't consider you a suspect for Zak's murder, because you were safely at The Zoological when the murder took place.'

'So, Smith must have been murdered by one of the family.' Laurence drew his attention away from the passing countryside to look at Kathryn. 'I suppose the police will be wondering now whether the same member of the family had arranged for Smith to murder Eva.'

Kathryn frowned, and slowed the car. 'That's Penwithen village up ahead. We could walk down there later, if you'd like. The church is worth a look.' The clumsy deflection was all that she could muster. 'Always supposing that Richard doesn't monopolise your time.' They had reached the entrance to the estate and she turned the car to the right, pulling off the main road to pass through an imposing, wrought-iron gateway. 'Good morning.' She mouthed the greeting silently to a uniformed police offer standing beside the gate, nodding as he acknowledged her. 'That's PC Richardson. I'm sorry to say that he's almost a regular visitor to the hall now. I suppose on the plus side I don't have to explain what I'm doing here every time I roll up to the gates.'

Laurence mumbled under his breath as the car began to pick up speed. 'I suppose it's too late to back up now, isn't it?' He stared out of the window as they trundled down the driveway. 'This place is going to be rather grand, isn't it?'

'It's wonderful. You'll get a good view of the house in a moment, just as we round the bend.' Kathryn kept the car at a slow and steady speed, and smiled to herself as the jungle of rampant foliage to their left gave way to a pristine, rolling lawn and a magnificent view of the manor house. 'I come here almost every day, and the sight of it still takes my breath away.'

It had a decidedly different effect on her passenger. Laurence jerked forward in his seat and banged his hand on the dashboard. 'Stop the car.' He hissed the words through his teeth. 'Please, Kathryn, stop the car.'

Startled, she braked abruptly, turning to stare at him as she pulled on the handbrake. 'What? What is it?'

'What the hell are we doing here?'

'Doing here?' She didn't understand. 'You're here to meet with the family.'

'But look. Just *look*.' He pointed through the windscreen. 'This is a crime scene. There are police vehicles everywhere.'

And so there were. Not to mention the numerous uniformed and plain-clothed police officers that went with them. Kathryn slumped back in the driver's seat with a sigh. 'I suppose I'm so used to seeing them that it doesn't really register anymore.' She ran a finger around the rim of the steering wheel. 'Is it really just the police presence that's causing your concern? Because I've spoken to Ennor, and he has no objection to you being here, providing we don't get in the way of the investigation.' She reached across and placed a hand gently on his arm. 'Or are you worried about meeting the rest of the family?'

'Not the rest of the family. But seeing all these policemen...' Laurence turned his deep, blue eyes towards her. 'I'm worried about meeting Marcus. Do you think he could have murdered Zak Smith?'

How on earth could she answer that? But then, how many more times would she be asked the same question in the days to come? 'What makes you think it would be Marcus?'

'Because he's murdered before, hasn't he? DS Marwick told me. He murdered his fiancée's lover.'

'It was manslaughter, not murder.' As if it made that much of a difference. 'And he's served his time. And knowing Marcus, and how easily he has settled into life on St Felix, I think it highly unlikely that he's going to risk being hauled through the legal system again.'

'Manslaughter is very often a crime of passion, isn't it? Not passion in the romantic sense, but triggered by heated emotions?' Laurence raised an eyebrow. 'It sounds as though Marcus has a temper and a tendency to lash out.'

'As far as I'm aware, he's lashed out once. At Philip McKeith. That doesn't mean that he lashed out at Zak Smith, although I can see that he might have done so if he knew that Zak had murdered Eva. And having done so, I suppose there would be nothing to stop him from lashing out at you, for not protecting her.' Kathryn felt a tinge of disappointment as she released the car's handbrake. 'But, I don't really think that he's going to do that in front of a house full of police officers. Even Marcus isn't *that* hot-headed.' She let the car roll down what was left of the driveway, her foot barely on the accelerator. 'Laurence, I hope I can call on you to be pragmatic? After all, it was your decision to come to Penwithen.' She brought the car to rest close to the neatly clipped yew hedge that flanked the turning circle in front of the house. 'Setting Zak Smith aside, the family are in mourning for Eva. And I think Richard has been quite magnanimous in welcoming you to Salvation Hall, despite his initial reservations.'

'Forgive me, Kathryn. I'm forgetting my manners. I suppose it must be my guilty conscience talking. I still haven't forgiven myself for letting Eva out of my sight.' Laurence bowed his head. 'Of course I'll be pragmatic.' He stretched out a hand to open the car door. 'And, hopefully, the same can be expected of Marcus.'

22

'They tell me that it's the housekeeper's room, but it feels more like a cupboard to me.' Price tucked the mobile phone into his neck as he spoke. 'At least I know where I belong – in the servant's quarters, close to the tradesman's entrance.' The spindle chair beside the housekeeper's desk was cold and hard and he shifted his weight as he spoke, searching in vain for a comfortable position. 'I suppose I should be grateful that they understand the need for a temporary headquarters for the investigation.'

'Frankly, given the amount of time you spend at the place I'm surprised you don't have your own interview room there.' Alyson Grant sounded almost cheerful at the end of the line. 'Anyway, you must be relieved.'

Must he? 'I guess it's a relief that Smith won't be able to hurt anyone else. And that you can draw a line under your case and give some closure to Geraldine Morton's family.' And perhaps a relief that the Lancefields wouldn't have to go on looking over their shoulders waiting for Smith to strike again, although that relief might well be cancelled out by the anxiety of wondering which of them was likely to be in the frame for his murder.

'Did the blond hair and mask really put you off the scent, Price?'

'I suppose they must have done. My gut was screaming that it had to be him, but the photographic evidence suggested otherwise.' He simply couldn't be certain. 'It didn't help that my gut had already let me down when it came to Eva travelling to Salvation Hall back in November.' And when a policeman begins to mistrust his gut, it's probably the end of the road anyway. He cast the thought aside. 'On the other hand, I guess we know now why Smith was happy to be caught by the CCTV cameras. He just couldn't resist it. If he'd just done the deed and walked away, the hair and mask would have been enough of a disguise to get away with it. But he didn't want to get away with it, did he? He just couldn't resist poking us in the eye.'

'Well, I always said that he looked like a cocky little bastard.' Grant muttered under her breath. 'Still, we can be pretty certain now that he was responsible for Eva's death. The camera doesn't lie. And you've been vindicated.'

Vindicated and devastated in equal measures. 'If we'd caught him before now, Eva might still be alive.' Price could hardly bear to think about it. 'And he won't be brought to justice to account for his crimes.'

'Ah, well, I suppose you could call it a kind of natural justice. He'll still have to account for his crimes to his maker.' Grant clicked her teeth. 'So, what do you need from me?'

'Nothing concrete, at this stage. We can't prosecute a dead man for the murders of Geraldine and Stella.'

'Agreed. But we don't know for certain that he was acting of his own volition. What if there was some truth to that claim that Marcus Drake offered him money to get rid of Eva?'

'Even if there was a grain of truth in that, we'd simply have no way of proving it. Not now he's dead. There would be no witnesses to the agreement and Marcus is hardly likely to admit to it.' Any more than he was likely to admit to murdering Zak Smith. 'No, I think the only course of action open to us is to close the cases against him for the murders of Geraldine, Stella and Eva.'

For a few moments, Grant was silent at the end of the line. Then she slowly drew in an audible breath. 'Did Marcus know that he was going to benefit from Eva's death?'

'I haven't had the opportunity to ask him yet. I came back here yesterday evening to discuss it with him but Smith's body kind of got in the way.' He knew what Grant was thinking. 'Eva didn't change her will to favour Marcus until after Geraldine and Stella were murdered.'

'I know. But just suppose that Marcus *did* know that the will had been changed. Regardless of the motive for the first attempt on her life, that inheritance could be a motive for the second attempt. And if Marcus did arrange for Smith to commit the crime so that he could inherit, that would be one hell of a motive for Marcus to murder Smith, wouldn't it? To keep him quiet?' She left the question hanging for a moment and then said, 'And don't you think DCI Greenway would be interested in that?'

'Joint enterprise for Eva's murder? To be honest, I think it's far more likely that DCI Greenway will just want to wrap this up as quickly as he can. He's already confirmed to me that Eva was dead when she went into the water. He's going to be as happy as a sandboy to learn that the blond assailant was Smith after all, and that his prime suspect is already dead. There will be no need to bring charges and comparatively little paperwork to complete. And what paperwork there is will probably end up on Marwick's desk.'

'You're still not a fan then?' Grant laughed. 'When are you going to tell him?'

'I've asked Tom Parkinson to give him a call. I've got too much on my plate here this morning. I've got a crime scene to analyse and several members of the Lancefield family to interview.' He looked down at his watch as he spoke. 'Before we end the call, is there anything else that you want from me this morning?'

'Yes, there is.' She sounded suddenly solemn. 'Don't take the easy route, Price. If there's any remote possibility that Marcus and Smith were colluding over Eva's murder, I hope you'll do everything you can to make sure that he doesn't benefit from her death. For Eva's sake.'

*

David Lancefield walked slowly over to the library window and stared out towards the ornamental lake.

From his vantage point, there wasn't a great deal to see: the wall that encircled the kitchen garden was too far to his left to catch the comings and goings of uniformed and plain-clothed police officers as they ducked in and out of the gateway. Occasionally, an officer or two would walk back towards the terrace, passing in front of the house as they went, their eyes respectfully – or perhaps cautiously – turned away from the windows as they passed.

It was difficult to know whether to be overjoyed or dismayed. Zak Smith had been found and the nightmare was almost over.

Unless it was just about to begin.

There was no question that DCI Price was a man intent on bringing justice, whatever the circumstances of the case. And David couldn't help wondering whether the man would sense an opportunity to right what he had long perceived to be a wrong: that if he could bring home the murder of Smith to a member of the extended Lancefield family, make it stick with a sentence that would be commensurate with the crime rather than a nod in the direction of the justice system, then Becca Smith might finally receive what she had long since deserved.

Something more than money in return for the loss of the man she had loved.

He narrowed his eyes and peered through the glass at nothing in particular. He knew that Marcus, sitting in an armchair beside the fireplace, was watching him closely. He could feel the weight of the young man's gaze on his back, and he knew that the brittle atmosphere in the room wouldn't ease until he spoke.

'Inspector Price will be looking at all of us.' He was standing so close to the window that the glass misted under his breath as he spoke. 'And he'll say that we all had a motive for getting rid of Zak Smith.' He wanted to say 'unless one of us confesses to the crime', but he didn't have the courage.

'How could Barbara have a motive? Or Kathryn?' Marcus spoke quietly, his voice unreasonably calm. 'Or Nancy, for that matter? Nancy, of all people, is the least likely to have a motive. She hated Stella. She probably thinks that Smith did her a favour.'

'She was on good terms with Eva.'

'Was she?' There was an unexpected inflection in the reply. 'I'm not so sure about that. I think the two of them hid it well, so as not to upset the family. All the venom was on Nancy's side, of course. Eva did everything she could to be friendly. But she confided to me that she suspected Nancy was play-acting to keep the peace.'

'Play-acting to keep the peace?' David, suddenly riled, banged his fist against the hard, wooden panelling beside the glass. 'Marcus, this kind of divisive talk really won't do.' He turned furious eyes to his stepson. 'We have to be strong, and support each other until the situation resolves.'

Marcus shrank back into his chair. 'I didn't mean to make you angry. But the reality is, Inspector Price will only be looking at three people.'

'You, me, and my father.'

'You and me, certainly. But no one could possibly conceive that Richard could murder a fit and healthy specimen like Smith, even if he had the motive.' Marcus ran his tongue around his teeth. 'I know it wasn't me, and I'm certain it wasn't you. So that only leaves Laurence Payne.'

'Laurence? How on earth could he be responsible for a death that took place in our potting shed?'

'I don't know yet. But you have to admit that it's a possibility.' Marcus leaned forward. 'Doesn't it strike you as odd that just hours after Laurence Payne arrives in Cornwall, Zak Smith turns up dead?' He paused, waiting for David to consider the suggestion. 'What if Laurence didn't come to Cornwall to meet with the family at all? What if he came here to meet with Zak Smith? What if he came here to pay him off?'

'To pay him off for what?'

'For killing Eva.' Marcus was growing animated. 'Think about it, David. What if Laurence Payne offered to pay Zak to murder Eva? He provides Smith with that garland to hang around her neck, so that he can claim someone was trying to point the finger at him. A double bluff, if you like. But he has no intention of paying up. He arranges to meet Smith here, at Salvation Hall, on the pretext of handing over the cash. But his real intention is to arrange for Smith to be murdered on Lancefield property, so that he can avoid paying him and put the blame for his death onto the family.'

David closed his eyes and leaned against the wooden panelling beside the window. 'I hadn't realised, until just now, what a fertile imagination you have, Marcus.' If it *was* just imagination, and not a loosening grip on reality. 'Who are you suggesting carried out the murder?'

'That's for Inspector Price to work out. All I'm suggesting is that if Laurence Payne paid Smith to murder Eva, he could quite easily have arranged for a third party to murder Smith.'

'In our potting shed?' David opened his eyes. 'My dear boy, I'm beginning to wonder if the pain of losing Eva is finally taking its toll. Why on earth would he arrange for the murder to be here?'

'I would have thought that was obvious.' Marcus narrowed his eyes. 'So that he could point the finger at me.'

*

DS Marwick closed the door of DCI Greenway's office behind him and stepped over to the desk. 'We've confirmed Laurence Payne's alibi for the time of Eva's murder.' He sat down on an adjacent chair without waiting to be invited. 'It's taken a lot of piecing together but fair play to the team, they've nailed it.'

Greenway, irritated, lifted his eyes from the document he'd been examining. 'You've done what?'

'Confirmed his alibi. Using CCTV footage.' It was hardly the thanks that Marwick had expected. 'We've traced him walking over the floating footbridge at eleven minutes past twelve on Friday night, and then picked him up at random points as he made his way back to his apartment.' The sergeant pulled a notebook from his pocket and flipped it open, running his eyes down the page with a familiar sense of disappointment. 'He crossed Cabot Square and turned down South Colonnade towards Upper Bank Street. Then minutes later we picked him up on a street camera close to his apartment building, and then five minutes after that'—he flipped the page of the notebook—'the cameras in his apartment building registered him coming into the foyer and entering the lift up to the fifteenth floor. There's no other way for him to exit the apartment building, so we viewed the footage from the foyer cameras for the following ninety minutes, up to the time that Eva was put into the water. There was no sign of him.' Marwick flipped the notebook shut. 'He didn't leave the building.' He waited for a moment, expecting Greenway to comment, and then said, 'I thought you'd be pleased. If there was no question of Payne returning to the crime scene, we can focus all of our attention on the blond man.'

Greenway's lip curled and he snarled at the sergeant. 'The blond man is dead.'

'Dead? Where the hell did that come from?'

'He's turned up in Cornwall. As a corpse.' The inspector flopped back in his seat. 'In the grounds of the Lancefield family's home.'

Marwick whistled softly. 'You heard this from DCI Price?'

'I heard it from DS Parkinson. Apparently the sainted DCI Price is too busy investigating Smith's murder to call me himself.'

'Ah.' At least that would explain the sudden bout of peevishness: Marwick had worked with Greenway long enough to know that even the remotest prick into his bubble of self-importance was bound to provoke a reaction. But there was still the obvious question to be asked. 'Zak Smith? I don't see the connection.'

'The blond man turned out to be Zak Smith after all. A blatantly disguised Zak Smith with cropped, dyed-blond hair and a smart suit. Wouldn't you think that Price would have seen through such a flimsy charade and recognised the man, even with dyed hair?'

Marwick wasn't about to remind Greenway that he himself had examined a photograph of Smith, compared it to the grainy CCTV footage from the camera outside Vincenzo's, and decided that it wasn't Smith but some unknown, random assailant. 'The mask didn't exactly help, did it?' An unbidden chuckle tried to make its way to Marwick's lips and he clamped them together to suppress it. 'Do you want me to stand the team down?' There would be no point in combing hours of CCTV footage to search for witnesses if the suspect was dead. 'I can draft out the documentation needed to draw a line under it. We can't charge a dead man. And it'll be the same for DCI Grant, up in Edinburgh. She can't charge a dead man, either, can she?'

'I'm not interested in how it affects her, only what it means for us.' Greenway was hissing through almost-clenched teeth. 'I don't for one minute believe that a rural hick like Smith would have known anything about Caribbean witchcraft. Someone had to either provide him with that garland, or tell him how to make one.'

'We already know that the information was readily available in Laurence Payne's book.'

'Then someone had to tell Smith that the book existed, and how that garland was relevant to Eva McWhinney.' Greenway snapped out the words. 'Or, more to the point, how it was relevant to Eva McWhinney meeting with Laurence Payne. And the most likely person to do that was Laurence Payne himself.'

'You still think he was working with Smith?'

'I still think it has to be investigated. Which is why we can't wind the team down too much.' Greenway stretched out a hand to pull a blank sheet of paper from the tray on his desk. 'Stand the team down from looking at CCTV footage and interviewing.' He picked up a pen and began to scribble. 'And mobilise them to start looking into Laurence Payne in more detail. I want to know everything there is to know about him: his financial situation, his fiancée, and any previous contact with Eva McWhinney.'

Marwick felt his spirits sink. 'As you wish, guv.' He stood up. 'Anything else?'

'Yes. Get someone to look at the components of that garland: the feathers and the bottle might be commonplace enough, but that animal skull? You can't buy those on every street corner. I want to know who sold it, and I want to know who they sold it to.'

And what about the obvious possibility? Marwick stepped towards the office door, and then paused. 'Is Laurence Payne in the frame for Zak Smith's death?'

Greenway scowled. 'I don't know. According to Parkinson, Payne has an alibi for the death. But Marcus Drake was on the spot.' Greenway chewed on the end of his pen. 'And we already know that Drake stands to benefit from Eva McWhinney's will.' The cogs in his brain were turning. 'There is always the possibility that the two of them know each other. We might not just be looking at a link between Payne and Smith. We might be looking at the three of them. We need to find out whether Laurence Payne had ever had any contact with Marcus Drake before he made his way to Cornwall.'

23

DCI Price had walked past the front of the Dower House on almost every visit he had made to Salvation Hall, but the day before had marked his first invitation to step inside. And today, the repeated privilege was making him feel curiously uncomfortable.

Perched on the very edge of a fading, chintz-covered sofa he found it difficult to look Richard Lancefield in the eye. 'We think that Smith died sometime between four and six o'clock yesterday evening. That means the body lay undiscovered for around four to five hours.'

The old man digested the information with a weary sigh. 'And at what time do you believe he arrived here?'

'Not much before that, to be honest. I didn't have the opportunity to discuss it with you yesterday evening. I did advise you that we had a lead on him, and that was the reason for sending an escort to The Zoological Hotel to accompany you back to Salvation Hall.'

'And the reason you were already here when David and I returned home?'

'Yes. I'd come to warn the family and make sure that everyone was safe.' Price cleared his throat. 'But I didn't have the opportunity to share details of the lead we'd received.' He looked down at his fingers. 'We received information, a little late in the day, that Smith was at his sister's new home in Truro.'

'Will that girl never learn?' Richard's eyes rolled with a smile. 'Did she finally see sense and give him up to you?'

'No. We arranged for Amber Kimbrall to visit her, because we thought Becca might open up to a friend, and to some extent that was the case. Smith had arrived at Becca's the evening before and he was in the house when Amber visited. But he had made threats against Frankie's safety and both girls were too afraid of the consequences to speak up until they had safely removed the child from the house.'

'I would expect nothing less from Amber. It would appear that I owe her yet another debt of gratitude.' The old man appeared to sense the policeman's confusion at his response. 'I realise that she could have raised the alarm earlier but you seem to forget, Chief Inspector, that Frankie is my goddaughter.'

Trust the old man to see the positive side. 'Well, I can reassure you that Frankie is safe and with Becca's mother in Helston.'

'And where is Becca?'

'Still at home in Truro. We'll be bringing her in for questioning, but we're donning the kid gloves until she comes to terms with her brother's death. She has a liaison officer with her at the moment, and DS Parkinson will be putting some gentle questions to her.'

'Then I hope she is able to explain just exactly what Zak was doing here at Salvation Hall.'

That was everyone's hope, but Price couldn't help thinking it was a forlorn one. 'You realise that I will have to ask everyone in the household for an alibi for the estimated time of death?'

'Yes. And I see no reason why we cannot assist you with that. David and I were both here at the Dower House. You are aware that we travelled to Penzance to meet with Laurence Payne yesterday evening, but we didn't leave until six thirty. Barbara was here with us until then, and she will be able to vouch for us. I'm sure that Marcus and Nancy will be able to account for themselves.' Richard narrowed his eyes. 'Tell me, Chief Inspector, what do you think Smith was doing here?'

'I'm keeping an open mind.' Mainly, on this occasion, because he wasn't yet ready to openly suggest that Richard Lancefield had a murderer in his household. 'It's possible that he was just planning to cause more trouble.'

'And by trouble, do you mean vandalism to our property or harm to our family members?'

'At this stage, we have no way of knowing.'

'Then it only remains for me to ask what we can do to assist in your investigation. I have already agreed that you may have free access to search the house and grounds. Is there anything else?'

'May we search any part of the house?'

'Of course.' Richard's lips twitched. 'I realise that the members of our household are the most obvious suspects for this latest crime, but I am quietly confident that the answer to Smith's murder lies outside of the family. It is possible that Smith unwittingly disturbed another intruder on the estate. Possible, even, that he did not come here alone, but with an accomplice who turned on him. That, of course, is for you to determine.'

Was Richard Lancefield warning him off? It would hardly be a surprise. And there was no question at all that Price was relieved now not to be in the old man's debt. After all, if he'd accepted Richard Lancefield's offers of help when his career hit the skids, his hands would have been tied when it came to investigating members of his family.

The question was, which member of the family was the old man particularly keen to protect?

*

'I don't know what we're doing up here, Barbara.' Nancy closed the door of the attic room behind her. 'I don't really have the time to spend on any more packing today. I have lunch to prepare for Laurence's visit.' She leaned against a packing crate and folded her arms. 'And even that is a stretch. I don't know what Richard was thinking of, inviting him to visit when the place is swarming with policemen.'

'We're here because I wanted to discuss the spinet with you.' Barbara had already crossed the room and was busy pulling the dustsheet from the small, delicate piece of furniture. 'I spoke to Richard this morning and he has agreed that it should be shipped back to St Felix. I thought you might be able to advise me on the best way of packing it for transportation.'

Nancy's lower lip began to tremble. 'He agreed that it can go back to Woodlands? Just like that?'

'No, not "just like that". I explained to him how important the piece was to you, and said that if you were to return to St Felix on a permanent basis then the very least he could do was to let you take the spinet back with you.'

If Barbara had expected an expression of thanks, she was only to be disappointed. Nancy frowned, and fixed her with questioning eyes. 'And if I am not to return on a permanent basis? Will the spinet still go back so that my mother can play it?'

'My understanding from Richard is that nothing has changed, and you are still to return.'

'But in the light of Eva's death, and Zak being found…'

'Why should that make a difference?' Barbara shook out the dustsheet and began to fold it. 'I don't really see that Zak's death is anything to do with you. I know that you found the body but that's just a matter of giving a statement to the police.' She turned to look at the girl. 'And Marcus will be returning to St Felix after Eva's funeral.'

'Even though he failed yet again to marry into the family?'

Barbara took a step back and examined the spinet. 'That comment intrigued me so much the last time you made it that I asked Richard whether he shared your opinion.'

'You breached my confidence?'

'I don't recall you saying the remark was made in confidence.' Barbara was beginning to tire of Nancy's belligerence. 'All I can say is that Richard doesn't agree with you. In fact, his actual words were "Marcus doesn't need to marry into the family, he is already a member of the family by dint of being David's stepson."'

'That is not the same as marrying into the family or being of the same blood.'

'Perhaps not.' Barbara lowered her voice. 'But it is still a legitimate relationship.'

The words, though softly delivered, hit the mark and Nancy let out a strangled sob. 'What exactly do you mean?'

'I'm not a fool, Nancy.' Barbara dropped the dustsheet onto a nearby chair. 'I know it's no coincidence that you've been trying to track down Abigail Woodlands in the family's documents. I don't know how you discovered that she was William Payne's mistress, but I can see how important it's become to you to make that connection.' She rolled her head towards the girl. 'You know, now isn't the time to make waves over this.' If there ever would be a time. 'You need to be patient.'

Nancy pulled a handkerchief from her pocket and lifted it to her face. 'You seem to understand.' She sniffed loudly into the soft, white cotton. 'Does Kathryn also know why I have been researching what happened to Abigail?'

'Of course she does. And no one blames you. Not when there is another connection between you and the Lancefields that hasn't been recognised.'

Nancy's eyes grew wary. 'Another connection?'

'Oh, come now. I can't believe you would really be bothered about the spinet and what it meant to your grandmother, if it was just about status and the fact that Richard's wife saw fit to remove it to England.' Barbara stepped slowly across the attic. 'I think your grandmother was fond of Richard.' She put an arm around Nancy's shoulders. 'Very fond of him.'

'Richard promised the spinet to my grandmother, but he did nothing to stop its removal.' Nancy dabbed at her eyes with the handkerchief. 'It was as though she had ceased to matter to him. It would have been bad enough if *he* had taken it away, but to let his wife do it?'

Her arm still around Nancy's shoulders, Barbara lifted her other hand and stroked the girl's hair. 'How long have you known?'

'That I am Richard's granddaughter? Since just before my grandmother's death. She told me herself.'

'So, your mother knows that she is Richard's natural daughter?'

'Yes. Angel didn't want to leave us without telling us the truth.' Nancy lifted moist, beseeching eyes to Barbara. 'It is too cruel, not to acknowledge us.'

'Well, I don't disagree with that. But I'll say it again: now isn't the time. Once Eva has been laid to rest and the police investigation into Zak's death is complete, then we can sit down and talk about the best way of moving forward. There is just too much disruption at the moment.' Barbara squeezed Nancy's shoulders. 'Will you do what I ask? Will you wait a little longer, until the time is right?'

'Will you help me to bring out the truth, if I say yes?'

'Of course I will.' Barbara smiled.

It wouldn't be easy, but that was no reason not to try.

*

Marcus sat back in the armchair and folded his arms.

Tension was throbbing in his temples, sending tiny sparks of pain behind his eyes, and he drew in a silent breath to steady his nerves.

It had been Kathryn's idea that he and Laurence should clear the air with a private conversation, and initially he had welcomed the suggestion. But now, sitting stiffly opposite the man in the library, he was filled with such a burning rage that he could barely focus on the moment.

Laurence, sitting equally ill at ease on the damask-covered sofa opposite, gave every appearance of contrition. 'Of course Eva mentioned you.' His brow furrowed sharply above the deep, blue eyes. 'She told me that she hadn't expected your relationship to develop so quickly, but that she was pleased that it had. She saw a future with you. A future that she hadn't expected. And she hoped that you felt the same.' He leaned forward, the hypnotic eyes full of regret. 'Marcus, if there was anything I could do, anything at all, to put the clock back and walk her to the door of the hotel, don't you think I would do it?'

'It's easy to say that now.' Marcus heard the anger in his own voice, the words spilling out in short, sharp bursts of fury. 'It was midnight, in London. She didn't know anyone. She was vulnerable, an easy target.'

'She was certainly an easy target for the man who had tracked her down and was hellbent on taking her life. How could I possibly have known that she was being stalked by a maniac who'd already tried more than once to kill her?' Laurence's voice was calm, but surprisingly firm. 'From where we parted, she only had to walk a few minutes to reach the hotel's entrance. And she turned down my offer to walk with her. But if I'd known about Smith, if she'd given me any indication at all that her life was at risk, I wouldn't have left her alone. Not for a second.'

'She wouldn't have expected Smith to turn up in London.'

'No, I suppose not.' Laurence looked troubled by the

thought. 'What did Smith have against her? What had she ever done to him, that he would go to such lengths?'

'Nothing. Except be related to the Lancefields. Smith had a grudge against the family because... well, I suppose you know why.'

'Yes, I suppose I do.'

'Did you hear about it from Eva?'

'No, from the police in London. The same way that I heard about Smith's attempts on her life.' Laurence seemed to sense his need to know. 'She didn't betray your confidence, Marcus. And for what it's worth, I don't think any the less of you for knowing what you did. You must have had your reasons. And you've served your time for the crime. It's water under the bridge.'

'Not as far as the Smith family are concerned.'

'So, that's why he was targeting Eva? To get back at you?' Laurence lifted a hand and tugged thoughtfully on his ear. 'Well, I'm pleased to hear there's no truth in the rumour that you offered him twenty thousand pounds to kill her.'

The statement caught Marcus by surprise and he laughed, a spontaneous cough of disbelief. 'No truth at all.' He swallowed hard. 'Is there any truth to the rumour that you provided the Obeah garland for Smith to hang around her neck?'

Laurence smiled. 'No truth at all.' He leaned back against the sofa's cushions and steepled his fingers. 'I suppose, when you think about it, we have a great deal in common, don't we?'

'Do we?'

'We both cared for Eva, and neither of us wanted her to die. But both of us will be suspected of having a hand in her death.'

Marcus took a moment to consider the theory, and then he said, 'Will we both be suspected of murdering Zak Smith in revenge for what he did?'

'No, I think that particular honour belongs to you.'

Laurence smiled, and then his face straightened. 'I apologise if that sounded flippant. The fact is, I wouldn't have known where to find the man. And in any case, I believe I was in Penzance at the time he met his death.' Laurence looked down at his fingers. 'You know, that's something that's been troubling me. How on earth could Smith have known where Eva was? There were so few people who knew that she was coming to London, let alone where she and I had planned to meet.'

'No one could have known that better than you. Isn't that the main reason the police were eyeing you as a suspect?'

'Possibly.' Laurence shrugged. 'Have you any idea why she didn't tell you about it? Given that the two of you were so close?'

A question for which Marcus didn't have an answer. And one which made his cheeks burn. 'It wasn't like her to hide things from me.' At least, that was what he believed. 'I can only think that she was worried I might accidentally give the game away. Let slip to Richard that she had gone against his instructions.' The conversation was taking an unwelcome turn and he braced himself. 'Why do you think she didn't tell me, Laurence? Did she think I would be jealous?'

'I doubt it. There was certainly no cause for you to be jealous. Eva was unquestionably attractive and utterly charming, but she was well aware that I have an equally attractive and charming fiancée of my own.' Laurence let out a barely audible sigh. 'A fiancée to whom I am devoted, as Eva was devoted to you.'

24

'I hope this won't take long, Inspector.' Nancy looked uncomfortable in the stiff, wooden chair in front of the housekeeper's table. 'I have lunch to serve.'

'I'm investigating a murder, Nancy, and you found the body. It will take as long as it takes.' DCI Price had the advantage of knowing the girl, though it occurred to him now that the Nancy sitting before him was different. She had always been feisty, and never afraid to challenge him. But her challenges usually arrived with a mischievous eye and an inscrutable smile, not the sullen, suspicious demeanour she was displaying today.

And he couldn't help wondering why.

'I wanted to talk to you again about yesterday evening.' He tried to make the suggestion sound casual. 'In case you had anything to add.'

'I'm sure I've already told you everything that's relevant.'

'And I'm sure that's what you genuinely believe. But when we spoke yesterday evening, you had only just discovered the body. You were still in a state of shock, which is quite understandable. It's possible that you'll remember a little more in the cold light of day.'

She leaned forward towards him. 'Well, perhaps I do remember one thing that I didn't mention yesterday evening.' She seemed to rally a little, and her smile was enigmatic. 'I do remember thinking what an astonishing coincidence it was that a police patrol car arrived just minutes after Zak's body was discovered.' She raised a perfectly sculpted eyebrow. 'And an even greater coincidence that a detective chief inspector turned up just ten minutes behind it.'

Now, there was the Nancy he knew. 'Neither of those events were a coincidence. There was no opportunity for me to explain at the time. But we'd had a tip-off that Smith was in the area, and I wanted to make sure that the family was safe.'

'You thought he was coming here to cause trouble.'

'No, I just wanted to make sure there was a police presence in case he did.' There was a notebook on the desk in front of him and Price looked down at it. 'You told me yesterday evening that you'd been at Salvation Hall all evening?'

'Yes. I watched a film with Barbara and then spent an hour in my room reading. But Samson needed his last walk of the day, so I took him out along the terrace and into the walled garden.'

'And is that something you do every evening? Walk Samson around the walled garden?'

'No. Sometimes I take him around the lake, sometimes we walk up into the shrubbery. Why do you ask?'

'I was just thinking that it was an astonishing coincidence that you happened to walk him into the walled garden when Zak Smith's body was lying in the potting shed.'

His words hung in the air for a moment, and then Nancy smiled. 'I suppose I asked for that.' She bowed her head. 'Had I known that Zak was in there, I would have made sure to head for the shrubbery.'

She sounded confident, but the Nancy of old would

have held his gaze while delivering such a riposte. And he couldn't help noticing that this Nancy's eyes were focused somewhere to his left. 'Tell me, where was Marcus while you and Barbara were watching a film?'

'In his room, I believe. We all had supper together in the kitchen, but he was tired and wanted time to himself. He and David are still feeling the effects of Saturday's overnight flight, as well as the pain of losing Eva. They haven't really had time to recover from either.'

'So, you didn't see him again until he came out to join you at the potting shed?'

'No. I'm afraid there will be no question of my providing him with an alibi this time.' She looked back at Price almost defiantly. 'Assuming that an alibi would be needed.' She ran her tongue around her teeth. 'Do you have any idea at all what Zak was doing in the potting shed, Chief Inspector?'

'No idea at all. Do you?'

'All suggestions gratefully received?' She forced another smile. 'I'm afraid not.' She put a hand up to her face and brushed a stray curl away from her cheek. 'David tells me that Zak murdered Eva. Is that true?'

'We're calling that our working assumption. We have video evidence that shows him with Eva in London.' It was all Price was prepared to say. 'It isn't my investigation, so it will be for DCI Greenway to confirm that he's satisfied that Smith was the killer.'

'I had no idea that his hatred of the family ran quite that deep. I mean, I knew that he hated the Lancefields. But not so much that he would go back on his word. It was a very cruel act if all he was doing was trying to punish the family for what happened to Philip.'

Is that what Smith had been trying to do? 'A cruel act it might have been, but he paid for it with his own life.' Price tapped his pen impatiently on the notebook in front of him. 'It might be for DCI Greenway to confirm who murdered Eva, but it's my responsibility to determine who murdered Zak Smith. When a murderer becomes a victim, he acquires a right to receive justice.'

'Despite his cruelty?'

'Regrettably, yes. Because I have to take into account the cruelty demonstrated by his killer.' Price twirled the pen around his thumb and then dropped it onto the notebook. 'Can you account for your whereabouts yesterday afternoon, Nancy? Between the hours of four and six o'clock?'

The girl's shoulders stiffened. 'Is that when you believe he was murdered? Towards the end of the afternoon?' She rolled her eyes. 'Everyone in the family was here at Salvation Hall, myself included. Kathryn, I believe, was with you.'

Price smiled. 'I wasn't asking where the other members of the household were. Just where you were.'

A flash of indignation registered in the proud dark eyes. And then Nancy smiled. 'I know it would make things so much easier for you if I were to say "I was in the potting shed, murdering Zak". But I'm afraid it wouldn't be the truth. The truth is really far more mundane: I was on my own in the library, packing up boxes of documents to return to St Felix.'

*

Barbara placed the tray down on the small, mahogany dining table at the rear of the sitting room. 'I suppose it was a foolish notion to believe that we could have a civilised family lunch together, given everything that's going on.' She peeled back the cloth covering the food. 'At least Nancy had already prepared everything, and laid it out in the kitchen. I've brought a selection over with me. Sandwiches, cheese and fruit.' She dropped the cloth onto the table. 'And over here, we're at arm's length from the police investigation.'

Richard, already seated by the table, looked up at her. 'Where is everyone? Are they coming over to the Dower House?'

'I wouldn't think so. Laurence and David have gone down to the village for a walk. David is keen to show him St Felicity's while he's here.' She lifted a plate of sandwiches from the tray and offered it to Richard. 'I saw them before they left. Laurence looked quite drained after his conversation with Marcus. David thought the fresh air would do him good.'

Richard lifted a ham sandwich from the plate. 'And what about Marcus?'

'In the library, with Kathryn.' Barbara helped herself to a cheese sandwich and dropped it onto an empty plate. 'And Nancy is still with Inspector Price. I don't think she'll be very pleased when their interview ends and she discovers that her lunch party has disintegrated.' Barbara sat down at the table next to Richard. 'She thinks you're trying to keep her away from Laurence.'

'Then she will find that she is mistaken. She will have the opportunity to speak to him this afternoon. David is arranging for him to spend another night at The Zoological, and he will travel back to London in the morning.'

'Is he staying here for supper?'

'No. David and Kathryn will be joining him at the hotel. I'm sure they would be very pleased to include you, if you would care to join them.'

'And Nancy?'

Richard answered with a scowl. 'Barbara, this has to stop. I have made my feelings about Nancy quite plain to you.' He waved his uneaten sandwich at her. 'Now, tell me what you make of Laurence.'

His cousin's cheeks dimpled. 'He seems charming. And he's certainly very handsome. His eyes are almost hypnotic.'

The old man growled. 'There has always been

something strange about that branch of the family. All that nonsense about Obeah. It is an unnatural, ungodly practice that caused no end of problems for our family. It is not an influence I would welcome.' He stared directly at Barbara. 'They dabbled, you know, on their return to this country. Arcane practices, mesmerism…'

'Just because something is mysterious doesn't mean it's nonsense, does it? Anyway, if it's someone's belief, what right do you have to judge?' Barbara bit into her sandwich and chewed on it thoughtfully. 'You're still uncomfortable with him being here, aren't you?' She flicked her eyes in Richard's direction. 'Are you sure it's because of the Obeah and not because he's of Creole descent?'

'Is this about Nancy again?'

'Only if you make it so.' Had he almost made an admission? 'She's related to the Payne line of the family, isn't she?'

'Is that what she told you?' Richard pushed out his lips. 'If the link truly exists, then it is so distant that it makes no odds.'

'It makes no odds to you, perhaps. But it matters very much to Nancy.'

'Nancy harbours a fantasy: that one day she will uncover a link to the Lancefields that will entitle her to a far greater role than that of my secretary.'

'Heavens, Richard, she doesn't have to go all the way back to Abigail Woodlands and William Payne to do that, does she? Do you really think that she doesn't know the truth?'

The old man's face contorted and his eyes, eyes that until now had only ever shown her kindness and consideration, suddenly darkened with an unfamiliar anger. And then he checked himself, and forced a smile. 'The truth about what?'

Barbara studied his face for a moment and then pursed her lips. 'Oh, very well. If that's the way you want to play things.' She took another bite of her sandwich and chewed as she thought. 'For what it's worth, I think that you will come to regret that stance in the long run. Blood will always out, Richard. You, of all people – so intent on tracking down what's left of the Lancefield bloodlines – should know that. I think you need to be prepared for bloodlines to come looking for you. And when they do, when the inevitable truths that you've worked so hard to bury all these years, come floating to the surface, I hope you'll be prepared for the consequences.'

*

The pristine living room of Becca Smith's new Truro home was beginning to fray at the edges. And so was Becca herself.

Huddled in one of the neat, grey armchairs, blonde hair hanging lank and lifeless around her shoulders, and her eyes red-rimmed from crying, she was hugging one of Frankie's new teddy bears tightly to her chest and refusing to look at DS Parkinson.

The sergeant, sitting opposite in the matching armchair, was sticking doggedly with his kid-glove approach. 'We're not trying to blame you, Becca.' Not at this stage, anyway. 'But I have to ask these questions. Were you giving Zak money when he was on the run?'

'Am I going to prison, Sergeant Parkinson?' She kept her eyes on the teddy bear's head as she spoke.

'That's not a question I can answer.' It was difficult to feel much sympathy when she was the engineer of her own downfall. But he was doing his best. 'Just tell me the truth. Were you giving him money?'

'Yes.'

'Then you knew where he was, all the time?'

'No. Not all the time. And I only knew which town he was in. I didn't have an address for him.'

'So, how did you send the money?'

'I mailed it to a newsagents' shop in Weston-super-Mare. Zak had an arrangement with the owner, that he would take in his post. He told the owner that he was estranged from his family and didn't want them to know exactly where he was living.'

Well, that part was probably true. 'You sent it in cash?'

'Yes.' She was still avoiding the policeman's gaze. 'I knew it was risky, but I disguised it. I sent some hidden in the pages of a book, and other times I sent a food parcel with the notes hidden in a box of biscuits.'

'Where did the cash come from?'

Becca had the grace to blush. 'I knew you would be looking at my bank accounts, so I took it from Frankie's savings account at the building society. I knew it wouldn't be so easy for you to trace transactions from a passbook account.' She sniffed loudly, a self-indulgent snort of self-pity. 'I always planned to pay it back when this was all over. Frankie won't lose out.'

As if that made it better. Parkinson turned his head away and stared out of the window. Beyond the glass, two uniformed officers were keeping a small gathering of onlookers at bay, and it occurred to him that Becca's dream of a fresh start in Truro was already beginning to tarnish. 'Look, I know this is hard for you. And I'm not going to judge what you've done. Zak was your brother, and you've lost him. But you need to help us now. The more you help us, the easier it will be for you in the long run.' He watched as she gave an almost imperceptible nod. 'Did Zak tell you, yesterday, that he was going to Salvation Hall?'

'No. He just told me that he was going out, and that he'd be back before bedtime.'

'Did he admit to you that he travelled to London, and that he murdered Eva McWhinney?'

'Not in so many words. But he didn't deny it.' Becca's face folded into a scowl. 'Do you have any evidence that it was him?'

'Enough to convince us that he was responsible. What we still don't understand is why?'

For the first time, she looked up at the sergeant. 'Because of Marcus Drake.'

'Marcus didn't offer Zak twenty thousand to murder Eva. Even you must have worked out by now that the story wasn't true.'

'Must I?' She lowered her voice to a whisper. 'I'm not talking about the original twenty thousand.'

'I'm sorry?'

'I'm talking about the additional twenty thousand. The twenty thousand that Marcus offered Zak to try again to do the job properly.' A note of defiance crept into Becca's voice. 'Marcus Drake is the reason Eva is dead. Forty thousand quid is the reason. Not that Zak ever saw a penny of it.'

Parkinson felt a flare of anger in his gut. 'And you're the one who gave Zak enough money to stay on the run until he'd finished the job. If you hadn't done that, Eva might still be alive.'

She let out a sob. 'You ask Marcus. You ask him about the money. Why else would he murder Zak?'

'Who the hell said he murdered Zak?'

'What other explanation is there? Zak must have gone to Salvation Hall to meet with one of the family. That's why he's dead. Because the person he went to meet murdered him.' She was crying tears of rage now. 'And it wouldn't have been David or the old man, would it?'

'Prove it.'

'Prove it? How the hell do I do that?'

'Let's start with the phones.' Parkinson stood up. 'You were using a burner phone to stay in touch with him, weren't you? Were there more?' He took a step towards her. 'We know he made a habit of using them. He used one the night he murdered Stella Lancefield. Are they here? Am I going to have to take the place apart to find them, or are you going to hand them over?'

She sank her head into her hands. 'I don't know what you're talking about. I only know about two phones: the one he bought for himself after he went on the run, and the one he sent to me. It arrived in the post a few days later. He'd already loaded his new number into it, for me to call him.'

Trust Smith to be that cunning. 'So he set up new phones for the two of you to stay in touch without being detected.' Parkinson looked up as the sitting room door opened and PC Wilmott's head appeared in the gap between door and frame. 'What?'

Wilmott jerked his head. 'You might want to see what we've just found in the bedroom upstairs.'

Becca rose to her feet. 'You shouldn't be searching up there. You haven't got a warrant.'

Parkinson rounded on her. 'We don't need one. You invited us in.' He could barely contain his anger. 'I'm going out into the hall to see what they've found. And when I come back, you're going to hand over that phone. Or I'll arrest you for being an accessory to the murder of Eva McWhinney.'

25

'I must admit, the irony isn't lost on me.' Marcus sounded weary. 'All those months you've spent searching for the man and he turns up at Salvation Hall.'

Price wasn't sure he would have called it ironic. Quite another word. 'Why do you think he came here?'

'How should I know? To gloat? To hurt another member of the family? To prove a point?' They were sitting in the small housekeeper's room, and Marcus looked around him as he spoke. 'They really have funnelled you through the tradesman's entrance this time, haven't they?'

'I try not to take it personally. The privileged classes have been trying to put policemen in their place ever since the force was founded.' If Marcus was trying to derail the conversation with petty jibes, then perhaps he had something to hide. 'What point might Smith have been trying to make?'

'Who knows? Perhaps he was just trying to say that he was smarter than the rest of us.' Marcus frowned. 'Why do you think he was here?'

'To meet a co-conspirator.'

'I hope you're not planning to revisit the idea that I offered him money to dispose of Eva? Even Eva herself could see how ludicrous that idea was.'

Ludicrous or not, it was still a possibility. 'We think that Smith arrived here sometime after four o'clock yesterday afternoon, made his way to the potting shed to meet someone, and met his death sometime before six o'clock.' Price paused to let the information register. 'I've been told that most of the household were here during that timeframe, so where were you?'

'Oh, I was here, Inspector Price. But only sometimes in the company of a witness to prove what I was doing. I'm sure you've already thought of that.' His lip curled. 'Can I ask, does Laurence Payne have an alibi for the timeframe you've mentioned?'

'Several alibis, as it happens. He was continually in the presence of either a police officer or a member of the Lancefield household from the time he arrived at Penzance station until he went to bed at The Zoological yesterday evening. With the exception of one, brief forty-five-minute period when he checked into his room, showered and changed. And he couldn't possibly have travelled from Penzance to Salvation Hall, murdered Zak Smith, and then returned to the hotel in time to meet his dinner guests. However extensive his magical powers.'

Marcus grunted and slumped back in his seat. 'Are you lining me up as a suspect for Eva's murder, or Zak's?' His smile was weary now. 'Or is it both?' He held up a hand. 'And before you answer that question, can I remind you that I cared very deeply for Eva, and was looking forward to a long and happy life with her. I had no reason whatsoever to want her dead.'

Price rested his elbows on the small table between them and folded his hands together. 'Apart from your inheritance.'

The words struck Marcus like a slap in the face. 'What inheritance?'

If he was acting, Price could only concede that he was making a good job of it. 'Before she travelled to London, Eva made a new will. David will inherit the contents of number three, Hemlock Row, and the three properties will be rolled into a trust and rented out.' Price lowered his chin to his fingers. 'With the rents, after costs, to be payable to you for your lifetime.'

The colour drained from the young man's face. 'I don't believe you.'

'Then you should. It's been confirmed by DCI Grant, up in Edinburgh, and I will have the documentary evidence for you by the end of today, all being well.' Price kept his eyes on the young man's face as he spoke. 'It will be somewhere between fourteen and fifteen thousand pounds a month, if the properties achieve market value. And it was the reason I returned to Salvation Hall yesterday evening – to ask if you knew she had changed her will in your favour.' He scratched his ear. 'Of course, I didn't expect to arrive here to find you all examining Zak's body.'

'Forgive me, Inspector, but it still doesn't prove that I murdered Eva.'

'No, but it gives you a motive.' Price felt suddenly uplifted. 'As to Smith, he died from a blow on the back of the head with a garden spade. The same MO that you used to murder Philip McKeith.'

Marcus stiffened. 'You won't find my fingerprints on that spade. I didn't touch it.'

'I know. We've already examined the spade, and it's quite obvious that the last person to handle it was wearing gloves.' The handle had already given up some tiny threads of fibre which might, just might, have come from the very gloves that the killer was wearing. But Drake didn't need to know about that. 'Did you invite Smith to meet you in the potting shed, Marcus?'

'Of course not. If I was involved in some way with that maniac, do you think I would have been stupid enough to invite him here, to Salvation Hall?'

Price shrugged. 'So, he just happened to break in and secrete himself in the potting shed, and you just happened to stumble across him?' The policeman unfolded his hands and sat back in his chair. 'Do you make a habit of popping out to the potting shed, Marcus?'

'I didn't see Zak until we discovered his body yesterday evening.' Marcus was growing angry. 'It seems to me, Inspector Price, that you can't quite make up your mind just what motive I might have had for murdering the man? Are you saying now that I came across him by accident and murdered him in revenge for killing Eva?'

'That's one possibility.' Price raised a single eyebrow. 'That, or perhaps you just didn't want to pay him the money you'd already promised him to do the job in the first place.'

*

The light inside St Felicity's was fading, but the stained-glass window at the end of the nave glowed golden with the last few rays of late afternoon sunlight.

'It was installed by the family to commemorate their links with St Felix.' David felt a twinge of guilt as he spoke. His father, he knew, would know exactly which members of the family installed it and when, but such details of the Lancefield's dim and murky past were still an anathema to him. Agreeing to take on the running of the estates was one thing. Willingness to fill his mind with the minutiae of a past that filled him with shame was another.

'It's quite beautiful, David.' Standing beside him, hands in his pockets, Laurence Payne was eyeing the tribute with genuine appreciation. 'Was it constructed by a local craftsman?'

'I believe so.' David turned on his heel and snapped his fingers softly. Samson, sitting patiently beside a pew, rose to his paws and padded quietly down the nave without further instruction. 'Most of these memorial stones are in remembrance of the family.' David pointed vaguely at the opposite wall as he followed in the terrier's wake. 'If you'd like to follow me outside, I can show you some of the family's tombs and headstones.'

If the invitation was a morbid one, Laurence appeared to be too well-mannered to say so. He followed his host out into the daylight, pausing in the doorway for a moment as the glare from a sinking sun hit his eyes. 'It seems bright out here after being in the church.'

'Bright, but the temperature is dropping.' David paused beside a familiar grave, the black-marbled resting place of his own late daughter, Lucy. 'This is where my girl was laid to rest.' He half turned towards Laurence without catching his eye. 'My darling Stella is over there.' He pointed towards an elaborate headstone farther along the path. 'I never thought to see both of them here before me.' It was difficult not to sound maudlin, though he hadn't brought Laurence to St Felicity's to burden him with sorrow. 'I suppose we may soon be bringing Eva here, if she made no other provision in her will.'

Laurence stepped forward to join him beside Lucy's grave. 'I realise that I'm the newcomer here, and I hope you'll forgive me for my directness, but you must have your suspicions about Marcus?' He bent his head to read the inscription on the tombstone. 'I don't think anyone could blame him for wanting Zak Smith to get his comeuppance.'

'I'm trying not to think about it. I can't deny that Marcus has a temper when pushed. He admitted as much after killing Philip McKeith. He saw Lucy's body on the ground and he lashed out at the man he believed was killing her.'

'So, in disposing of Zak Smith, history would be repeating itself? He would have murdered the man he believed responsible for Eva's death?'

'Possibly.' David shivered. 'But if that were the case, how did he know that Smith would be in the potting shed?'

'Perhaps he invited Smith to meet him there. Or Smith broke in and invited Marcus to go down to the potting shed to have it out with him?'

'Don't both of those hypotheses assume that Marcus and Smith already had some way of contacting each other?' It didn't make any sense. But neither did discussing such a brutally private matter with a virtual stranger, even one distantly connected to the family. 'I don't believe for one minute that Marcus would have wished any harm to Eva. He was far too enamoured of her, whatever the gossips would have us believe. If Smith murdered Eva, he did so of his own volition.' David lowered his eyes and scoured the surrounding paths for Samson. 'Come on, boy. Time to go home.' He began to stroll slowly down the path. 'We really should have something to eat, Laurence. I've enjoyed our walk, but we've stayed out much longer than I had intended.'

Laurence fell in behind him, slowly following as David made his way towards the lychgate. 'I suppose if Marcus was responsible for Smith's death, it would put the family in a very awkward position.'

'To see him go back through the legal system again?'

'No. I was thinking about the estates. Eva told me that Marcus had gone out to St Felix to manage the Woodlands plantation. He won't be able to do that if he's facing a second murder charge.'

'I don't think that would be awkward for us.' David unlatched the gate and pulled it towards him. 'It had never been the intention for Marcus to stay out there indefinitely. But it will break my father's heart if he discovers that Marcus has been lying.' The conversation was becoming far too personal. 'Have you been out to St Felix yourself, Laurence?'

'Only once, as a boy.' He took hold of the gate as

David stepped through. 'I went with my parents, but I don't remember a great deal about it. I have a vague recollection of driving past the St Aldate's estate and my father saying that it felt surreal to think that our family once owned it.' Out on the pavement, he let the gate swing shut behind him. 'Do you spend much time out there yourself?'

'No, I can't say that I do. I have never shared my father's affinity towards the Caribbean, or the family's heritage, come to that. In fact, I only agreed to take on the running of the estates after his death because I came to realise just how much it would mean to him for me to do it.' David held up a hand. 'We turn right here, back down the lane to the house. Perhaps when we get back we can find a quiet corner to have a late lunch, and I can tell you a little more about the family?'

'Yes, I'd like that. Your cousin Barbara seems delightful. You must be pleased that she was happy to form a connection with the family?'

Pleased? If David had the whole of the week in which to do it, he could never fully express his appreciation for the unflinching support that Barbara had offered him. 'She has been a godsend.' The sister he had always needed. 'Marcus you have already met, and my father, of course. And Kathryn.' He smiled at Laurence. 'But there is still one member of the household that you haven't had the pleasure of meeting, and we must put that right as soon as we get back to the house. She is as indispensable to the smooth running of Salvation Hall as Samson is to the warming of our hearts.'

Laurence turned to look at his host. 'A glowing testimonial, indeed. I take it that you're speaking of Nancy?'

*

'I thought we would never get the opportunity to speak.' Kathryn sounded weary, challenged by the day's events. 'Do we really have to go as far as Marazion? Can't we just park up in the village to talk?'

Price had brought the car to a halt at Salvation Hall's high, wrought-iron gateway. 'No. I need to get away from the Lancefield's sphere of influence.' He pulled the coupe onto the main road and turned left, away from Penwithen. 'I need to keep a clear head. Another murder at Salvation Hall looks very much like another opportunity for me to screw up if I don't tread with absolute care.'

Kathryn pouted, and leaned her head against the cool glass of the car's window. 'Is that why you and the other officers have had so little contact with the family today?'

'Partly. I've tried to separate the crime scene from the family's domain. We've been concentrating on the potting shed, trying to gather as much evidence as possible.' Not that there was that much to gather. 'I have spoken briefly to Richard, Marcus and Nancy. But I still need to speak to Barbara and David, and I'm hoping to do that when we go back.' Along with another very important task, but he was keeping that to himself for the moment.

'I suppose I should be thankful that I was in Penzance yesterday afternoon, so you don't need to question me.'

'Are you trying to say being questioned by me is an unpleasant experience?'

'That depends on whether the questioning develops into an interrogation.'

'I don't interrogate people. I'm a kid-gloves sort of detective. I thought you would have worked that out by now.' He felt a sudden pang of disappointment. 'To be honest, it's not looking good for the family. The stolen motorbike abandoned outside the rear gates to the estate tells us how Zak arrived at Salvation Hall, and there are signs that he climbed over the gates to gain entry to the estate.'

'But you still don't know why.'

'Don't we?' Price depressed the brake as the car approached a junction, and flicked on the indicator before turning left. 'Look, Kathryn, this is completely in confidence: and only because I need your help.' Again. 'Smith had a mobile phone on him and it shows two calls to another mobile number yesterday afternoon – one before he left Truro, and one an hour later. We can't get the timings absolutely nailed, but we believe that second call was made when he reached the estate.'

'You think he was calling someone at Salvation Hall.'

Did he really need to answer that? 'The number doesn't belong to anyone we know. We've already checked it against his family's numbers and the numbers of everyone in the Lancefield household.' He forced a smile. 'And before you ask, yes – we checked it against yours.' He flicked on the indicator again and slowed the car. 'If you don't want to go all the way to Marazion, this layby will do.' It was a small inlet in the verge, vacant of any other vehicle, and he brought the car to a halt and switched off the engine.

'How did you know that Zak was in Truro?'

'We persuaded Amber to pay Becca a visit, and she learned that Zak was already there. Becca had been funding him while he was on the run. He turned up at her place two days ago looking for a place to hide out. She coughed up to Tom Parkinson that they've been using new pay-as-you-go phones to stay in touch, so we couldn't trace their calls.' Price ran a finger around the rim of the steering wheel. 'We think the number he called yesterday was another burner phone.'

'You still haven't found the original burner phone, have you? The one that Zak called after he'd murdered Stella by mistake?'

'I don't think we ever will find it. It'll be buried in a landfill site by now. Or lying at the bottom of the sea.' Or possibly an ornamental lake, though this wasn't the time to contemplate another trawl of those murky, inhospitable waters that Richard Lancefield referred to as his waterlily collection.

Kathryn huddled deeper into her seat. 'I suppose you have a suspect in mind?'

'We do.' Price knew he would have to choose his words carefully. 'Do you think we've all misjudged Marcus?'

'Misjudged him?'

'He's always held to the story that Philip murdered Lucy. But what if that wasn't true? What if Marcus murdered both Philip *and* Lucy?'

'Marcus loved Lucy.'

'I know he did. But just because you love someone doesn't mean you can't be jealous. It doesn't mean you wouldn't lash out in rage if that person hurt you.'

'I'm not sure I'm following you. If – and it's a big if – Marcus did murder Lucy, why would that lead him to murder Eva?'

'Perhaps he was jealous.'

'Because she went ahead and met with Laurence Payne behind his back? I'm not buying that. Anyway, Zak made his first attempt on Eva's life before Marcus had even met her. Why would he bribe someone to kill a woman that he'd never met?'

'Revenge.'

'Revenge? For what?'

'For being used.' Sharing his thoughts was making Price feel uncomfortable. 'You asked me why I wouldn't let Richard help me when my career was on the line. And it's because I didn't want to be beholden to him. I didn't want to be in Richard Lancefield's pocket. And before you say anything, I have a great deal of time for the old man. I have nothing against him as a human being. But if I'd let him help me, he would have expected something in return. There's no question of that. And it may well have been something I couldn't or wouldn't give, which would have caused friction.'

'I still don't see how this relates to Marcus.'

'What if Marcus resented being in Richard's pocket? What if he agreed to hold up his hand to Philip's murder to make things easy for the family, but flatly refused to accept responsibility for killing Lucy? What if he resented the fact that Richard even thought he could be bought in such a way? What if the resentment festered, but he squared it with himself by taking on the role of Lancefield heir, convincing himself that Richard and David would leave everything to him? Until Richard decided to start digging up blood relatives of the family. Relatives who might have a stronger claim to the Lancefield estates than Marcus ever could.'

'The first cousin that Richard turned up was Barbara. And she looks alive and well to me.'

'No. The first cousin was Dennis Speed. But Jason Speed's greed led him to remove not just his father, but himself from the race. Barbara isn't the threat that a younger person would be. And she has no heirs to follow her. She's the end of that particular line of the family. But Eva?' Price pushed out his lips. 'Eva was young, pretty, clever; everything that Richard valued. And above all she was connected to the Lancefields by a bloodline.'

'And you think Marcus saw her as competition?'

'I think it's possible. Of course, when he met her he came up with a much better plan. Why not just pretend to fall in love with her and marry her? Then no one else has to die.'

'So why is she dead?'

'Maybe changing her will to favour Marcus wasn't such a good idea after all. Maybe Marcus found out about the bequest and saw Eva's money as his ticket to walk away from the Lancefields for good.'

'You're clutching at straws, aren't you?' Kathryn shifted in her seat. 'What do you want from me?' Her words dripped with disappointment.

And the disappointment stung, but he couldn't stop

now. 'Before we left Salvation Hall I instigated a search of the main house. Richard has already given his permission to search without a warrant. Any room that we choose. I need you to be on hand if we find something. You're still my link between the case and the family.' He depressed the car's clutch pedal and pushed at the ignition button to start the engine. 'I don't want this to drive a wedge between us, Kathryn. I know how close you've become to the family. But I have to do what I think is right. Whatever it means for the Lancefields. And if you don't think you're going to be able to help me with that, then now is the time to speak up.'

26

Laurence watched in silence as David Lancefield made his way out of the kitchen and then offered Nancy an uncertain smile. 'Why do you think Sergeant Parkinson wants to speak to David?'

'I really have no idea. I thought they were busy searching our rooms.'

'Searching your rooms?' Laurence whistled softly through his teeth. 'You don't seem unduly put out by the idea.'

Nancy smiled. 'It will be the third time they've searched my room – first after Lucy's murder, then after Stella's, and now this.' She picked up her tea cup and sipped from it. 'I suppose there's no need to be put out by it when one is certain there is nothing incriminating for the police to find.'

She seemed to accept the situation with a detachment that bordered on disinterest and Laurence wasn't quite sure what to make of it. What to make of *her*. Earlier in the day, David had suggested to him that Nancy was confident, capable, self-assured. But the young woman sitting at the other side of the kitchen table seemed possessed of a composure that was almost clinical in its coolness. 'Well, I suppose you'll be stuck with me now until David returns. I hope you don't mind having to keep an eye on me.'

'Is that how you see it?' Nancy fixed him with dark, probing eyes. 'I rather thought it was an opportunity for us to get to know each other a little better. After all, this is the first time today that we have been able to have a free and frank conversation.'

'Do we need to have a free and frank conversation?'

She hesitated, and then let out a laugh, a spontaneous ripple of genuine amusement. 'Tell me, have you found your visit to Salvation Hall to be worthwhile?'

'Worthwhile?' It was a curious choice of word. 'Well, it's been a pleasure to meet everyone. Although I would have preferred it to be in happier circumstances.' He considered the question further. 'Do you mind my being here, Nancy?'

'Why would I mind?'

For any one of a myriad of reasons: he hadn't been invited; he had arrived in the midst of another murder investigation; his very presence was an unnecessary distraction. 'I know we've only just met, but I can't help feeling that my being here makes you feel ill at ease.'

She sipped again on her tea. 'Eva has been murdered and her killer's body has been found here, within the grounds of Salvation Hall. Wouldn't that be enough to make anyone feel ill at ease?'

'It would. But I have a sense that you disapprove of my coming here.'

'It's not for me to approve or disapprove. But I will admit that I was surprised to hear that Richard had invited you to spend the day here. He had been quite clear that he didn't want to extend the family further after Stella's death, and Eva was asked not to get in touch with you. It was ignoring that request that led to her death.'

Was she trying to accuse him of something? 'Nancy, I'm as devastated about Eva's death as the rest of the family. If there was anything I could do, anything at all, to put the clock back, I would do it. I didn't know that her life was at risk. And I couldn't possibly have known that Zak Smith knew she was travelling to London and planned to follow her there.'

'Well, clearly someone told him about her plans. And you were the only person who knew of them.'

'Ah, no. I'm the only person who can't deny that he knew she was travelling to London, because there are witnesses to our meeting at West India Quay.' Laurence watched Nancy's face as he spoke. There was no question that she was following his train of thought. 'Anyone else in the family might also have known, but not be prepared to admit it.'

'It would have to be someone who knew about the Obeah garland, though, wouldn't it? Which narrows the field quite considerably.' She placed her teacup down on its saucer and ran a thoughtful finger around the rim. 'I'm told that your line of the family has always been interested in Obeah.'

'Are you interested in Obeah, Nancy?'

'I'm interested in your line of the family.'

The unexpected declaration threw him. He turned his head to look out of the window, unable to disguise his discomfort. 'I'm not quite sure what you mean by that.' He leaned back in his seat, his face still turned away towards the garden. 'Why would my line of the family be of interest to you?'

'Because I believe there is a connection between the Paynes and my own family on St Felix.'

'You think that we might be distantly related?'

'I'm certain that we are.' Her voice was growing stronger. 'I have traced my family tree with a great deal of care, and I believe that we have a common ancestor – Jeremiah Woodlands. His daughter, Abigail, was the mistress of William Payne and I believe that she was the natural mother of your ancestor George Payne.'

Laurence put a hand up to his forehead and rubbed at it. 'I haven't heard David or Richard mention that. Perhaps we could talk about it further this evening, when we all meet up for supper?'

The girl bridled. 'That would have been nice. But I have not been invited to join you and the rest of the family at The Zoological. I am to stay here this evening and keep Richard company.' She blinked, fluttering her long, dark lashes. 'But I think you already knew that.'

'Did I?' Perhaps he did. 'Does Richard always require someone to stay here with him? Is he uncomfortable being alone at Salvation Hall?'

'No, just uncomfortable with the idea of you and I having a conversation.'

'But we're having a conversation now. Why would it make Richard uncomfortable? Surely he doesn't think that it's an issue, you and I being so distantly related?' The question was absurd. 'Just look out there. What do you see?' He waved a hand towards the window. 'Police officers, scene of crime investigators, all milling about, all trying to find the evidence that will point to Smith's killer. And all you and Richard have to worry about is whether or not there is a link between your family and mine? A link so distant that it has absolutely no relevance at all?'

Nancy's shoulders tensed, and then she smiled. 'Of course it has no *real* relevance. But I had hoped that you might have been at least a little interested to hear about it.' She pushed her chair away from the table and stood up. 'I hope you won't think me rude, but I really must clear the table now. I'm planning to make an early supper for Richard and myself.' She lifted her cup and saucer from the table. 'Perhaps you could make your way to the library, and wait in there for David to return?'

It was a summary dismissal. Laurence watched as she carried the china over to the sink, certain that he had just been the victim of an ambush, and yet totally at a loss to understand just what Nancy's motivations might have been. 'I'm sorry if I've offended you in some way. I'll go over to the library, as you suggest. I think I can remember the way.' He rose slowly to his feet and cleared his throat. 'Nancy, you do know that I had nothing at all to do with the garland that was found around Eva's neck?'

*

'Why have you brought me to Marcus's room? Is it really necessary for us to speak in here?'

'Yes, I think it is.' DS Parkinson could understand the man's reluctance. Considering the task in hand, he was feeling a degree of reluctance himself. 'Has Marcus mentioned Eva McWhinney's will to you, Mr Lancefield?' He closed the door behind him and leaned against it. 'Did he tell you that DCI Price had made him aware of the contents?'

'No. I understood that the terms of the will would not be disclosed until the formal reading next week.'

'The contents were revealed to us in the light of the police investigation into Eva's death. I can advise you that you are a beneficiary, and so is Marcus. His bequest is significant, and will provide him with a very substantial income from the letting of her three properties in Hemlock Row.' Parkinson didn't want to reveal any more than was necessary. 'It will amount to something between fourteen and fifteen thousand pounds a month.'

'How much?' David let out a soft gasp. 'I knew that they had grown close, but I had no idea she felt that strongly about him. Why are you telling me this now, when the information is confidential?'

Did the implications of the bequest really evade him? 'Certain items have been found at Becca Smith's house which tie her brother to Eva's murder. We have discovered a bag containing a copy of a book on Obeah, written by Laurence Payne, and the remains of a pack of artificial feathers with a receipt showing that they were bought from a craft shop in Weston-super-Mare. There is little doubt now that Smith was responsible for making the garland and hanging it around Eva's neck. Payne's book provided him with the description. The illustration on the relevant page was circled with a pen to highlight it.'

'Why on earth would he do that?'

'We think it was a crude attempt to throw suspicion onto Laurence Payne.'

'And how do you think Zak knew where to find her?'

'We believe he was given the information by someone who knew where she was going.'

'The only person who knew that was Laurence.'

'Not necessarily. Several of Eva's work colleagues in Edinburgh knew, although we have no grounds to suspect that any of them had a motive for her death. And where one person might have known about her plans, so might another.' He paused to give David time to think about it. 'And there's something else.' The sergeant folded his arms. 'We've already examined the mobile phone found on Smith's body. It made a call to an unregistered, pay-as-you-go number at four forty-three yesterday afternoon. The call lasted less than two minutes and we believe it was made to tell an accomplice that he was either on his way to the potting shed, or perhaps already in it.'

'Forgive me, Sergeant Parkinson, I'm not quite sure why you're telling me all of this?'

'I'm telling you because we have found the mobile phone that the call was made to.' The policeman stepped away from the door and walked over to a bookcase beside the bed. 'We found it about twenty minutes ago, hidden under the bed in this room.' He lifted a clear plastic bag from the top of the bookcase and held it up so that David could see it. It contained a small, cheap mobile phone. 'Do you understand now?'

Evidently not. David stepped forward and lowered his eyes to examine the item in the bag. 'Why would that be in here?'

'This'—Parkinson shook the bag to emphasise the point—'has only ever received two calls: one yesterday morning, and another in the afternoon.' He paused, and then added, 'At four forty-three yesterday afternoon.'

The penny was beginning to drop. The colour drained from David Lancefield's face and he raised his eyes to the ceiling. 'Oh, Marcus, what the hell have you done?' He lowered his eyes back to the policeman. 'You have found only that phone. Nothing to actually implicate Marcus?'

Wasn't it enough? 'I've already apprised DCI Price of our findings and he's on his way back to Salvation Hall to question Marcus.' Parkinson returned the plastic bag to the top of the bookcase. 'Do you know where your stepson is? Because we can't find him anywhere in the main house.'

'Have you tried the Dower House?'

'Yes. Your father is there with Barbara, but they haven't see him.'

'Then perhaps he's gone for a walk down to the village.' David took a step backwards and sat down on the edge of the bed. 'Sergeant Parkinson, I think you're making a terrible mistake. Marcus didn't know that Eva was going to London.'

'Are you certain of that?'

'It's what he told me. And I believe him.' David looked close to tears. 'He wouldn't hurt her. He loved her. He was planning his future with her.'

'And are you certain of that?'

'I know him.'

'He's a convicted killer. He killed Philip McKeith.'

'That was a crime of passion and he has paid the price for it. It doesn't mean that he would kill again.'

'Do you have an alternative suggestion for our findings then?' Parkinson lifted his hand and pointed to the plastic bag. 'Perhaps you put the phone under the bed?'

'Me?' David recoiled.

'Or your father? Or Nancy? Or Barbara? It could have been any of you. You were all here at Salvation Hall yesterday when Smith was murdered.'

'You already know that my father and Barbara were together at the time. They have provided each other with an alibi.'

'And that would be quite convenient, if they worked together to kill him.'

David snorted. 'That is the most ludicrous suggestion I have ever heard.'

'Of course it is. I'm trying to show you that all of the other explanations *are* ludicrous. There is only one viable possibility.' Parkinson paused to give him a moment to think about it. 'Mr Lancefield, I cannot begin to tell you how sorry I am that the family is going through this again. But you need to help us. We need to find Marcus Drake, and we need to find him now.'

*

The sleek, silver BMW slowed to a halt just a few metres from the high, wrought-iron gates. The two uniformed police officers standing guard did nothing to acknowledge its approach but Kathryn, hands sunk deep into the pockets of her coat, stepped forward to stand beside the car's passenger door, bending her head to peer in through the window.

The driver kept his hands firmly on the steering wheel, his clear blue eyes staring blankly through the windscreen, even when she pulled a hand from her pocket to tap sharply on the glass.

'Marcus?' She waited a moment for him to acknowledge her and then, frustrated by his obstinance, she pulled on the door handle. 'I need to speak to you.' She slipped into the passenger seat, pulling the door shut behind her. 'I'm sorry, but they're not going to let you leave the grounds.'

'I have to go into Penzance. And they have no grounds to keep me here.'

'Ennor thinks that they do.' She spoke as softly as she could. 'They've found a mobile phone under the bed in your room, and he needs to speak to you about it.'

'He must be mistaken. I have my mobile phone with me. It's in my pocket.'

Kathryn sighed. It wasn't the first time she'd had a conversation like this with Marcus. The last time they had been sitting in the shrubbery at the far end of the garden, and he had calmly confessed to her that he had murdered Philip McKeith. But then, his confession had been a willing one. There had been no need to confront him, to question him, to apply any sort of pressure to tease out the truth.

Unlike now.

'This isn't about your regular mobile phone. The one they've found received calls from Zak Smith yesterday.'

The young man visibly stiffened, and then his face contorted. 'I don't know why you've agreed to do DCI Price's dirty work for him, but I can tell you now that I have no intention of going through this charade for the Lancefields a second time. If a phone has been found in my room, then it must have been planted.'

'And who would have planted it?'

He looked at her with expressionless eyes. 'It's not my responsibility to work that out. It could have been anyone in the household. Even you would have had the opportunity. The door to my room is never locked.'

She placed a hand gently on his arm. 'For what it's worth, I'm not here to do Ennor's dirty work, as you put it. I volunteered to be the one to speak to you.' Although now, she was beginning to regret the decision. 'Even if someone did plant the phone, it would be your word against theirs. So it really would be better if you just came back to the house and spoke to Ennor. Just tell him the truth.'

Marcus turned his eyes upwards. 'Please tell me that you don't think I had anything to do with Eva's death. You know me, Kathryn. You know I wouldn't have hurt her. She meant the world to me.'

'I know she did. But this isn't just about Eva. It's about Zak.'

'He deserved to die. And I know what you're thinking. You're thinking this is just like Lucy and Philip. You're thinking that I murdered Zak because he killed Eva. Just like I murdered Philip when I thought he was hurting Lucy. But I didn't do it. I know I had a motive – Zak deserved to die for what he did to Eva – but I swear I didn't do it.'

'This isn't just about revenge. Becca Smith has told them that Zak confirmed to her that you had offered him twenty thousand pounds to kill her before she came to Salvation Hall.'

Marcus coughed out a laugh. 'For pity's sake, everyone knows he was lying about that. Even Eva found it funny.'

'Becca also told Sergeant Parkinson that you offered him double the money him to try again. And the police suspect you may have killed him to avoid making the payment.'

'Do you believe that?'

'What I believe doesn't matter. It's what the police believe, coupled with the evidence they've obtained.' Kathryn drew back her hand. 'Becca has agreed to make a sworn statement. And, taken with the phone found in your room...'

'And what about that ridiculous thing that was hung around Eva's neck when they found her? How does that come into it?'

'A ploy to point the finger at Laurence. They know Zak

had a copy of Laurence's book describing the garland. They found it in his overnight bag at Becca's. They think he got the idea from you.'

'So, just to be clear, I'm supposed to have induced him to murder Eva, offered him a bribe to come back and finish the job and then murdered him in cold blood to avoid paying him off?'

'And possibly to avoid any further confrontations or demands.'

'And how did I know where he could find her?'

'They think Eva confided in you that she was going to London to meet with Laurence, but that you agreed to keep it a secret from Richard and the rest of the family. And that you've continued to keep your knowledge of it a secret to protect yourself.'

'So, on top of everything else, I'm a liar?' Marcus bent his neck and rested his forehead on the steering wheel. 'It isn't enough that I've lost her, is it? I haven't even been permitted to see her body. To see for myself that she's really gone.' His voice was almost a whisper. 'Let alone bring her home to Salvation Hall.'

'Would it help if I said that I believe you?'

'You believe me? You think that the phone was planted?' He lifted his head. 'Or are you just saying that to encourage me to face up to DCI Price?'

Could she answer that question with any real sense of conviction? 'I don't know how the phone came to be in your room. But I saw for myself how much you cared for Eva. And I can see any number of flaws in Ennor's argument. Apart from anything else, if Eva confided in you about her trip to London, she could just as easily have confided in someone else. And that someone else could have decided to share the information with Zak Smith.'

'I give you my word, Kathryn, that I didn't do it.'

'Then you don't have anything to fear by speaking to Ennor.' Kathryn twisted in her seat and reached over her shoulder to pull on the seatbelt. 'Which is why we have to go back to the house now. So that you can tell him the truth.'

27

'I'm not hungry.' Richard's tone was tart. 'I'm too anxious for Marcus's wellbeing.'

'But it's your favourite seafood curry.' Nancy placed the supper tray down on the dining table. 'Surely you're not going to ask me to eat alone, after everything that's happened today?'

The old man stared at her through rheumy eyes. 'You are welcome to sit here and eat yours. It's probably as well that you stay here in the Dower House anyway. I cannot imagine that Inspector Price would welcome your presence in the main house.' At least, not while he was interviewing Marcus. 'Have David and Laurence left for The Zoological?'

'Yes. Barbara is with them.' Nancy sat down at the table. 'At least I was able to have a conversation with Laurence before he left. There have been times today when I could have sworn you were trying to keep me away from him.'

'Nonsense. What reason could I possibly have for doing such a thing?' Richard flicked his eyes in Nancy's direction. 'You are free to come and go as you please, and speak to whoever you please.' Why did she have to be so belligerent? 'I assume you took the opportunity to let him know that you are very distantly related?' He watched her face as he spoke, and caught the faintest hint of annoyance in the clear, dark eyes. 'Was he impressed by your knowledge of the family's history?'

'I didn't expect him to be impressed. I simply wanted him to know that we are all one family on St Felix.'

So, she had failed to skewer Laurence on her hook. Perhaps it was just as well. 'Did you tell him that you were about to return to St Felix?'

'No, because I didn't think it had anything to do with him.' She lifted a bowl of curry from the tray and placed it down on the tablemat in front of her. 'Anyway, you will still need me here, now that Marcus has been arrested again.'

'I wasn't aware that Marcus had been arrested.'

'But he soon will be. He has to be. He murdered Zak Smith.'

'And how do you know that?'

Nancy hesitated, the lid from the tureen still in her hand. 'What other explanation do you have for Zak's body being found in the potting shed?'

'That someone other than Marcus murdered him.' Richard wafted a hand towards her. 'Eat your food, Nancy. It will be going cold.'

The instruction fell on deaf ears. Nancy put the lid back on the bowl and picked up her napkin. 'How could you say that? How could anyone else have murdered him?'

'Very easily. I might have done it myself.'

'Richard, this is not a joke.' She shook out the napkin and dropped it into her lap. 'Marcus has committed another murder. He has let the family down for a second time. Surely you are not going to defend him again?'

He had expected her to protest, but still it came as a disappointment. 'I don't think there will be any need for me to defend him. Because I do not believe the good chief inspector will find enough evidence to charge him. And I do not believe that Marcus will confess to the killing, as he did to killing Philip. After all, the only reason he confessed so willingly to that murder was because I asked him to.'

Nancy bridled. 'You asked him to? Why would you do that?'

'In order to save the family the ordeal of a prolonged investigation.' Richard dropped a hand to the side of his chair, where Samson lay quietly dozing. 'Of course, he flatly refused to admit to murdering Lucy. Because he didn't kill her.'

'You still believe that Philip murdered Lucy?'

'I still believe that it is wise for us not to consider the alternatives.' Richard rubbed his fingers into the fur of Samson's neck as he spoke. 'As it is wise for us not to spend too much time contemplating who might have murdered Zak Smith. For now, we should be content to believe that it wasn't Marcus.'

'But the phone that was found in his room?'

'Circumstantial evidence. For all we know, Smith may have entered the house himself to leave it there before he made his way to the potting shed.' Richard chuckled under his breath. 'I might have left it there. So might David. Or Barbara. Or Kathryn.' He licked his lips thoughtfully. 'Or yourself.' He didn't expect her to take the bait. 'Of course, this is all conjecture.'

Nancy lowered her head. 'I'm not quite sure what point you are trying to make. But I would like to know what you expect to happen next.'

'My dear girl, the answer to that is simple: multi-faceted, but simple. David and Barbara will remain here with me at Salvation Hall, as planned. Barbara will move into Holly Cottage once the refurbishment is complete. After Eva's funeral, Marcus will return to St Felix to run Woodlands and you will go with him to begin setting up the foundation. Kathryn, I hope, will be persuaded to remain here as our secretary after your departure.' Richard tilted his head with a smile. 'I intend to recruit DCI Price to my cause there. I can only think it would be in his interests to persuade her to stay.'

'You seem to have everything clearly mapped out.' There was a hollow note in Nancy's voice. 'I fear that if I return to St Felix, I might not have the pleasure of being with you again.'

'You need not worry about that, my dear. Because I only intend to remain at Salvation Hall for a very short space of time. There is one very particular thing I have to do, and when that task is complete I shall return to St Felix myself.'

Nancy gasped — a tiny, spontaneous intake of disbelieving breath. 'You are returning to live at Woodlands? But the doctor forbade it.'

'The doctor advised against it. But I have reached the age now where the doctor's advice really counts for very little.'

'Then we will be home together, you and I?' The girl's eyes widened, and then they began to fill with tears. 'I had no idea.' Her voice wavered. 'Will it take very long, this task that you have to complete?'

'I hope not. I simply have to make sure that DCI Price stops looking at the family in his search for Zak Smith's killer.'

*

'Tom's taken him down to the station, but we'll need hard evidence to charge him. Finding that phone in his room is just circumstantial.' Ennor looked at Kathryn as he spoke, but she was avoiding his gaze, her eyes fixed down towards her hands. 'I'm grateful that you were able to persuade him to come back and speak to me. It might have turned ugly otherwise.'

'You don't think it's ugly, anyway?'

'I suppose it depends how you look at it.' They were sitting on the sofa in the library, just a few inches apart.

And yet, if he judged the situation by the tone of her voice, he couldn't help thinking a gulf was opening up between them. 'You did the right thing, Kathryn. It's better that he faces up to what he's done.'

'Always supposing that it actually was Marcus who committed the murder.' She clearly didn't agree with him. Her brow was deeply furrowed, her lips drawn down by an overwhelming sadness. 'I didn't bring him back to admit to the crime. I brought him back to tell you the truth.'

'And you believe him? You believe that he didn't bribe Smith to murder Eva? Or that he murdered Smith to keep him quiet, or to avoid paying him off for carrying out his instructions?' She didn't have to say anything for Price to know the answer. 'This is going to come between us now, isn't it?

'I don't know.' She lifted her eyes to look at him. 'I hope it isn't. But I know what it would mean for you to have Marcus all trussed up as the solution to the crime. It would solve everything for you, wouldn't it? Marcus would go to prison again for murdering Zak, Grant and Greenway would be able to wrap up their investigations and your career would be back on track.

'Would you begrudge me that, after everything that's gone before?'

'Oh, Ennor, of course not. But if your career has to be back on track, then let it be for the right reason. Let it be because you've caught Zak's killer, not because you've strung Marcus up on the basis of circumstantial evidence.'

The stark accusation hit him in the gut. 'You don't really know me at all, do you? I thought you understood that I played everything by the book. If all I cared about was my career, I would have accepted Richard Lancefield's offer to intervene and speak to senior officers on my behalf. I would have played the "old boy's network" card.' If nothing else, it would have saved him from giving up most of his life in favour of unpaid overtime. 'Much as I would love to thrash this out with you now, I'm afraid I'm going to have to go back to the station. I only have twenty-four hours to question Marcus and the clock is ticking.'

'Will I hear from you tomorrow?' Kathryn looked up at him as he rose to his feet. 'Will we still be friends?'

'Well, I suppose that depends on what happens in the next twenty-four hours, doesn't it? Will we still be friends if I charge Marcus with murder?'

'Of course, if you have the evidence to charge him and can prove that he did it. We've weathered that storm once in the last twelve months. I can't see any reason why we couldn't do it again.' She bit on her lip. 'You know that if you charge him, Richard will do everything he can to make sure it doesn't end in another prison sentence.'

'You mean he'll try to play the system a second time? I wouldn't expect anything less.' Ennor turned on his heel and began to walk slowly towards the door. And then he turned back to look at her. 'It will be a lot more awkward if Marcus doesn't confess. Unless we can turn up something concrete before our time runs out, I'll have to let him go. And that means every minute of my day and night will be taken up with searching for evidence to prove that he did it. And I won't rest, Kathryn. I hope you know that.'

'Marcus will return to St Felix if he isn't charged.'

'And I will make sure that the local force keeps him under constant observation until I have enough evidence to bring him back. You know…' Ennor was almost reluctant to speak. 'When you and I first met, when I had to find Lucy and Philip's killer, you did everything you could to help me. You were my eyes and ears at Salvation Hall. And I thought you did that because justice mattered to you.'

'Justice does matter to me. That's why I don't want to see Marcus convicted for something that he didn't do. He held his hand up to Philip McKeith's murder. He might have been under pressure from Richard to make a clean breast of it, but he never denied the responsibility. But this is different. Marcus told me that he didn't murder Zak.

And I believe him.'

'Then perhaps there is something that you can do to help me. To help *us*.' Ennor stepped forward to stand beside the sofa. 'If you truly believe that Marcus isn't guilty, you can help me to find the real killer.' He crouched down beside her and lifted his hand, placing it gently under her chin, guiding her to look at him. 'If Marcus wasn't the killer, then it must be someone else within the family. And I don't know anyone else who knows the Lancefields like you do.'

'You want me to spy on the family?'

'I want you to do the right thing. If you really want justice to be served, Kathryn, and you believe that Marcus didn't murder Zak Smith, show me that I got it wrong.'

ABOUT THE AUTHOR

Mariah Kingdom was born in Hull and grew up in the East Riding of Yorkshire. After taking a degree in History at Edinburgh University she wandered into a career in information technology and business change, and worked for almost thirty years as a consultant in the British retail and banking sectors.

She began writing crime fiction during the banking crisis of 2008, drawing on past experience to create Rose Bennett, a private investigator engaged by a fictional British bank.

St Aldate's Magick is the fourth Lancefield Mystery.

www.mariahkingdom.com

Printed in Dunstable, United Kingdom